THE ST. CROIX INCIDENT

To Bill
Merry Christmas 2005

Jim L. Traveler

THE ST. CROIX INCIDENT

Jim L. Traveler
with
William O. Bryant

Writers Club Press
New York Lincoln Shanghai

The St. Croix Incident

Writers Club Press
an imprint of iUniverse, Inc.

For information address:
iUniverse, Inc.
2021 Pine Lake Road, Suite 100
Lincoln, NE 68512
www.iuniverse.com

ISBN: 0-595-25406-3 (pbk)
ISBN: 0-595-65153-4 (cloth)

Printed in the United States of America

This Book is Dedicated
To
William O. Bryant

A trusted friend, editor, dedicated co-worker
And Author Of
Cahaba Prison And The *Sultana* Disaster
The University of Alabama Press, 1990, 2001

CHAPTER 1

Monday, August 24, 1970, 5:00 p.m., Greenwich Mean Time Minus 4 Hours

The bar at the Buccaneer Hotel and Country Club near Christiansted, St. Croix, in the U.S. Virgin Islands, provided a cool, dark haven against the sweltering tropical heat outside. Dark paneled walls and a huge mahogany bar created an atmosphere reminiscent of staid old clubs in London except for the big ceiling fans whirring softly overhead. Four well-known men were at the bar, engaged in happy and animated conversation, verbally replaying each stroke of a round of golf just completed. Sweat still stained their shirts.

Nothing about the board meeting that preceded the golf entered even briefly into the conversation. Both of the companies represented by the gentlemen were profitable, growing, and under competent managers. Business simply was of no concern in the post-game ritual of drink and laughter. The other three members of the board of directors, who, declining golf, had departed after the meeting, received little mention. Golf and only golf was important at the moment.

The only other customer in the bar, a big man of strange and striking appearance, sat across the room at a small cocktail table near the large dark-tinted windows, nursing a beer in a once-frosty mug. Through vivid blue eyes partly covered by bushy red eyebrows, he watched the men with considerable interest. A heavy red beard and mustache covered much of his face, which was a stunning white and without freckles. A cascade of red hair flowed to his shoulders. His suit, a true navy blue, was well tailored and expensive. The coat concealed his massive shoulders and arms nicely, but not the large hands with stubby fingers that occasionally explored the bowl of mixed nuts. The redhead wore no tie with his white silk shirt.

The bartender leaned against the back of the bar watching television. He displayed no interest in anything else and ignored his customers unless summoned. On the screen, a happy tune was whistled as Andy and Opie walked down a rural road carrying fishing rods while Opie paused to toss pebbles. It was just past 5:00 p.m.

The two entrances to the bar suddenly burst open and three yelling armed men raced into the room through each door, wearing military-style camouflage uniforms, berets, and dark sunglasses. They brandished Armalite 180 semi-automatic rifles. Their shouts through heavy black beards, apparently in Spanish, were indecipherable to the customers of the Buccaneer Bar. After one quick look at the intruders, the bartender immediately dropped to the floor behind the bar. The astonished golfers froze in place, staring open-mouthed and with total disbelief at the six men.

One of the intruders, the one with a white star on his beret, barked an obscenity in broken English and opened fire on the golfers. His companions joined in and a brutal fusillade ripped into the four men. The first thirty or forty rounds tore their torsos apart as they collapsed in a shower of blood and flesh to the floor. Then the last cartridges in the magazines were fired into heads and throats. All four golfers were dead before the whistling on the screen ended.

The man with the white star turned to the redhead still seated at the table, snapped a new magazine into the 180, shrugged, and blasted the redhead's ashtray, bowl of mixed nuts, and beer mug. He then shattered the large window with a final shot. "Hey, mon," he said, "you too fucking ugly to shoot. Killing you be a relief of you misery." He smiled, saluted, and whirled about. He dashed through the door leading to the golf course and was quickly followed by the others. One stopped briefly to get off a quick round in the direction of a cook who had rushed from the kitchen. The cook quickly reversed his course.

The hairy and bearded redhead stood and calmly brushed the glass and beer from his suit. He walked slowly over to the victims at the bar. He stared a moment at the bloody mess on the floor before turning away. "Son of a bitch!" he muttered. "I should have asked for more details. Hell, I would have picked another place to drink beer." He stalked deliberately and heavy-footed out of the door leading onto the golf course. On the television, Barney and Gomer, lights flashing, siren blaring, pulled Mayberry's patrol car up at the fishing hole to summon Andy for a big emergency.

❦   ❦   ❦

Charlotte Amalie, USVI, July 4, 1980

Why I am sitting here telling this unlikely story, I do not know. I know, and have known, Washburn for several years, but do not understand him. He's a world-class accountant, a CPA, brilliant, scrupulously honest. Yet he's parked on the front porch of a dinky little house stuck on the side of the hill overlooking the port of Charlotte Amalie, St. Thomas, U.S. Virgin Islands. Nice view. Sure for a couple of hours. But for ten years? Hell's the matter with Washburn? Hell's the matter with me? Washburn is happy. So is his wife. Me, I been running all over the world looking for something to make me happy. Washburn says if you can't find it in the Virgin Islands it doesn't exist. Oh, yeah, I know the shrink says you gotta make yourself happy. No one else can do that for you. Big frigging deal. Fat lot he knows about anything.

Nigel James Alasdair sat on the porch with his friend, Washburn. He had not yet begun to speak. He was thinking of Washburn and the story he was about to tell the accountant. His thoughts ran on.

Washburn moved here from Atlanta maybe ten, maybe twelve years ago. Helluva jump from that plush office in Buckhead. To my knowledge he has not left the island. How can a man live for ten years on an island only fourteen miles by seven miles? It is ridiculous, unthinkable, out of the question. Yet there he sits, completely satisfied with his lot. This very minute he is staring at Water Island and I am sure he has never hopped a boat to go over there. Better yet, I'll bet he has never visited the Royal Mail Hotel only three or four minutes from the dock across from the Windward Passage Hotel. A boat leaves every thirty minutes. Washburn is only fifty years old. That is not old, but Washburn is old. Look at him, bare feet stuck inside a pair of worn sandals, ragged shorts, ancient golf shirt, worn out old straw hat. Hell, I am sneaking up on forty but I do not look like Washburn and I never will. I am young and virile, not old and worn out, and I won't be when I am fifty.

"Wake up and listen, Washburn, if you want me to tell about my last venture into the world of legitimate business," Alasdair said. "Legitimate business is too dangerous for me. It damn near got me killed, it did.

"It all started the day Richard Nixon appointed that guy, Evans, governor of the Virgin Islands. An old political friend invited me down for the inaugural festivities. Did Nixon appoint him or was he elected? Both. I came for the party to celebrate his election. Doesn't matter. That is why I am here except for having to visit you quarterly. Hell of a party, as I recall, but that is incidental to the story. It was just after Bill Brock beat that old fox, Albert Gore, out of his seat in the U.S. Senate, representing Tennessee. Surprised everyone, it did. No one more than Gore. Thought he ruled by divine decree. Never thought about all the voters lurking in the shadows, quietly waiting to give him the boot. OK, Washburn, stop rolling your eyes. I'll get on with it.

"During the inaugural festivities, I met Stephen O'Rielly, that accountant from St. Croix. I liked him the minute I met him, all six feet, four inches of him. Big smile, lots of white teeth, a sense of humor I could not believe. I, of course, have none, sense of humor that is, but got on well with Stephen. He enjoyed telling me how he gave new meaning to the phrase 'Black Irish.' Black as the ace of spades, he is. He tried to change me. 'Lighten up,' he would say. 'Smile. It is not as tiring as frowning.' It never worked. I always had to do what I had to do, and no relaxing until it was done. Then there was always another something that had to be done. He kept saying things like, 'You can be a nice guy if you try. Say a kind word to someone on occasion.' I couldn't, wouldn't, didn't. He offered to get me a good job at Tilly's Funeral Parlor as a mourner. Be good for business for me to just stand around.

"You know me, Washburn. Am I that bad?" Alasdair asked.

"Damn right you are," Washburn said. "If it wasn't for what you pay me for accounting, I would not put up with you for ten minutes."

"Hell's the matter with you? Hell of a thing to say to your only friend. We can't even go to a decent restaurant because you got nothing to wear. Look as if you live in a refrigerator box, you do. A smile doesn't do anything for you. A shave might, now that I think about it.

"Why the hell is it so hard to buy Scotch whisky in the islands where untaxed whiskey is a major industry? They got your bourbon, that sour mash crap, and all the clear stuff, but no Scotch whisky," Alasdair said.

He sipped a bit of the brown liquid laid in at both Washburn's and his suite at the Windward Passage, and began to think seriously again about the story he had agreed to relate. He silently vowed never to engage in legitimate business again.

Washburn stirred in his chair and said, "You begin to bore me friend Alasdair. It is well known that you and O'Rielly opened an insurance office in Palm Passage. The great Nigel James Alasdair, an insurance agent in Charlotte Amalie, St. Thomas, U.S. Virgin Islands! A ludicrous idea to anyone. Tell me what the hell were you doing that caused so many deaths in so short a time?"

"Relax, Washburn. I must give you all the background before you can understand the occurrences of which you speak. It is not a simple story to give you in a few words. Lots of people have been after the story for years that I am giving you today. We have time, all afternoon and night.

"Stop rolling your eyes, Washburn. You are my accountant and know everything about me, and you know damn well there is nothing illegal with any of my businesses, and that includes the Belize airport deal. You read too many newspapers. Stick to Value Line, you don't need any news. You searched every expense and purchase on the airport project. Did you find any evidence of kickbacks? Hell no, because there were none. No matter what the newspapers churned out, I did nothing wrong. Quit rolling your damn eyes. Beginning to look like a sick calf in a thunderstorm.

"OK, OK, back to the story. Here it is, near as I am able to recreate."

CHAPTER 2

August 24, 1970, Christiansted, St. Croix, 9:03 p.m. GMT–4

The redhead slipped on a pair of sunglasses to protect his sensitive eyes as he walked, plodded really, out of the Buccaneer Bar toward a Chevrolet Belair sedan. He shucked off his coat and tossed it onto the back seat before squeezing behind the wheel. His eyes were fastened intently on the six men who piled into two decrepit station wagons and quickly departed. He followed at a discrete distance as they left the busy city street for the quiet highway toward Blue Mountain. He knew the airport would be closed shortly and the ruptured ducks would be grounded. Ruptured ducks. Strange name, that, for the seaplanes which served the island. The Coast Guard soon would have sufficient boats on the water to board any craft seeking to depart. The shooters would be trapped on the island for quite awhile, giving him as much time as he needed to complete his work.

At the foot of Blue Mountain, the station wagons turned onto an unpaved road leading up the mountain by the easier ascent. He followed. After three miles, the road split into two going around the mountain in opposite directions. It seemed wise to turn around at the fork. He knew where they were going. There was no point in further risk. Swinging the Belair in a circle on the wide area at the fork, he began the return trip to the Caravelle Hotel.

In his room, he locked and chained the door, then unlocked the closet. He removed a large hard-bodied case, and from that an insulated case, which he placed on the bed and opened. He looked for a suitable work site and decided on the combination vanity, chest of drawers, and TV stand. Pushing the television aside, he removed a box from the insulated case and placed it on the spot vacated by the television. He scooted the straight-backed chair forward and seated himself. He went to work with his big but delicate hands.

The clock on the night stand gave the time as 9:03 p.m. when he stood and stretched for the first time in over an hour. In his heavy, plodding way he walked to the bathroom and stripped off the white latex gloves. He methodically cut them into small pieces and dropped them into the commode. After three flushes, satisfied no traces remained, he returned to the bedroom and removed a leather briefcase from beneath the bed. He gingerly put the three small packages he had completed in precise slots cut for them in the case's foam liner. From the insulated suitcase on the bed, he removed a glass bottle containing twelve ounces of an opaque, viscous liquid. He placed it in the indention also made for it in the foam. Satisfied everything met his requirements, he closed the top, snapped the locks, and set the briefcase beside the door. Deliberately and methodically, he returned to the box all bits and pieces left over from his work, all unused material and his tools. He closed the box and placed it in the insulated suitcase. He studied the case a moment, then put it into the big hard-bodied case. Making sure it was securely locked, he returned it to the closet and locked the door. With a bottle of spray cleaner from the bathroom, he cleaned the work area and returned the television to its proper location.

He removed his clothing and, after brushing his teeth, carefully began dressing for the evening. On the inside of his left leg, he strapped on an ankle holster containing a Smith and Wesson .38 Special with a two-inch barrel. He added a pair of baggy tan trousers, heavy socks, and a good pair of hiking boots. He slipped a tan T-shirt over his head, taking care not to overly muss his hair. He carefully slipped on a leather holster with straps that looped over his left shoulder and around his chest. It fit perfectly because he had made it himself in Italy. It held a S&W .38 revolver with a longer barrel snugly in place under his arm. A sheath, Velcro-strapped inside his left forearm, concealed and protected a star dagger with a six-inch blade and T-grip, also of his own design. Over it all he wore a dark brown bulky shirt with long sleeves. Smiling at himself in the mirror on the bathroom door, he flipped his lustrous red hair over the shirt collar and nodded his approval. He checked the room carefully to make sure everything was tidy and in order. From the drawer in the night stand, he removed a belt which included a pouch intended for money or other valuables, the type tourists wear. The contents of his pouch consisted of 40 spare hollow point rounds for the S&Ws. He slid the belt around so the ammunition lay on his right side, balancing the weight.

Down Cay Street to Island Rentals required about two minutes. He rented a convertible and drove to the Top Hat for dinner. Walking there would have been quicker but he needed the car. He remembered the blonde rental girl and her friendly smile. He appreciated her kindness, especially her "Goodbye, Mr. Walther, and thank you."

August 24, 1970, San Juan, Puerto Rico, 9:03 p.m., GMT–4

In his room on the tenth floor of the Americana Hotel in Puerto Rico, Cosgrove waited impatiently for the telephone to ring. Alternating between pacing and flopping on the queen-sized bed, he nervously smoked cigarette after cigarette. The TV droned on with some asinine program, doing little to ease his nervousness. Cosgrove, a small-time hood from Miami, worked for his brother-in-law, a big-time hood in New Jersey. This job was way above his head and he was worried. Why didn't the phone ring? He looked at his cheap watch and then shook his wrist vigorously. Perhaps the watch had stopped. The formerly luminous dial read 9:03 p.m. The last time he had looked it read 9:00 p.m. and that was at least half an hour ago. He turned his attention to the bottle of bourbon and then suddenly to the television as the broadcast increased in volume and switched to urgent news. The great seal of Puerto Rico appeared on the screen, then the identifier of the station, which slowly faded to a serious-looking male news reader. Cosgrove gave his full attention.

"Good evening, ladies and gentlemen. This afternoon, at approximately 5:00 p.m., six reportedly drug-crazed Vietnam veterans stormed the bar of the Buccaneer Hotel in Christiansted, St. Croix, screaming obscenities and accusing the patrons of being Vietcong sympathizers. Using automatic weapons, they gunned down the bar patrons and made their escape, leaving an unknown number of victims either dead or wounded. Details are few at the moment, but we will keep you informed as we learn more. Our man, Ramon Ramano, is on his way to St. Croix by our helicopter. As soon as he reports, we will bring it to you live. Our sources at the hotel think the victims are all golfers, maybe local, and not guests of the hotel. Now back to our regular programming."

Cosgrove took a long pull on the bourbon bottle, then grabbed the telephone. He gave the operator a number in New Jersey and waited while she dialed. The bourbon was beginning to taste much better. At last the number answered.

"It's me. It's done. It's all over the news here. You probably see it on your TV any time now," he said.

"Shut up and listen to me. How many? Was it all seven? That's important."

"I don't know. No details released. The news guy talked like it might have been a bar full. No details."

"Then get off the phone and wait for Whitestar to call. Then call me back." Cosgrove was treated to a dial tone.

Cosgrove did not understand how he was supposed to know how many. He had found the crazy Puerto Ricans. He got them to St. Croix and gave them the information furnished him from New Jersey. What more could he do? In his bourbon-soaked brain, Cosgrove decided to return to Miami with the money as soon as Whitestar called. What more could he do? He had paid Whitestar half the money and promised the other half on the shooters' return to Puerto Rico. How the hell were they going to get back to Puerto Rico? St. Croix is an island and the police and the Coast Guard will cut it off from the rest of the world for at least a month. By then they will have found the damned Puerto Ricans. Cosgrove himself needed the other twenty thousand dollars more and, as he told the bourbon bottle, he deserved it.

The insistent ringing of the phone roused Cosgrove from a stupor of bourbon and sleep. It was Whitestar. "We got them, we reelly got them," he said. "You shoulda be there. They surprised, mon. They reelly surprised. Then they dead. All four of them."

"What do you mean four? There were seven. You were supposed to get all seven."

"No, mon. We got them all four. You said watch and when they come in off de golf to get them all. They was four and we got them all four. Dats all was in de place except some weirdo wid red hair. We scared de shit out o' him. But that all was in de place. I didn't even see no bartender. We gots them all. Now you come wid de rest of our money. We OK here. Them dumb cops still running in circles out at de Buccaneer Club. They never find us. After it cool off, we go home. Then it be over."

"Sure, I will bring the other payment, but where shall I leave it or will you meet me?"

"Hell, I meetcha, mon. That place where I'm holed up, it got a phone. This is de number. When you get here, call me and I meetcha. You come quick, de mons wants they money."

Cosgrove cradled the phone and flopped back on the bed. He could see in his soaked brain the one big project for which he had hoped falling to pieces about him. Where were the other three men? Why weren't they at the golf course as planned? They had a tee time. They had partners all set up. He had that information from the man in New Jersey. He had checked the tee time with the club pro-shop. He knew the schedule and the time required to play eighteen holes. What happened? For no particular reason he remembered a high school coach telling him that just because he had sneakers didn't mean he could play basketball. His brother-in-law, Franco, was going to be pissed. This was a big-money deal to him and involved important people. He did not want to call Franco, but he had no choice. It would soon be on the news. He gave the number to the operator and waited.

"There was only four of them, Franco. Only four and, no, I don't know where the other three are. I am in San Juan. I'm not in St. Croix. I just told my people to get the group you said would be playing golf."

"What the hell do you mean they only got four?" yelled Franco. "Did they miss the other three? How the hell could they do that?"

"No, No. They didn't miss anyone. The others weren't there. They never played golf. There was no one else in the bar except some redhead weirdo and he had nothing to do with your group. Whitestar said the four were the only ones, the only ones on the golf course and the only ones in the bar. You fucked up, not us."

"Don't tell me who fucked up. Tell Whitestar to get the other three and get them quick, or he will never see his money. Nor will he ever get off St. Croix. You tell him that and you tell him now. We are not messing with no Saturday night pushers, we messing with big people and they mean business. They don't like problems. You picked Whitestar, I picked you, and they picked me. If there is a problem they won't be looking for you or Whitestar, they'll be looking for me. Me, who is right here and handy. Do you get my drift? When it's a problem for me I will make it a problem for you, so you better make it a problem for Whitestar. You got it?"

"It is not my fault, Franco. I told them to get the golfers and they got them." Cosgrove again was treated to a sudden dial tone. Dejectedly he gave Whitestar's number to the operator and waited. The telephone rang on the other end, but there was no answer. He determined that he had done all that possibly could be expected of him. "I'm going back to Miami. Fucking brother-in-law can't talk to me like that. Let him sort the shit out himself. I'll call Whitestar from the airport or Miami." After one more visit with the nearly empty bourbon bottle, Cosgrove scooped up his clothes and toilet articles and stuffed them into a small bag. He completed the in-room checkout form and caught a taxi for the airport. The table clock said 10.42 p.m.

҂   ҂   ҂

August 24, 1970, Nashville, Tenn., 8:58 p.m. GMT–6

The airliner rolled to a stop at Gate 1 of Nashville's Berry Field as the usual gaggle of people clamored to retrieve their light luggage, mostly junk, stowed in overhead bins. Flights from the Caribbean always produced bins full of junk and booze. Passengers in first class are not immune to the junk craze brought on by the tropical sun. Nigel James Alasdair slid his worn suede briefcase from under the seat in front of him and made his way out of the first class cabin and down the walkway to the terminal, hoping as he walked that his wife would meet him. One of Nashville's taxis did not appeal to him tonight. Glancing at his watch, he became aware that today had started early. It was almost 9:00 p.m., Nashville time. He was not sure of the time difference but it probably was two hours, making it almost 11:00 in the islands. He regretted not calling his wife before boarding the plane. She would bitch. That would be normal, but she also would bring the big, comfortable car, and for that a little bitching was acceptable.

As he passed through the secure section exit, he saw her standing in the middle of the aisle, studying each passenger as if she were meeting a stranger. Sometimes she thought he was a stranger.

"Hi, stranger," he said. "I didn't expect to see you. I forgot to call. How did you know to meet me?"

"Stephen called."

"Stephen called? Whatever for?"

"Come on. Here's the bar. You better have a drink. We need to talk. Here, this table is fine." With a sense of urgency that almost shocked Alasdair, she had pulled him into the nearly deserted plastic and Formica lounge. She motioned wildly to the nearer of the two waitresses leaning against the bar.

"I don't want a drink," he protested. "They have free booze on the plane. I am tired and I want to go home. What is it with Stephen? We were together all morning."

"Two double Dewars, and hurry, please, lady."

"I told you I don't need a drink, certainly not a double. Hell's wrong with you? What did Stephen say to cause you this much concern? I know he never told you about the multitude of women I have in the islands. Even if he had, that wouldn't get you into double Dewars. Come on, out with it."

"OK, here's your drink. Thank you, lady. Bring him another in about three minutes, then leave us alone. OK, here it is. It's your partners, Jim."

"What about my partners? What the hell Stephen call you about?"

"They're dead, Jim. They are all dead. That's what Stephen called about." With that, Mrs. Alasdair gulped down a third of the Dewars in her glass. "After the golf game at the Buccaneer Club, they were murdered in the bar. Shot to death. Brutally! Several times each. By a bunch of crazy war veterans, the news says. High on dope, the news says. Stephen says no. He says the two of you are lucky there was no time for golf. Of course, anyone who knows you knows you never play golf. You were scheduled, Stephen said. The tee times were in yours and Clarence's names."

Visibly shaken, Alasdair looked to the bar for the three-minute Dewars. His glass was empty. "OK, give this to me again. A bunch of dope heads crashed the bar and shot the patrons who happened to be our board members. No one else? Just our board?"

"According to Stephen, it happened at a slow time in the bar. No other customers so far as he knows. Clarence and his group completed their round and, because of the big water show, nearly all the guests were on the beach watching. Stephen said Clarence, Balboa, Phillip, Rico, and Brookings are dead. You need to call Stephen. He is at Cyril's house and is sure the killers are after him. I think he and his family are going to stay at Cyril's until you figure out what is happening."

Alasdair searched, without success, for a more comfortable position in the plastic chair, sipped his Scotch, and asked, "Why me? What do I know about this? Why does he think these freaks would be after him or me? We are not anything, just a crummy little insurance agency and a two-branch bank. Stephen must be losing his mind or he is into something I don't know about. I need to go to the office or home to call him. If American's counter is still open, I'll make reservations to return tomorrow. No choice."

❦   ❦   ❦

August 24, 1970, New Jersey, USA, 10:40 p.m., GMT–5

Franco was paranoid and attributed his paranoia to a burning desire to remain alive and healthy. Thus far it had worked well. Now he had a problem. His wife's brother was an idiot. Why he had decided to use him in this job, he could not remember. It was now an unmitigated error. First, Cosgrove hired a totally unreliable bunch of junkies and they had fucked up the well-planned hit. How could they let three of the targets get away? Next, he called on Franco's home phone and blurted out all sorts of damning information. Worse, in his concern and anger, Franco had allowed the conversation to continue. Who knew who might be listening on his phone? Franco never placed a long-distance call from his home phone and he never accepted one. Cosgrove could call and ask to speak to his sister, and arrangements could be made. Did he do that? No, he blurted out everything. Did Franco stop him before he went too far? No. He, in fact, furthered the breach by joining in and losing his temper.

Franco backed the Ford out of his garage and drove slowly around, making a couple of U-turns to confuse and expose a possible tail. After twenty minutes, he turned into the parking lot of the downtown Holiday Inn. He sat in the car for five minutes, watching all vehicles coming into the lot. Satisfied no one had followed him, he entered the hotel through the rear lobby door. In the hallway to the right of the door was a bank of phone booths. Selecting one he had never used before, he made his call with a credit card number he had stolen from an out-of-town businessman who had been calling a massage service. He glanced at his watch while waiting for the ring to be answered. It blinked the time at him: 10:40 p.m. Franco shivered over what this call might bring. He never screwed up with the big guys. It didn't pay. No way would he lie. The man was too smart and had too many contacts. He could spot a lie in ten seconds.

"This is Thad."

"Its me, Thad. I just received a report from the islands. There was a mess-up somewhere along the line. Unfortunately, only four of the seven played golf. Our men got them. The others were not there."

The voice was cold and without emotion. "Unsatisfactory, Franco. We made no provision for errors. What corrective measures have you taken?"

"I told them to finish the job and finish it quick. The problem is they don't know the names of the targets. I am sending my man in

Puerto Rico to help. He can point out the johns for them or do it himself. We will finish the job, Thad."

"Of that I have no doubt, Franco. It would be most unfortunate if you left any loose ends. I suggest you might be well advised to get your ass down there and make sure. Now explain to me what happened."

"Well, as you told me, the Reynolds and Alasdair guys had tee times ten minutes apart, 1:00 and 1:10 p.m. They were the first groups after noon and no other group was within half an hour of them. We figured they would finish about 4:30 p.m. The guys were in two vehicles at the rear of the club with a view of the last hole. They were to wait until the golfers went into the bar, then go in and take them out. They waited and watched until the first foursome came in, then waited for the threesome. There was no threesome, so they went in and took out the foursome. That's it. The other three did not play. I don't know where they were and I don't know which ones we got. All I know is four. Jeez, Thad, I don't know what to say. There was no backup plan for a no-show."

"Were there any witnesses?"

"I'm told there was one, a weirdo with a bunch of red hair. They said they scared the shit out of him but did not hit him."

After a long pause, during which Franco was struck with a sudden and urgent desire to urinate, Thad said, "Franco, go to the airport and get to St. Croix and finish this job yourself. Whoever is left will be taking care of families and that sort of thing. Maybe you have not scared them into hiding. This didn't look like a hit, did it? I mean it was supposed to look like a dope-crazed random shooting. Too bad there weren't a few customers or maybe the bartender to shoot. What happened to the bartender? Didn't they at least shoot him?"

"I don't know, Thad. I told you all I know. I will get down there and straighten the mess out. I don't know when I can get a flight, but I am out of here. Perhaps the welfare redeye is running about 1:00 a.m."

"You do it, Franco. You get the other three and you get them quickly. Your future is at stake, so be careful. But be sure you get them. Our client was only specific about two items and perhaps those items have been taken care of already. If so, you must return at once. If not, do not return until they are no longer a source of embarrassment for you and me. Those two items are Brookings St. John and N.J. Alasdair. Do you understand me?"

"Yes, sir."

"Good. And Franco, try to locate that weirdo with red hair and speak to him about what he witnessed."

After Thad severed the connection, he swiveled his big chair slowly from side to side as he looked out the window high above the lighted city. Now an old man, he held the power more strongly and more selfishly than when he was younger. Ramrod straight, thin, but still strong, addicted to snugly tailored black suits with white shirts and black silk ties, he was a well-known person in certain elite circles. With a full head of neatly trimmed, almost snow-white hair, he was often mistaken for the distinguished senior partner in an important law firm, or one of those fancy gentleman stock traders with his name foremost in the company name. He was neither.

He removed a cigar case from an inner pocket of his black suit coat and selected a thin panatela. Instantly, one of the two young men in the room with Thad was at his side with lighter burning. "Thank you, Lou," Thad said in his low, icy voice. "Have either of you ever heard of Brookings St. John or N. J. Alasdair?" The two shook their heads.

"St. John is unknown to me but the name Alasdair I have heard in more than one conversation. They have angered a very rich and very powerful man with an ego larger than his brain. St. John will present no problem for him or me, but Alasdair is a different and troublesome commodity. Franco has made a mess of the operation that we had very carefully planned. I have sent him to set matters straight. However, my confidence in him is shattered. He used his brother-in-law, a cheap pusher in Miami, and I was stupid enough to allow it. Now I have my tit in a wringer over a very simple operation. I am up to my ass in Murphy's Law. It could and it did. Now I have to send in more men to clean up the mess. Lou, get my man in St. Thomas and tell him to meet Franco at the airport tomorrow and look after getting him a place to stay. Orlando does not know anything about our involvement with the St. Croix incident and does not need to know. Just put Franco up at some small out-of-the-way motel and let us know where. You tell him you will call him as soon as you know what flight Franco is on. Then find Walther and have him call me. He need not worry about waking me. There is no need for Orlando to know about Walther. I want this done quickly. Call our client and get the name of the person who gave him the information on the tee times. That person caused me more trouble than all the idiots I have working on this project."

 ❀   ❀   ❀

August 24, 1970, St. Croix, 11:30 p.m., GMT–4

Walther had known since he was a child that he was different from other people. First, it was the flaming red hair. Few women and no men to his knowledge had such beautiful hair. Next was the almost milky white skin with no freckles, none, a common occurrence in women but rare in men. He had little tolerance for the sun, so he seldom exposed his skin. Last was his size, especially the shoulders, arms, and hands. Walther was big, although neither tall nor overweight He was only five feet, eight inches in height, but had those massive shoulders. He was truly a strong man.

Over the years he became accustomed to people staring at him, even laughing. Few dared to insult him and those who did soon regretted it. In the Top Hat tonight, he felt on display. Quite a few black West Indians were there and, to them, he was like nothing they had ever seen. They were friendly and not insulting, just amazed. He enjoyed the attention. He also enjoyed the Aquavit and the almond cakes, as well as everything else he ate. The Top Hat served good food and the redhead was grateful for the opportunity to try several selections.

Outside, the night sky was beautiful, a large half moon giving more light than he preferred. But it posed no significant problem for his night's work. He drove the rented convertible along at a nice, comfortable clip. He was going almost due west toward Frederiksted. All too soon the road to Blue Mountain led north, a slightly different route than last time, but all roads end up in the same place on an island. He turned right onto the unpaved road that led up the easy side of the mountain. He paused at the wide spot where the road forked, then took the left trail. Exactly two miles later he passed a small cabin set back in a clump of trees and bougainvillea bushes. He noticed what seemed to be a party in progress. Island music floated over the convertible and voices could be heard but not understood. The party was a good sign and would offset the disadvantage of a moon that was a bit too bright. One of the station wagons he had followed from the Buccaneer Club was parked near the house. Walther drove on until he came to the other cabin that he sought. It was dark and empty. There was no car. Strange, he thought. They were not supposed to leave the cabins until the man came with the other half of their money. He dismissed the thought because there was always tomorrow.

He turned the convertible back toward the first cabin and drove past it, parking a quarter of a mile down the road. Taking the briefcase in his left hand, he walked back to the cabin. After looking around carefully, he went to the station wagon, moving slowly and quietly, in the shadows as much as possible. At the vehicle's right rear, he checked to see if the fuel cap had a lock. It didn't. He removed the bottle from the briefcase and emptied it into the fuel tank. He put the bottle back into the briefcase. Moving slowly, he circled the dark end of the house and located a door on the backside, a kitchen door most likely. He took one of the packages from the brief-case and fastened it to the door with a strip of duct tape. He made adjustments to the package, then made his way back to the road. He noticed women were in the cabin. This was another breach of the contract to which these people had agreed, or so he had been told. "It is too bad for the women," Walther thought. But the presence of women did not much bother him. He would complete the contract to the letter. He always did. He waited.

It was only five minutes, although it seemed forever when waiting. But Walther was a patient man. The blast came exactly on time. The rear of the house erupted and then the rest collapsed. The windows and the front door blew into the yard, followed quickly by two women and one man. They picked themselves up and leaped into the station wagon with shouts and screams, but without a backward glance. With a screech of rubber and flying gravel, they roared down the road in the direction of Walther's convertible. Walther walked to the remnants of the house to check inside. He found two men and one woman in the rubble. One of the men groaned and moved. Walther took the .38 from the shoulder holster and pressed the long barrel against the base of the man's head. He pulled the trigger. The other two people already were dead.

As he walked toward the convertible, he could see the glow of the station wagon as it sped down the hill. Fire was coming from around the hood and wheel wells. Then the flames engulfed the entire vehicle. Before it could stop or anyone get out, it exploded in a fireball of great size and intensity.

Walther put his briefcase into the convertible and drove slowly to the burning station wagon. It was not blocking the road and he moved slowly past the inferno without stopping.

Back at the Caravelle, there was a note on his door asking him to call his brother. He glanced at his watch: 1:15 a.m.

✤   ✤   ✤

August 24, 1970, St. Thomas, 12:00 p.m., GMT–4

Stephen answered the telephone in Cyril's study on the first ring. "Hell's going on down there, Stephen?"

"I wish I knew, Jim. All I know is three Virgin Island senators and a Senate lawyer, all members of our board, are dead. We can determine no reason. Cyril is as confused as I am in trying to understand a motive. There is nothing in the Senate, no bill or anything that is controversial. The Senate deals with Virgin Island problems, not war veterans. There is no reason for veterans, doped up or otherwise, to kill senators. If this were some sort of coup attempt, it would take more than three senators from Cyril's chicken party. One other thing, I can't locate Brookings. He is not at home or at any of his other haunts. Did he mention anything to you about any plans?"

"Nothing I recall. I do know he was meeting someone in Jamaica about getting some deposits from a rum maker. I think that meeting is scheduled for next week. Mrs. Alasdair understood Brookings was killed also. That is not true, correct?"

"Correct, Jim. Brookings did not play golf. Has it occurred to you what would have happened if you and I had not had other things to do? We'd be dead also. Have you thought maybe the people were actually after you? You are the only controversial person in the group."

"Hell's the matter with you, Stephen? You trying to say I am to blame? I only come to the damn islands every three months. Who the hell would want to kill me? Somewhere else perhaps, but I don't know of any enemies in the islands. I did not pick anyone for the board. Hell, I didn't know any of them. I don't think many people know I have any interest in either the agency or the bank. We never announced my name. There is no billboard saying, 'Nigel James Alasdair put up the money for your insurance business.' Hell, who knew we were having a board meeting? Who the hell knew we would be playing golf at the Buccaneer Club?"

"I know, Jim. No reason for us to blame each other. Perhaps it was just a random shooting by a bunch of crazed vets, like the police say. You get down here tomorrow and help me sort this out. God, have we got family problems to deal with. You know what us black folks do when it gets hot. All you have to do is come to my house at dinner to see ten of the results. Cyril had a damn fit when he saw my load arrive. I put the kids at a hotel with my wife and three policemen. I think Cyril's old lady would have had a stroke if my brood moved in. Those four board members have fifteen, maybe twenty children. No way to estimate how many grandchildren, brothers, sisters, uncles, aunties, cousins, in-laws, or whatever. I need help."

"You better see Tilly. He's the man who deals with funerals and mourners. I don't do that. I am on an American flight tomorrow morning, 9:00 a.m., Tennessee time. It has a long stop in Miami. I'll call you from there with arrival time and to get any new information you may have by then. Keep cool and be careful until we get an idea of what is going on."

Stephen O'Rielly and Cyril King talked until the early hours about the past and their now-perilous present and future. Cyril would be governor of the islands now if the democrats had stuck with him, as they should have. Jealousy, envy, and pure pig-headedness let the republicans take over. It always brought a chuckle to the two of them to observe the expression on Alasdair's face when people greeted King on the street, especially women. Cyril King was a tall, thin man with a striking appearance. On the street he was regal. His handsome black face with the snow-white hair seemed to give women the shivers. Always they ran to him and always they greeted him the same. "My King, my King!" Alasdair said it made him sick.

Disgusted with the democrats, King's supporters organized a new party to nominate and elect him governor in the next election. The new party needed a symbol. The republicans had an elephant and the democrats a donkey. The new party chose a chicken. Cyril King planned to beat the hell out of them both with a chicken. The U. S. papers said it was voodoo. King thought it great fun.

❦   ❦   ❦

August 25, 1970, St. Thomas, 1:23 a.m., GMT–4

Orlando Rondino left Camden, New Jersey, five years ago for a two-week vacation in the Caribbean tropical paradise of St. Thomas. His friends and the travel agent assured him that two weeks in the Virgin Islands was the answer to his depression and anger. Orlando did not want to end his depression and anger. He wanted to kill the "grease ball." Orlando's friends were afraid he would do exactly that, and intended to prevent it if at all possible. The first step was to get him out of Camden, and during his absence, reason with the grease ball.

Joey Bonito, the dispatcher at Orlando's City Cab Company, and Pete Seevers, Orlando's banker, were responsible for convincing him to take the vacation. They loaded his 300-plus pounds onto the American Airlines flight to St. Thomas never suspecting it would be their last sight of Orlando. They assured him he would be a new man when he returned in two weeks.

Joey and Pete drove directly to the cheap little weekly-rental shack-up motel to talk with Eula and the grease ball. Joey and Pete pleaded with Eula to explain to them what the hell she was doing. They reasoned with the grease ball, or tried to reason with him, about the risk he took by moving Eula in to live with him. Orlando, married to Eula for fourteen years, was "connected." Didn't the grease ball know that? Didn't he realize Orlando could have him floating face down in the Delaware River? He did not. It was his considered opinion that everyone in New Jersey claimed they were "connected" but none was, certainly not a fat-ass taxi operator in Camden. He liked Eula and she liked him and that was that.

Driving back to the City Cab Company garage, Joey realized nothing could be gained by further reasoning with the pair, although he supposed a futile effort better than no effort. The grease ball was enamored of the 160-pound voluptuous Eula and she was enamored of his extra large schlong. It was a situation made in hell. The grease ball erred in thinking Orlando Rondino was not "connected."

Orlando did not return in two weeks, or at the end of three weeks. Joey then received a telegram: "If you want the taxi company get with Pete and work out the details Stop Send me as much cash as you and Pete can work out and you can owe me the rest Stop This place is heaven and I ain't coming back Stop The bank has a branch here so Pete can send the money to me there Stop Orlando."

Orlando now owned Paradise Taxi Company operating on both islands, St. Thomas and St. Croix. Paradise Taxi provided land and water taxis, and one airplane for rent to fly to any of the near islands. During the five years, he lost one hundred pounds and found himself a young enchilada. They lived in a little house on Bogeyman Court. Orlando actively supported the Chamber of Commerce and other civic activities promoting the islands. His connections remained strong and he occasionally was called on for information or assistance with some minor inconvenience. Once, Orlando was asked to work out a particularly unpleasant inconvenience in Puerto Rico. The package Orlando recovered and sent by private messenger to Newark, N.J., contained a few thousand dollars in excess of five hundred thousand. He added a short note that said simply, "You owe me one." One month later, the grease ball was found floating face down in Delaware Bay near his capsized fishing boat. It was considered another tragic accident that sometimes occurs when fishermen refuse to use safety equipment. The grease ball was an inexperienced fisherman and should not have been out alone without wearing a life jacket.

It was 1:23 a.m. when Orlando's phone rang and Lou said hello.

"Yeah, what is it?"

"Orlando, it's me, Lou. I am sorry to wake you but Thad asked me to call."

"OK, Lou. Don't you and Thad ever go to bed? It's two o'clock in the morning here. Very well, what is Thad's problem? It must be bad or you wouldn't be calling me at this ungodly hour?"

"Our problem will not be a problem for you, Orlando. Thad just needs a little help. Franco Casale is on his way to St. Croix and is bringing some piece of shit brother-in-law. They will arrive in the late morning, we think. When I know for sure, I'll call you so you can meet them. We need for you to get two rooms in some dumpy, out-of-the-way motel. Beyond that, stay away from them. He really screwed up and Thad is some kind of upset. Stay away from Franco after you get him a room. Orlando, don't get involved with Franco. If he asks or begs for help, stay away from him. He has to solve his own problem and correct his own mistakes. It should only take him a day or so, then he has to go to San Juan. All clear?"

"Goodbye, Lou."

Orlando folded his arms behind his head and lay back on the pillow, his eyes open but seeing nothing. He did not know Casale but he knew Casale could never repair any breach created with Thad. Thad always was an unforgiving bastard. He hoped Casale could make it to San Juan. If he did, he might have a chance to survive.

❧   ❧   ❧

August 25, 1970, Frederiksted, St. Croix, 12:30 a.m., GMT-4

After Hector Whitestar completed his conversation with Cosgrove, he stood with his hand resting on the telephone for a long time as he contemplated the dirty wallpaper of the tiny bar on the outskirts of Frederiksted. He had a bad feeling about Cosgrove. The man seemed almost drunk or high on his own dope. Cosgrove was a pusher but did not appear to Whitestar to be a user. However, something didn't feel right. He began to worry about getting the balance of the money due him and his men. Perhaps he needed to go to San Juan to get the money tonight. It was not smart to be separated from his money by so much water. But leaving St. Croix anytime in the near future was impossible without creating suspicion. Hector had planned on being confined to St. Croix for at least a month but had not expected problems with the last payment of his fee. Without the freedom to come and go granted those with white skin, the risk of being noticed by customs officials was too great until the search for the shooters cooled off. With a shrug of his shoulders, he walked to the corner table and joined his two friends.

They had disposed of every item of clothing worn at the Buccaneer Hotel by putting it into the garbage bins outside behind the bar. Hector divided the clothing among the four containers, pushing it into the center of the worse of the slops from the kitchen or whatever other mess the bins contained. Now at the table, they ate "old woman's fish," which was whatever fish the "old woman" happened to catch, and drank beer. Hector told his two fellow shooters that Cosgrove would fly over from San Juan with their money tomorrow. After they met with Cosgrove, Hector would take all five of his group to the Cruzan Rum warehouse near Christiansted. Jobs had been arranged. The work was not too hard and the pay reasonable. With jobs and the two cabins for addresses, they would easily disappear into the mass of rum workers and create nothing to cause them to be noticed any more than any other citizen of the islands. Shaving the beards and cutting the long hair would give them the look of ordinary Virgin Islanders.

The old station wagon clanked and rattled but steadily made its way toward Blue Mountain. Inside, the three occupants, well-fed and with a beer buzz, talked only occasionally, preferring to relax and enjoy the ride. As they approached the intersection of the road north to Blue Mountain, Whitestar noticed a convertible turn left out of Blue Mountain road and leisurely disappear in the direction of Christiansted. Well up the mountain where the road forked, Whitestar wheeled the vehicle onto the left fork. "I gonna check on the others. Make sure they OK. Then we go to our cabin."

"Hey look at dat," said the passenger in the front seat with Whitestar. "Something burning up there."

Whitestar slowed the vehicle and carefully approached the smoldering mass on the left. "Hey, mon, that used to be a car, a station wagon I think. Hell, mon, that our other station wagon."

Whitestar slammed on the brakes and everyone leaped out almost before the wagon stopped. They dashed to the smoking wreckage. "Look at it, damn thing blew up, by God. What a mess. There's one person over by that tree and it look like a woman.

They's two more in de car and I think one of them is another woman. What de hell is gone on here? I know that our car, Whitestar. We better get up to de cabin right now."

Nodding agreement, Whitestar leaped into the vehicle and they sped toward the cabin less than half a mile ahead. Whitestar whipped the old wagon into the cabin yard a few moments later. "Oh shit, mon. Look at that, the damn cabin, it blew up too. I'm going inside." Whitestar and the other two men raced into the remains of the cabin and found Ramon dead on the floor near the door. The other man and a woman were partially covered with debris from the back wall and roof. Both were dead.

"What de hell happen here, Whitestar? Where these womans come from? We not s'posed to have no womans. How this happen?"

"Hell mon, we got here at the same time. How I know any more than you do? Damn! Look at Ramon's head. It a real mess. Something mustta fell on him. Damn, we better get de hell outta here. If anyone heard all that racket them dumb-ass cops be here soon."

"Come here, Whitestar. Look at Ramon's head. Somebody shot him. Look at that big hole. He done it with a big gun and with a 'sploding cartridge. We better get outta here now. Maybe he ain't done yet. Maybe he still in them damn bushes."

Whitestar and his friends rushed to the other cabin and found it undisturbed. He half filled three glasses with Ole St. Croix dark rum, divided a six-ounce Coca Cola among them, and dropped in a few pieces of ice. Sipping the rum and Coke, Furillo, Estavo, and Whitestar tried to analyze their situation. "Cosgrove hired us to do a job on seven johns that would show up in de bar after a round of golf," Whitestar said. "For this Cosgrove pay us twenty thousand dollars and promised another twenty when de job was done. Cosgrove also arranged two cabins for us to use until de heat's off and jobs to use as cover while waiting to leave. We waited and watched. Only four golfers turned up. I made de decision to take them out and we did. When Cosgrove learned we only got four he was pissed but agreed to bring de other twenty to St. Croix. Now think about dis. On the same day we took out de golfers, someone who knew about the cabins took out half of us and a bunch of whores. By going to Frederiksted to call Cosgrove we done missed being blowed up and burned like de other mons."

Whitestar had to face the fact that someone on the island knew who they were and where they were, and planned to shut them up, either to save the twenty thousand or to get rid of witnesses, or both. They knew Cosgrove was not involved in that plan. He was not smart enough. Hope to ever see the other twenty thousand faded, but knowing that someone on the island had a contract to get rid of them was worse. From what they had seen, he was certainly competent to do the job.

Suddenly Leon Furillo spoke up. "If all that true we better get outta here. He appears to be in a big-ass hurry to get us and may come back tonight. I don't want to be blowed up."

"I don't think so, Leon. He be worrying about the cops up here tonight and maybe we should, too. I think we better go back to Frederiksted for de night. We may have to sleep on de beach but that better than getting blowed up or rousted by the cops."

Taking the other road around Blue Mountain, they arrived back in Frederiksted at 2:30 a.m. They camped on a strip of beautiful white beach.

CHAPTER 3

Tuesday, August 25, 1970, St. Thomas, 7:00 a.m., GMT–4

Maddie Willis was graduated from business school at age nineteen and immediately applied for a job at the William Peace Bank & Trust Company. The bank hired a new officer on the same day. He needed a secretary and Maddie got the job. During the ensuing years she remained with him and moved through the desks behind Brookings St. John until he was in charge of all branch banking, and she was his executive assistant and the number two person in branch banking. When the bank decided to establish a substantial presence in the Caribbean and selected Brookings St. John, it seemed logical she would accompany him and assume the same duties there as in Pennsylvania.

When Brookings moved to the new Island Bank he and Alasdair started with Stephen O'Rielly and Cyril King, he did not bother to ask her. He merely set up an office for her and sent people to collect her and her personal items. She did not question but merely complied.

Now the clock on her desk gave a small chime indicating the passage of an hour. She glanced at it although she knew it to be 8:00 a.m. After all, she had arrived at 7:00 a.m. as she did each morning and had for the past twenty years. The coffee, freshly made, sat untouched on her desk. Brookings was late again, the bastard. He had played golf yesterday and today he had missed their daily coffee. Usually he missed when he visited one of his whores. Maddie, a tall curvy blonde, was arguably the most beautiful woman who ever worked for the Peace Bank and definitely more beautiful than any whore Brookings might find in the islands. But he showed little interest. He had golfed in St. Croix, meaning the whores he visited in Christiansted had once again enticed him into bed. It never took much enticing with Brookings. In a meaningless gesture, Maddie threw his coffee mug into the waste basket beside her desk.

Why, she wondered as she had countless other times, do I put up with this, me the most beautiful employee of the Island Bank? She had realized she loved him at the end of her first week of working for Brookings St. John. Twenty years later, with never so much as a kiss on the cheek from him, she wondered if she now loved or hated him. Her tolerance had begun to collapse years ago and now each time he missed her coffee for some scruffy whore, her anger grew. Soon she would put an end to his ignoring her. She would not be humiliated over and over any longer. Today she would have it out with the bastard.

She spent more and more time now wondering about her strange attachment to Brookings, trying to understand herself and the intensity of her feelings over so long a period. Some people said Brookings was physically ugly and lacked any feature endearing to women. Maddie admitted he did not meet the standards commonly set for male good looks, but to her he was beautiful. It was unbelievable that at age thirty-nine she had settled for a cup of black coffee with Brookings St. John at 7:00 a.m. six days a week as the prime feature of her love life. It was unbelievable but true. It also was unbelievable but true that for all those years Brookings had believed her to be a lesbian. But Maddie was unaware of this second impossibility that was strange reality. Fellow employees at Peace Bank thought her weird if not crazy. The people at Island Bank had known her only a short time but were developing the same feelings. Already they knew not to disturb her when Brookings missed his coffee without a reason acceptable to Maddie. Thus she did not know, and no one told her, about the incident in St. Croix. She resigned herself to doing without her coffee date and isolated herself in her office to catch up on work. She found it hard to concentrate.

At 10:34 a.m., her private line rang. Aggravated at being disturbed, she snatched it up and barked "Hello!" into the receiver. There was a pause before the caller spoke. "Maddie! This is Roy Devoe. I know you are upset but I only just heard about the shooting at the golf course in St. Croix."

An ice-cold shaft of fear stabbed Maddie, causing an audible gasp. "What shooting? When? What are you talking about, Roy?"

"You don't know, Maddie? How could you not know? Someone shot your board of directors, at least four of them, at the golf course yesterday. You told me a few days ago about the meeting and the golf afterwards. What about Brookings? Was the bastard hurt? He was not among the dead."

Gasping and sobbing, fighting off panic, Maddie broke the connection by throwing the receiver to the floor. What did the people out on the banking floor think of her? None of them had shown enough concern or common courtesy to tell her. No one gave a damn about her or Brookings. Shouldn't the bank be closed? No, banking regulations included nothing to cover the murder of directors. If Brookings were alive why hadn't he called her? Maybe he was not in a whorehouse, maybe he was in a hospital near death. "That's it. He's hurt. He needs me."

Maddie quickly repaired her face in her private powder room and changed into jeans, heavy walking boots, and a Sapphire Beach golf shirt. She put on sunglasses to shield her reddened eyes and dashed outside without a word to anyone. She leaped into her BMW and headed to the Paradise Water Taxi. On board the taxi, she noticed the owner, Orlando Rondino, sitting near the front. He was a good customer of the bank and a friend of Brookings. She took the rearmost seat. She wanted to speak with no one. In an obvious effort to get acquainted, the middle aged man with gray hair seated next to her asked the time. She glanced at the Rolex on her wrist and announced the time to be 10: 47 a.m. She ignored the man otherwise.

❧   ❧   ❧

August 25, 1970, Christiansted, St. Croix 8:00 a.m., GMT–4

Walther began his morning ritual later than usual because of getting to bed late the night before. First, he did thirty minutes of push-ups, sit-ups, and weights before plodding off to the beach for thirty minutes of slow jogging. For weights, he used two stainless steel dining room chairs. After completing his routine, he showered, washed and conditioned his lustrous red hair, and trimmed his beard and mustache. He called to order a breakfast of tropical fruit, four eggs scrambled hard, and two six-ounce patties of ground beef cooked well with fat removed. His breakfast was waiting when he arrived at the dining room. Walther ate no bread but drank tea with milk. He preferred it to be half tea and half milk. He nodded to the waitress, smiled, and decided he would take his time about responding to the message left on his door the night before.

Walther drove the red convertible back to the Island Rentals office and surrendered it in good order to yet another smiling blonde. How can there be so many beautiful blonde women on islands inhabited primarily by black people? Walther did not know the answer, but that did not bother him. He smiled his thanks for her thanks and lumbered outside. The pay phone beside the rental building caught his attention. It was convenient. Why not make his call there? Walther placed the call, leaned against the building and waited, enjoying the view of the harbor.

"This is Thad."

"This is Walther."

"Yes, Walther. I wanted to speak with you. I hoped you would call last evening. My calls are rather urgent."

"I was out very late last night and only got your call this morning. But here I am."

"Yes, indeed you are. The six packages I requested you pick up for me, they are not ready and will not be for another day or so. Please wait until you hear from me again before going to pick them up."

"Well, I'll do that except I already picked up three of them and sent them on their way. I didn't know they were incomplete. That is why I was out late last night. I went by to pick up the other three but they were not where you said they would be. I planned to go back this evening to get those three."

"You mean you already sent three of them home, Walther?"

"That is what I mean. And there were three other packages with them. Since I had no instructions and no one to advise me, I sent them on home with the first three. You are getting six packages and three of them will be a surprise if you didn't know about them. They appeared to be designed for women. Did you expect any women-type packages?"

"No, certainly not. I must say you are very efficient to have handled this in so timely a manner. Wait to pick up the others. The first shipment was short three containers and I have sent someone down to collect those three containers. I suggest you look him up, if possible, and check on the progress he is making. He will be in about noon today, and I forget his name, but he will probably be the only person on the island wearing a black silk suit. Once he and his friends locate and deliver the three containers, you need to bundle all of them together and send them home. Try to not send any more packages that are not specifically addressed with delivery instructions."

"I understand. Sometimes I am impulsive and make decisions that seem necessary or desirable at the moment. If those are containers you did not request, I will stand the expense involved with my error. But I want to be clear on the containers your man is coming here to locate. I am to only wait until he has delivered them, then collect my other packages and bundle them and his and send them all home in one container, as it were."

"That is true, and any additional shipping charges will be paid by my company directly upon receipt of your invoice."

"Thank you. I planned to be out of here by tomorrow. Do you think I will be able to go by the end or the week? I have another problem requiring my attention rather urgently."

"If it is not straightened out by the end of the week I will turn the entire matter over to you. I have been paid for the parts and need the shipment to be made ASAP. Good morning, Mr. Walther."

Walther watched a seaplane land and taxi up the ramp and disgorge its three passengers, none in a black silk suit. He gave a moment's thought to riding one of those ruptured ducks, but not much thought. He wanted to get off the island, out of the islands. They were too small and confining. He came from a big country where a man could feel free, be free. He also liked big airplanes, lots of room, lots of engines. He didn't like "cleaners." Thad was sending in a cleaner to clean up the mess made by the shooters at the Buccaneer. The Latino dope heads had messed up the deal. They were supposed to get seven and only hit four. Thad had been paid, the dope heads had been paid, and now Thad was having to spring for a cleaner before the client got too hot. Thad had made a mistake using amateurs to save money. Now he was sending in a cleaner, really the guy who hired the amateurs, again to save money. Another mistake. After he got the other three, Thad wanted to add the cleaner to the "packages" Walther was to "send home." Thad was trying to save too many fees and Walther did not like that. Thad would never have made such a mess a few years ago. But Walther decided that when the cleaner cleaned up the mess, he, Walther, would take care of the cleaner for Thad, for old times. Clean the cleaner. Walther liked that.

Having suddenly received a free day and maybe two, the redhead had no plans for the unexpected time off. His life always had a plan, a schedule, and a goal to accomplish by a specific time. As much as two days with nothing to do would require some time and thought to work out. Slowly but determinedly, he walked past where the sea-plane sat draining and dripping water. A hundred yards ahead, directly in front of the water taxi stand, several benches overlooked the pier used by the taxis. The benches would be a satisfactory place to sit and work out a plan for the next two days. Once he formulated the plan, relaxation would follow and life would return to normal. For thirty minutes Walther remained motionless, seated on a bench, looking far out to sea, seeing very little. Slowly, plans for the following days materialized, allowing his mind and body to relax. The plans were simple but necessary for Walther's well-being and peace of mind. With them he once again was relaxed and ready for what might come as he waited for further directions.

"Oh, I'm sorry, sir. I thought you were asleep and wanted to tell you the water taxi is arriving." It was an employee of the Paradise Taxi Company.

"Thank you. I appreciate your concern and interest. I may have been asleep. The view is so beautiful and the water so relaxing. Thank you, indeed, but I am not taking the taxi."

He glanced at the water taxi gliding into the slip and suddenly noticed a shock of blonde hair. He stood and stared. Another beautiful blonde. Why did this island have so many beautiful blondes? A closer look revealed this one to be perhaps the most beautiful he had seen. She appeared irritated. Why would anyone so beautiful be irritated? It did not seem possible to Walther that anyone with her assets could ever be upset. She was first off the taxi. The middle-aged man with the gray hair nearly fell while trying to debark as near to her as possible. The other passengers showed only slightly more than passing interest, obviously intent on doing whatever they were here to do.

Maddie noticed the redhead. Her dark green eyes connected with his pale blue ones briefly, fleetingly, but long enough for both to be startled. Maddie recognized the redhead's stare as the pure enjoyment of looking at something of exquisite beauty. His stare had no sexual overtones, no hint of desire, only enjoyment of beauty. He stared as he would stare at a huge bougainvillea in full and magnificent bloom. It made her feel good despite her anger-tinged fear for the health and whereabouts of Brookings St. John, made her feel clean, not dirty as so many men made her feel with their leers. She flashed him a wide, white-toothed smile as she passed. Walther appreciated that.

❦   ❦   ❦

August 25, 1970, JFK Airport, NYC, NY, 1:28 a.m., GMT–5

In its effort to look after the poor and unfortunate, New York managed to develop a welfare program allowing recipients to live elsewhere and collect benefits in New York. This program became so popular that some airlines ran "welfare flights" to Puerto Rico during the first week of each month. Flights generally left New York or Newark airports at 1:00 or 1:30 a.m., to arrive in San Juan five hours later. The flights were cheap, no frills, with tight seating; no food or drink, no first class, no business class, just common no class. Franco Casale found that unsatisfactory but he had no choice. Wedged firmly between body odor on the left and garlic breath on the right, Casale prayed to the Virgin Mother for sleep. Sleep did not come in the midst of continuous loud talking in a foreign language that enveloped the entire cabin. He vowed on his solemn oath to kill Cosgrove the minute he saw him in San Juan. Allowing Cosgrove to participate in any project larger than selling dope on a street corner in Miami speedily developed into a monumental disaster. The breach with Thad seriously threatened Franco's future with the outfit, maybe his future itself. Why did his wife have an idiot for a brother?

In the lobby waiting area of the airport at San Juan, Franco located an air-conditioning vent and stood directly under it, hoping it could blow his rumpled suit clean of body odor and garlic. Breathing in the cool clean air gave him time to look about the lobby. The architectural design, if any, could be described as early functional. The waiting area rapidly filled with people anxious for the early morning flight to Miami. The TV screen indicated the flight would begin loading in thirty minutes. Feeling cleaner, he headed through the waiting area to the luggage pickup island. He had brought only a small bag with a few essentials, including a 9 mm pistol on a Colt .45 frame and a box of fifty Winchester Super X cartridges. He didn't trust the Spic baggage handlers not to rifle his bag but had not wanted to bring it on board as carry-on luggage. Sometimes carry-on bags were searched randomly for dope, usually on flights from San Juan. Franco did not want to run the risk.

A small commotion set off a round of laughter which attracted Franco's attention. A sleeping passenger had slipped out of a plastic chair onto the tile floor and, with difficulty, was struggling to rise. Franco stood for a moment in stunned silence. This scarcely could be believed. It was Cosgrove, his brother-in-law. "Why is he here?" He asked the question of himself but did not want to accept the answer he knew to be true. "The son of a bitch is going back to Miami without paying the final payment to the Latinos. He plans to steal the other half or the money. The dumb fuck doesn't know what will happen to him. He can't hide in Miami."

Quickly he walked over to Cosgrove and lifted him to his feet. "Stand still you dumb son of a bitch. What are you doing here? Damn! I believe you are drunk. If you have a bag, get it. You are going with me."

"Going where? How did you get here, Franco? Why are you here?"

"I am here because of you and my stupidity in dealing with you. Now let's go. We are going to St. Croix."

Cosgrove carried the small bag he had stowed under the plastic chair and followed Casale to the baggage area where they retrieved Casale's bag. Leading and dragging Cosgrove into the airport café, Casale sat him down and ordered coffee. "We are gonna eat some breakfast and you are gonna talk to me. I want to know what the hell is going on with you. Are you sober enough to talk to me? You dumb bastard, why are you drunk at six o'clock in the morning?"

"I am not drunk, Franco. I have been asleep. I'm going back to Miami because there is nothing more for me to do here. The thing in St. Croix is not my problem. You told us seven people would show up, but only four turned up and my boys took care of them. What did you expect us to do? There were no other people, just four. We didn't know any names, so what could we do? As for the Latinos, they will never get off the island, and besides, they only did half the job so they only get half the money. You and I can split the other half."

"You are stupid beyond belief, Cosgrove. I am not touching any of that money and neither are you. This deal is so messed up we may never get out of it. We are going to St. Croix to work it out and we better do it quick. Unless we finish the job we are finished and there is no place for us to hide. So sober up your ass and get ready to work."

"I am not going to St. Croix, I am going to Miami. You take the money and pay off the Latinos if you must. To me it is a waste of money rightly due us, especially due me. I did what I was asked to do while the Latinos only did half of their work, so they are only entitled to half the money."

Casale stared at Cosgrove in amazement and disbelief. Did he actually believe that because his shooters, through no fault of their own, only completed half the job they forfeited half their pay? Cosgrove bordered on being an idiot. If he kept the money, either the Latinos would kill him or the outfit who furnished the money would make Casale take him out. "Why," he wondered again, "was I stupid enough to rely on Cosgrove?"

Riding to the seaport in an old taxi without air-conditioning through streets piled high with rotting and stinking garbage, proved to be a hot and miserable experience. Another of the seemingly continuous garbage workers' strikes virtually brought San Juan to its knees. Rubbish of every conceivable type kept people indoors and, in many places, crowded automobile traffic out of the streets. This particular strike spared Old San Juan and the driver made as much of his journey as possible through there. Casale, correct in thinking the trek through the old city unnecessary except for the garbage, grumbled about the route while remaining at the driver's mercy. During the long, hot, smelly ride he attempted to explain to Cosgrove the purpose of going to St. Croix. "We will go to the mountain where the Latinos are staying and pay them half of the remaining half of the money and promise the balance after the other three people are taken out. High profile people such as these are no problem to locate. O'Reilly is experienced in island funerals. He will be in charge and visible at police headquarters, the hospital, and the funeral parlor. Alasdair and St. John are certain to be at his side. A close watch on the funeral parlor is apt to provide an opportunity if it is not located in a too-congested area. The details will fall into place."

Their flight in the Grumman Goose, 1930s edition, was smooth and uneventful. Cosgrove slept. As he crawled out of the plane upon landing and stepped down onto the concrete, Casale noticed the retreating form of a broad-shouldered, red-haired man walking slowly down a street. He wondered if that could be the weirdo who witnessed the shooting at the Buccaneer Club. His watch indicated a few minutes past 1:00 p.m. St. Croix time.

※   ※   ※

August 25, 1970, Miami, 12:22 p.m., GMT–5

Nigel James Alasdair slouched behind a desk at the Admiral's Club in the Miami airport, drumming his fingers on the walnut top. The newly lighted Baccarat Luchadore cigar pointed skyward as he clenched his teeth and regretted the two-hour wait for a flight to St. Thomas. His conversation with O'Reilly had produced little new information other than the complete disappearance of St. John. The bank had reported his failure to turn up for his morning meeting with Miss Willis, which resulted in a general trashing of his office coffee equipment and a few other personal items. No bank property was damaged. "For God's sake," Alasdair mumbled to himself, "who gives a damn about bank property." Also, the bank reported Miss Willis had left at ten o'clock without speaking to another employee. Their impression that she was angry was borne out by the screeching of tires and the roar of engine as the BMW left the parking lot. Stephen O'Reilly had expressed little doubt that Maddie was aware of the incident in St. Croix. An employee reported hearing her private telephone ring shortly before she stormed out, leaving the receiver on the floor where she tossed it into the midst of her broken coffee pot and cups. Employees also reported a trail of sugar packets leading to her powder room and directly to the commode, where several remained floating. "One pissed off woman," Alasdair said to the cigar.

The phone call, it seemed clear to Alasdair and O'Reilly, notified her of the shooting of the directors and the absence of St. John. There could be no doubt she went to St. Croix. Either she knew where to find St. John or she panicked because she did not know, and at this moment was checking the hospital. She knew his schedule and assumed that, if he could not be found, he had suffered injuries and would be at the hospital. That meant she did not know he had skipped the golf. "Hell's the matter with the people at the bank. Why didn't someone stop the blonde bitch and talk to her? They know her weird fixation on that ugly bastard, St. John. Hell's the matter with him? Got the most beautiful woman in the Caribbean tagging after him like a Cocker Spaniel pup and he pisses off to some damn whorehouse. Good banker but an idiot otherwise."

The possibility existed that St. John had taken a flight to Jamaica, although Alasdair thought that doubtful. Possibly, St. John completed whatever he needed to do and returned to the Buccaneer in time to have a drink with the golfers. If so and he is not among the dead, has he been kidnapped? Is that likely? Alasdair did not think so. Kidnapping on an island the size of St. Croix made no sense. Cops could sweep the island in a couple of days and find any hiding place. No, it was unlikely that St. John languished in some dark cellar, the victim of kidnapping. More likely he lay unconscious in a hospital bed unidentified, or having heard of the shootings, secluded himself in one of his favorite whorehouses until contact with O'Rielly or Alasdair could be made.

Alasdair used the telephone on the desk to place a call to his office in Nashville. The front-desk woman with the orange hair glared at him over the pink lenses of glasses perched near the tip of her generous nose. Obviously she felt it her exclusive right to make all calls for the patrons of the club. She found it inconceivable that a patron would dial his own calls, a usurpation of her authority and responsibility and another step toward her eventual replacement by some plastic-enshrouded mechanical or electronic device. In Nashville, the lovely Jean Saturday answered the telephone, caressing Alasdair's ear with her cheerful, lilting voice that transmitted her smile to the caller. Jean served exactly the purpose Alasdair wanted and projected the image he needed at the Nashville office. She was friendly and helpful, but wonderfully ignorant. He pictured her in his mind. She would be seated primly in her chair, long sensual legs crossed with lots of thigh showing from the pulled-up mini skirt, smiling at her newly painted nails which she held to the right side so her view was not blocked by the rather large unencumbered breasts seeking escape from a slightly too small sweater. She brought three assets to Empire Industries, extreme good looks, a beautiful voice, and complete loyalty. Her lack of knowledge of anything remotely important was monumental and perfect. Alasdair knew her innermost thoughts and her one and only desire. She often summed it up in the form of a question, "Are we gonna get naked and get in a pile?" Alasdair usually replied, "Not before lunch, Jeannie." She never took it as a rebuff, merely a postponement. She asked the same question this time and Alasdair provided the same reply. Then he asked for Sue. Equally pretty, equally friendly, but eminently more intelligent, Sue handled Alasdair's personal contacts, money, schedule, and nearly all else.

Sue quickly explained how she had cleared his schedule for the next ten days and made necessary arrangements for someone to represent him, if absolutely required, to complete two of his urgent projects. Everything, she assured him, ticked along quite nicely in Nashville in his absence. She was there and in charge and Jean was handling all the calls and visitors in her own way, leaving them completely happy and thrilled by their visit to the corporate offices of Empire Industries. Alasdair was pleased. He knew that it often took the normal visitor anywhere from thirty to forty-five minutes after leaving to realize that he had accomplished exactly nothing during his meeting. Jean had so mesmerized him he had forgotten the purpose of the meeting which, so far as he could remember, might never have occurred. Alasdair smiled. Sue understood Jean and Jean understood nothing.

The corporate office in Nashville served as a private office for Alasdair's convenience. Its staff consisted of five financial officers, each with a private secretary, along with Jean, Sue, and Alasdair himself. Individual companies making up the corporate Empire Industries were located throughout the United States and Europe. The

Virgin Islands venture was a private Alasdair deal with no connection to the main company. It was mostly a toy, a toy presently occupying too much of his time.

"One other item I must tell you about," Sue said. "Mr. Carlotta called from the construction company in Atlanta. You recall his main office was broken into two or three months ago and a few items were taken, mostly just office junk and a TV. This morning one of the accountants working for Mr. Washburn called Mr. Carlotta and asked him for some information on the Belize airport contract and the Belize cannery contract. Both files are missing and Mr. Carlotta thinks they were taken in the burglary and that they were the real targets of the burglars. No one ever looks in those files because everyone has a copy of their own. Mr. Carlotta would not have looked either except he was in the file room when he took the call."

"Hell's going on, Sue? Latino dope heads kill my friends, my office is broken into. What's next? Who would want those files? Reporters have given up on a story there. The court dropped the lawsuit brought by that bastard in Knoxville. Why the hell didn't he keep his ass in Pennsylvania? Everyone in Belize is happy and everyone in Tennessee would be if he moved back to Pennsylvania. Just because he played football at U-fucking-T, second string it was. The water boy had more playing time than he did. I am clean as a hound's tooth on those projects. What makes Carlotta think the two files and the burglary are connected?"

"I don't know, Mr. Alasdair. He seems to feel that way, so perhaps you need to speak with him. I will connect if you want."

"No, I think not. It's one o'clock here. My plane will leave shortly and I have other things to think about."

♦   ♦   ♦

August 25, 1970, Central Belize, 10:00 a.m., GMT–6

Esquiverl lifted his right arm and motioned for his men to be silent and to move closer. Together they looked over the scene below. At least two dozen men, half of them with chain saws, worked steadily, cutting trees, shrubs, bushes, everything. Five huge bulldozers uprooted the stumps and shoved them into piles. Two big forklifts topped off the piles with the smaller trees that once stood on the stumps. The piles of wood being burned dotted a vast expanse of land. Esquiverl cared nothing for the gigantic chunk taken out of the virgin forest. He did notice that any tree which could produce a good log escaped the fire. The limbs and branches were removed and the log cut and loaded onto one of the big carriers. Then the limbs and branches were added to the piles. He and the fifteen men with him studied the scene and wished for guns. While machetes were highly efficient for close work, it was going to be difficult to get close to the workers below unobserved.

Esquiverl decided to move his group through the trees to the area where the men were working and to simply get as near as possible before attacking. He still wished for a few rifles although he knew the workers had no weapons. Coming in from Mexico as he did allowed him no opportunity to bring firearms. The border guards strictly enforced the anti-gun law in effect in Belize. The workers, subject to the same restrictions, had no guns but did have axes and chain saws. A chain saw could be a formidable weapon against a machete. Esquiverl held no false hope of the workers being without machetes, although he had observed none. For his fifteen men to be successful against the twenty-four workers, surprise had to be with him.

Reaching the last trees nearest the men, Esquiverl huddled his team to discuss strategy. "We must stay unseen until the last moment. Then we must all charge and get at least one man each with our first swing of the blade. Whether they are dead or not, we must attack the others before they have time to get organized to resist. After the second rush, we can go back and finish off the wounded. We must get them all to give us time to get out of Belize before they are discovered. Now get ready to charge when I give the command." Moments later all work stopped and the workers walked over to water kegs and took out cigarettes. Esquiverl rejoiced. He had not expected a work break to cause the workers to leave their chain saws and axes behind. He did not notice the figure seated in one of the huge tractors.

Earl Fontana, from Bovill, Idaho, had almost graduated from the University of Idaho when he decided to enlist in the U.S. Army. He readily volunteered for combat duty in Vietnam. He thought it was for one year. Instead, after considerable combat, which he didn't seem to mind, he suffered for two brutal years in a Vietcong prison camp. The interviews with psychiatrists indicated a mind unsteadied by combat and POW experiences. The report said Fontana might become a danger to friend and foe alike, prone to attack whatever he perceived, rightly or wrongly, as an enemy. Back in Bovill, he had a very difficult time adjusting to normal life.

Emmett Dashell, in a telephone conversation with Alasdair, a long-time friend, wondered whether Alasdair needed a guard for either of his projects in Belize. A young son of a logging foreman near Bovill, Idaho, seemed unable to shake off the POW experience he had suffered in Vietnam and needed a change. "Jim, he is one mean son of a bitch," was Dashell's recommendation. "Maybe he is all there but needs to be in a hot, steamy jungle instead of Idaho forests." Alasdair sent a ticket to Bovill and now Fontana sat in the cab of the tractor used to move the log carriers. Fontana kept to himself and brooded over whatever bothered him day and night. Though not disliked, he was not a camp favorite. He had no close buddy, no confidant, no friend or enemy. He was a fixture, a piece of equipment, and as such, required no special feeling or concern. The mostly brown and black workers did not evoke any reminders of the Vietnamese. Fontana did no manual labor unless an emergency arose requiring one more man's strength. He sat in the tractor listening to country music tapes and watching for intruders. None ever appeared and none was expected. The project entailed the clearing of fifteen hundred acres to be planted in beans for the cannery being built nearby. "Who," Fontana often asked himself, "gives a shit about beans?"

Fontana noticed the men taking a break and felt the need to empty his bladder. He slid out of the huge tractor and stood facing the cleared area with his back to the tractor. He did not see Esquiverl and his fifteen men rush out of the trees and attack the workers.

Esquiverl's first slash decapitated the foreman of the work crew. The workers stared in horror at the gush of bright blood spouting eighteen inches into the air from the foreman's still-standing body. It was their last view before the military fatigue-clad Mexicans were upon them. The sounds of yelling Mexicans, screaming Belize workers, and disturbed and frightened birds filled the mid-morning air. The first onslaught of Mexicans left twenty of the workers either dead or disabled. Esquiverl and his Mexicans turned on the last four, viciously hacking and slicing them to a bloody mess.

Fontana was zipping up his fly when he heard the first screams. He wheeled about and dashed to the front of the tractor in time to see the last four men chopped to pieces. It was not a new scene to him. Dark-skinned men in dirty uniforms covered with blood transported him back to the jungles of Vietnam. Opening the tractor door quickly, he grabbed the AR 180 with a thirty-round clip in place and snapped off the safety. Snatching up another clip and shoving it into his pocket, he raced around the front of the tractor in time to see the Mexicans bunched up among the fallen workers, killing any who still lived. With a yell of his own, Fontana became the killing machine he was trained to be. With well-aimed bursts, he put at least one .223 caliber round into each of the sixteen surprised Mexicans. Fontana shoved a new clip into place as he moved closer. He methodically gut shot each man again. Despite wounds in his stomach and chest, Esquiverl clumsily charged Fontana, waving his machete. Fontana yelled, "Fucking Vietcong bastard," and shot him in the face. With ten rounds remaining in the second clip, Fontana waded through the carnage and again gut shot dying Mexicans. He knew the slow and painful death from a bullet in the guts and wanted these "Cong bastards," to experience it for themselves. Two of the raiders staggered to their feet. Fontana, out of ammunition, picked up a bloody machete and slashed their throats. "Bastards won't attack me again, I'll betcha." Back in the tractor, Fontana stuck a Dolly Parton cassette into the player and listened with closed eyes. When the tape stopped he looked at the clock as it blinked 11:00 a.m. "Bloody mess out there but I need to stand guard until relieved." He searched for another clip of ammo and reloaded the AR 180. At the time he hired on he had explained that a guard needed a gun and ammo or no guard was needed. He was glad the big boss agreed with him. He jerked out the Parton cassette, flipped it over, and stuck it back into the player. A feeling of peace swept over him as she sang of her coat of many colors.

Fontana awoke at 1:30 p.m., and realized he was no longer in the Vietnamese jungles and rice fields, but somewhere in Central America. Nonetheless, there were a lot of bodies strewn about in the field before him and he wondered how that had happened. Memory came back slowly, and suddenly he knew what had happened. "I better radio for some help in case there are more in the woods," he said to himself. The radio worked and he requested help.

"What's the problem?" It was the drawling South Georgia clerk at the cannery construction site.

"I had to shoot a bunch of Mexican bastards and I think I need help. Everybody is dead but me."

There was only silence from the construction office and Fontana clicked off the radio. Almost an hour passed before he heard the helicopters.

❧   ❧   ❧

August 25, 1970, London, 6:00 p.m., GMT+2

Don Keaton leaned back in his leather chair, clasped his hands behind his head and smiled at Deana Dobbins, his long-time assistant, as she tidied up his desk. "Another one wound up today. Alasdair strikes again. A battery factory in Kenya to make eighteen million size C and eighteen million sizes A and AA alkaline batteries annually is exactly what the Dark Continent needs. Kenya wanted it, Alasdair wanted it, and we, you and I, did it. We deserve a bottle of good champagne. Come on, we'll go downstairs and get a bottle."

The London office of Empire Industries was on the second floor of a five-story building at 121 Mount Street, above an Italian Tratatoria which was, itself, above a great and popular pub in the basement. In the five years Keaton frequented the pub he never noticed its name. Keaton had worked for a small construction company in Africa. He was a structural engineer. There he met Alasdair in 1966. Remodeling the British Caledonian Airline terminal and passenger check-in area, he invited himself to join for lunch what seemed to be the only other American in the Jomo Kenyatta airport restaurant. He felt the need to talk with a kindred soul. An hour later Keaton realized he had spilled his entire life story to a total stranger who, in return, barely gave him his name.

Keaton completed the work for British Caledonian two weeks later, wondering where and what his next job would be. He knew the company had submitted a tender to remodel the BCAL terminal facility in Lusaka, Zambia, but did not know whether the offer was successful. His wife and kids hoped to return to the U.S., especially his wife, who wanted better schools than the one furnished for foreign children. Zambia looked good to Keaton. The president, Kenneth Kaunda, who took over after independence in 1964, showed every intention of doing all he could to improve life for Zambians. Unlike the selfishness of many others in his position, he seemed determined to improve the country rather than line his pockets with the people's assets. A telex from the president of his company, who was also the owner, settled his uncertainties about Zambia, but created a new set. The telex, terse and to the point, changed Keaton's life in three short lines.

"I have sold the company to Empire Industries a US corporation interested in establishing a presence in Africa. Please contact Mr. Carlotta in the Atlanta Office of Empire at the number below."

No goodbye, no thanks for a job well done, just call Atlanta. No indication of a continuing job or any indications of termination or rehire, no explanation or introduction to Empire Industries. Just call Atlanta. It turned out well. "It was the lunch," Mr. Carlotta told Keaton. "Alasdair wanted you and bought the company, figuring he could offer you an opportunity which would make it worthwhile for you to stay."

Less than four years later, he headed a construction company head quartered in London with work in Africa, the Middle East, Wales, and England. His biggest project yet was a plant manufacturing and processing rock wool for a gigantic company in Wales, near Bridgend, his favorite place in the world. Nearly every weekend, or any time when they were free, he and his family took the road to Bridgend for fun and relaxation. The kids loved it and so did Ethyl, his wife. Often they invited Deana and her husband to join them. Deana had no children and enjoyed romping with Keaton's four boys, as did her husband, Jeff. What a difference one lunch can make, he often remarked to Ethyl.

Keaton stumbled down the narrow flight of stairs as he tried to keep up with Deana. She bounced ahead of him to the street. Perhaps, she suggested, the Conaught Hotel, only a block and a half from the office, would be an interesting change. He thought not, too stuffy, too quiet and over-priced for him today. His mood was light after closing the huge battery job, too light for stuffy upper crust Brits when he wanted to laugh and drink some of the damn Frenchies' bubbly.

"Look at that," Deana said, pointing to the Rover parked in front of the Tratatoria. "Poor sod is clamped."

Clamping of the front wheels was the British punishment for illegal or overtime parking, and this guy was in for a big ticket. He was not in a parking space. There was no parking on Mount Street. Keaton and Deana Dobbins stopped by the Rover to think of times when one or the other of them had been clamped and the problems it caused. There was a stack of paperwork, a large fine, and a tongue lashing by either a Bobby or a judge. Keaton laughed, put his arm around Deana and guided her toward the steps to the pub one second before the Rover exploded. It was an earsplitting, horrendous explosion and it blew Keaton and Deana through the plate glass window of the Tratatoria and across the dining room, raking customers and tables with them until they slammed against the back wall separating the dining area from the kitchen. So violent was the explosion that windows of the Tandoori Restaurant and most of the other buildings across the street exploded inward, leaving a block of Mount Street in ruins. The cries of the injured began immediately. Many were impaled by shards of glass from huge windows. Falling walls crushed some and others were thrown against walls and columns, leaving them with broken bones. In the pub below the Mount Street Tratatoria, someone said, "Fucking IRA bastards."

❦   ❦   ❦

August 25, 1970, Christiansted, St. Croix, 12:10 p.m., GMT–4

Orlando Rondino spoke briefly with his employees at the water taxi pier before taking the short walk to the seaplane port. The next flight from San Juan arrived thirty-six long minutes later. Rondino did not relish this assignment but he could not refuse Thad. Watching the passengers climb out, he had no problem recognizing his New Jersey guest. A typical goon dressed in a black silk suit, identifying a low-level member of the outfit, wanting everyone to know his importance. The suit told Rondino the wearer had no importance. The rumpled Cosgrove surprised him. Nothing indicated him to be anything other than a half-sober drunk. What possessed Thad to become involved with this pair he could not imagine. At least he had instructions to stay away from them and that he planned to do. He watched until the two of them became as nervous as he thought possible and looked totally out of place and out of options. He walked rapidly toward the pair. "You, you in the silk suit. Are you Franco?"

"Yeah, I'm Franco. Who are you?"

"Look up the street. About two blocks is the Caravelle Hotel. Next door is a coffee shop. Go get you and the drunk a cup of coffee and I will meet you there in about five minutes."

"What the hell's the matter with you?" Franco said. "Nobody talks to me like that, nobody. Now get your ass out of my face. Say, how did you know my name?"

"Thad told me, you ass hole. Now get in that damn coffee shop before I beat the shit out of both of you." Rondino walked back toward the seaplane and gave it a long appraising look until the two goons made it to the coffee shop. He intended to make sure anyone who saw him thought he was answering questions for directions. It shocked Rondino to think Thad had degenerated to working with those two. No way did he want anyone to know he had any connection with them. Their days were numbered. No matter if they completed their job, they were as good as dead. "Get them out of Christiansted and out of sight, and get your ass back to St. Thomas as quickly as possible," Rondino said to himself. Shaking his head, he strode purposefully toward the coffee shop.

"OK, Franco. It is not necessary for us either to like each other or to know each other. Thad asked me to meet you two, and put you in a safe place. I have made those arrangements. Go to the Island Rentals office and rent a car. Take the Blue Mountain road toward Frederiksted to the intersection with an unpaved road near the foot of Blue Mountain. Directly across from that intersection, on the left, is a small motel, the Sombrero Inn. where you have reservations. The Miami Oyster Company made them for two sailors here to take a look at an oyster boat. Feel free to use whatever name suits you. The hotel is American plan and paid in advance for ten days. I will not see you again. Do not look for me, do not try to identify me, do not try to contact me. If Thad wants me to make contact I will locate you. If I find you making any inquiry about me I will kill you both. Understood? I asked a question. Answer me now, both of you. Understood?"

Startled, upset, and confused, Franco almost snapped back at Rondino, but after a second thought, merely answered, "I understand." Cosgrove grunted his understanding. Rondino strode out of the building and disappeared inside the Caravelle Hotel. He walked through the lobby, past the bar and into the men's room. He began to wash his hands vigorously. Looking at his reflection in the mirror, he thought of the changes in his life since leaving New Jersey. A few years ago he eagerly associated with, actually sought out, goons like them as friends. Now he suddenly wanted a shower after being with them for a few minutes. He settled for a good washing of his hands. Rondino was no longer a fat-ass taxi operator from Camden, N.J.

"Who does that bastard think he is?" Franco said. "One of Thad's high-priced honchos, too good for you and me? I don't like him,

Cosgrove, and when this is over I'm gonna show him he don't talk to Franco Casale that way. The son of a bitch is as good as dead. Don't look for me! Bullshit. What kinda crap is that? Me, I am Franco Casale, and no frigging Sicilian gonna talk to me like that. He's gonna be mine, Cosgrove."

"Yeah, I noticed how you stood up to him. Like a fucking wet noodle, it was. We better get our asses out of here and get on with whatever it is you want to do. Thad sent him and I'll bet he told him to blow your ass away unless you did what he told you to do. You got me in the middle of your screw up. My guys did exactly what they were instructed to do. You had the bad information about the golf, not me."

Casale maintained the grip on his small bag while paying for the coffee. He kept just as firm a grip on the bag as he did in Newark, forgetting the islands were not yet full of thieves and bag snatchers of every sort. Together they walked to Island Rentals to get a car. Franco rejected the red convertible, turned in only a couple of hours earlier, and opted for an ugly blue sedan with four doors and in need of paint. Cosgrove protested in favor of the convertible.

Standing in the motel parking lot Cosgrove looked across the highway at the unpaved road to Blue Mountain. "I know where we are, Franco. That road leads right up to the two cabins I rented for Whitestar and his gang. They belong to a friend of mine in Miami and I was here two years ago. We are only four or five miles away from Whitestar. We can go see him after we check in."

"What? What did you say? You dumb son of a bitch, did you rent from someone you know? You can't be that stupid. What an ass hole. If the cops learn where these guys were staying, and they will, they'll be on your ass 'toot sweet.' What a dumb fuck you turned out to be." Casale pondered Cosgrove's bleak future. Thad would be very upset when he found that a trail ran from Cosgrove to his doorstep in Newark. It became obvious Cosgrove would have to go. Either that or Casale knew he himself would go. A sick feeling inched through his body.

❧   ❧   ❧

August 25, 1970, Christiansted, St. Croix, 12:15 p.m., GMT-4

Maddie almost ran to the Paradise Taxi stand near the pier. She noticed Rondino going in the opposite direction. Sensing her urgency, the driver rushed her to Christiansted's only hospital. There were a few clinics or doctors who maintained facilities for overnight stays, but only one hospital of consequence. There she encountered paperwork, inefficiency, lack of concern, and general confusion. An irritating young woman at the inquiries window shoved a sheaf of forms at her. "You hafta complete these forms before we release information concerning any patient." Upon learning the supposed patient was a possible gunshot victim, the young woman shoved an additional set of forms through the window. Maddie's yelling brought a black doctor in a white coat and two burly security guards. "I only want to see if my friend is in the hospital, that is all," said Maddie. "I think he played golf with those people shot at the Buccaneer Hotel yesterday. We cannot find him. Please help me. I can't stand here and fill out forms while he may be dying." Maddie broke into sobs and collapsed at the doctor's feet, sending papers and forms flying.

The doctor called nurses and used ammonia to revive Maddie. He spoke to her with a calming voice, assuring her that no gunshot victim, male or female, was in the hospital's care. "Miss Willis, we had our last gunshot victim here over thirty days ago. Gunshots are very rare on this island. I will help you any way I can, if that will ease your mind. There is nothing more the hospital can do for you. All the gunshot victims from the Buccaneer are in the morgue awaiting autopsy. I will take you there if you wish, but they have all been identified by friends or relatives."

"No, I do not want to see them. I just wanted to be sure he wasn't in the hospital." The dull luster in her eyes cleared and lightning blazed instead as she again became alive with intensity. Glaring, her voice an octave higher and shriller, she shouted, "I know where the son of a bitch is. I only wanted to make sure. When I find him he will answer to me, he will, by God." She stomped out of the building.

"When she finds that man he will wish he were in the morgue with the other stiffs," the larger of the two security guards said. "That woman is some kinda mad and I think she's flipped her lid." The doctor and most of the onlookers nodded in agreement.

The taxi driver noticed a different Maddie getting into his taxi than the Maddie he had delivered a few minutes earlier. There were no sniffles and sobs now. Anger had replaced them. He complied quickly when ordered to take her to Island Rentals.

The pretty blonde at the Island Rental counter, the one Walther so admired, wilted at the sight of an angry Maddie bearing down on her and waving a credit card. Taking a deep breath to meet the charging woman, she froze her smile too late. "I want a car and I want it now," Maddie yelled.

"Yes, ma'am. What type car do you prefer?"

"I don't give a damn, just a car, and don't ma'am me, you silly goose."

"I'm sorry, ma'am. We have a nice red convertible setting out front, full of fuel and turned in only a short time ago. It's a very nice car. The keys are still in it."

Maddie flung the credit card on the counter and spun on her heel as she headed toward the door. "Do whatever you have to do to the frigging card. I will be back later." The swinging glass door rattled on its hinges as she left.

"Ma'am, you must fill out forms. What about the forms, ma'am?"

Maddie waved goodbye, "I am filling out no more frigging forms today." She leaped into the red convertible without bothering to open the door and roared out into Cay Street. Maddie knew where she wanted to go and set the most direct course for East Point. She followed the curvy, hilly North Shore Road, driving too fast. The view of ocean on the left and beautiful countryside on the right, not yet spoiled by development, flew by unnoticed. This was not the leisurely drive of a tourist but rather the attack of an enraged female lioness. It was ten miles to East Point. Maddie crested the last hill and looked down on East Point almost thirty minutes after leaving Island Rentals. Her rage had abated somewhat during the drive. Fervently she hoped she would not find St. John there. "Let him be on a trip to Jamaica, anywhere, please, God, but not on East End piled up with some scruffy whore." Maddie did not think she could survive another dose of humiliation when people noticed St. John missing his coffee for two or more days. Her mind was firm, no more humiliation by St. John. If it meant going back to Peace Bank, so be it. Devoe would hire her tomorrow. She had fought off his advances in the supply room, hallway, office, and every office party or convention of any sort, back home in Pennsylvania. If she went back she might not fight him. It would serve that bastard, St. John, right. Her anger flared again as she thought of him and some Hispanic whore. The red convertible leaped ahead as she pushed the accelerator to the floor.

On the right, 150 feet off the road, stood a three-story Victorian house with white weather boarding, looking freshly painted and glistening in the sunlight. The gingerbread work bright red and green, a bit garish for conservative decorators, stood out against the white background. The roof of gray weather-beaten wooden shingles covered not only the house but two porches and one turret. In spite of her anger, Maddie noticed it was a beautiful house. A small discrete sign near the road announced it to be Auntie Monica's Inn. Tires squealed and gravel flew as the convertible spun into the drive, coming to rest in Monica's favorite flower bed. Maddie vaulted out of the car and raced to the front porch. She did not pause to knock or ring the bell before marching through the unlocked front door. She found herself in the 'lobby' of the inn where she, on other occasions, had retrieved St. John when Auntie Monica called to say he wished to be picked up. It was a huge room with three Victorian sofas, side chairs, end tables, tiffany lamps, and a great crystal chandelier suspended from a large exposed beam twenty feet above the room-sized oriental carpet on the floor. Against the wall near the front door stood a counter adorned by a guest register, a tome of innumerable pages, and a feather-topped quill in a quart size ink well. Maddie did not pause but took the stairs two at a time, turned right at the hallway and pounded to the last door on the left at the end of the hall.

The doorknob failed to turn at Maddie's grasp. She lifted her right leg and pulled her knee up and back, cocking the leg like the hammer on a shotgun. When she dropped the hammer, the booted foot crashed into the door inches from the knob. The wood of the door facing splintered, the lock and inner knob bounced across the room, and the door crashed against the wall. Maddie bounded into the room and froze in stunned silence as she stared at the startled occupants of the big bed. Three naked people were in a group, all more or less connected to each other in some manner. One hand, maybe the only unoccupied one, was poised to pour champagne into the only unoccupied mouth. Maddie recognized the back of St. John's head if not the bare buttocks presently pointing at the small chandelier hanging over the bed. When the door crashed, the young Hispanic girl's legs wrapped around St. John's head relaxed, flopping over his shoulders. It was her mouth that was to receive the champagne. Auntie Monica's head lay under St. John's lower midsection, her post-like legs pointed to the ceiling. The bottle in her upraised right hand poured champagne blindly. St. John managed to have a brown breast in his left hand and a black one in his right. Maddie was almost sick. She began to scream again and to beat the bedmates with long swings of her shoulder bag. The Hispanic girl and St. John pulled sheets around themselves while Auntie Monica rolled onto the floor, laughing uproariously.

"You slimy bastard," Maddie shouted. "You left me sitting in that office being laughed at for the last time. I am leaving, but before I go I am going to tell you a few things. I thought you were in the hospital and I cried my eyes out. I knew you were dead or dying, and then I find you in an orgy with two scruffly whores. I wish you were dead."

"Watch your language, Blondie," Auntie Monica snapped. "I may be a black whore but I ain't scruffly and you better know it. I'll get up off my ass and beat the shit out of you. You may be pretty but you ain't nothing but a damn dike, damn lesbian. Stupid bitch, don't like nothing but women. Brookings told us all about you."

"Brookings told you what? What did Brookings say? You…Brookings, did you tell her I am some kind of freak? You better tell me she is lying, you ugly son of a bitch. Tell me she is lying."

"What the hell are you doing here, Maddie?" Brookings shouted. "Quit yelling at me. Hell yes I told her about you liking women and not men. It's true. You sat in my office for years, your skirt pulled up to your ass to tease me, but not once did you even thaw enough for me to put my arm about you. You teased me, you laughed at me, and you only fuck women, not men. Plus you are a frigid bitch, no feelings, no heart. I did everything for you, and you repaid me by moving in with that damn little teller. You bitches deserve each other. I don't want you around any more. I have had it with you."

Screaming, Maddie jumped into the bed with Brookings and began pounding him with the shoulder bag. "You sorry bastard, you lying bastard. I am going to beat you to death." Swinging the purse viciously, she accidentally caught the Hispanic girl full in the face, knocking her out of the bed. Angered even more, St. John grabbed Maddie's wrist with his left hand and pulled her toward him. He slapped her with the flat of his hand, and hit her in the face with his fist. He struck hard, sending her flying off the bed and crashing into a chair. Brookings leaped off the bed and onto Maddie, his left arm around her neck and his right hand pushing her jeans down. He tore at the crotch of her panties. She screamed and clawed at his face until he abandoned her panties. He slapped her viciously until she stopped struggling. "I've wanted to do this for years and now I'm gonna do it, you bitch."

Auntie Monica began to laugh again. The Hispanic girl stood by the bed wiping blood from an injured lip. "Fuck her, Brookings. Fuck the queer bitch good," the girl said. Auntie Monica yelled, "I'll help you if you need me. My daughter will help us."

Maddie Willis heard the taunting, smelled the rum on St. John's breath, felt the hand again snatching at her panties, and gained enough strength for one big push. She screamed and shoved and flopped St. John over onto his back. She broke free. Scrambling to her feet, she quickly stood over St. John and kicked him as hard as she could in the crotch. St. John screamed and Auntie Monica stopped laughing.

"You're going to help him rape me are you, you piece of shit? Help him now while he needs you. Look at the ugly bastard while he rolls on the floor naked and not worrying about covering his ass. Help him now, you damn ugly whore."

Maddie Willis, a different Maddie Willis than the woman who earlier had sat lonely by the coffee pot, retrieved her bag from the floor, unsnapped the flap, and removed a little .25 caliber Beretta semi-automatic. The Hispanic girl saw the gun and scurried under the bed. Auntie Monica jumped to her feet and charged. Maddie shot her three times. Small dark holes appeared between the flopping breasts. Turning quickly to St. John, she fired the remaining four rounds into his chest. With no thought of the Hispanic girl hiding under the bed, Maddie tossed the gun onto the bed and, sobbing hysterically, ran out of the bedroom, down the stairs, and out the front door.

CHAPTER 4

Tuesday, August 25, 1970, 1:30 p.m., GMT–4. Caravelle Hotel, St. Croix

Walther plodded back to Cay Street and on to the Caravelle Hotel. The lovely blonde from the water taxi occupied his mind. She had smiled at him and he appreciated that. Walther appreciated kindness, and in his way expressed kindness and friendliness whenever possible. Usually Walther would not allow a woman to dominate his thoughts. That could be a highly dangerous distraction in his profession. But now, sitting on the side of the bed in his room, he found himself dangerously close to permitting the woman from the water taxi to do just that. He decided he'd better get back outside for more fresh air.

He expected no work during the afternoon, but one never knew. He strapped the knife to his forearm and left the other weapons in the room except for the briefcase, a constant companion. The old Belair started easily and, since it already pointed east, Walther drove east. He had no destination, only needing the drive to clear unaccustomed thoughts from his brain. Walther did not know who Thad would send to clean up the mess the Latinos made at the Buccaneer Bar, but he wished Thad had told him when the shooting was to take place. He would have gone elsewhere for his beer. When the Latinos had burst into the bar, he had thought he would probably have to send them home to protect himself. As he looked the leader in the eyes, he knew, and maybe they both knew, their final meeting was yet to come. Walther easily could have sent them home but hesitated because of the attention he would have gotten. It was a gamble, but eyes reveal the inner soul and inner thoughts. He had held in his hand under the table the power to send them home, but had waited. There would be another time for the man with the white star on his cap.

Suddenly the road required his full attention. It curved and snaked alongside the ocean at times, and then over hills and through woods. The stretch he drove now curved and crooked along steep bluffs and deep gorges. With his mind clear, Walther enjoyed the view as he navigated the dangerous section. The water on his left was a deep blue except for coral reefs or sand bars that changed the color to various tints of light green. The trees on the right flashed different shades of lush green as they swayed in the wind. Bougainvillea and other shrubs glowed with red, pink, yellow, and purple blossoms in the sun's brilliance, sometimes causing Walther to gasp at their beauty. Walther appreciated all beauty.

The road dipped suddenly and snaked downhill in a long graceful curve at East Point, the end of the island, and then headed west. As he made the turn, Walther saw the large white Victorian house with the red and green gingerbread woodwork around the eaves and porches. He admired the tall turret and its bright gingerbread. Then he saw the red convertible and instinctively applied the brakes and stopped the old Belair. He remembered the convertible from the night before when he had rented it, and wondered who had driven it here. It was simple curiosity over the coincidence of someone renting the same vehicle that had caused him to stop. He released the brakes and began to move forward again when the door to the house crashed open, banging against the wall, and the beautiful blonde from the water taxi dashed across the porch, down the steps and across the lawn toward the convertible. Walter pulled into the drive and stopped. The blonde sobbed hysterically and screamed and pulled at her hair. When she saw Walther, she changed her course and dashed toward him. Quickly, he set the brakes and got out of the Belair barely in time to enfold her in his arms as she rushed to him. She wrapped her arms tightly around his neck and buried her face against his neck. The screaming stopped but the sobbing continued. Walther held her tightly and gently patted her back. Slowly the sobs stilled, the shaking subsided, and she was quiet. Maddie lifted her head and leaned back but did not loosen her grip on his neck. Walther saw her lip, split and bleeding, and noticed red welts on her jaw. They looked like a handprint. Anger flooded his body and he determined to make someone pay for doing that to her. Her dark green eyes locked with his light blue ones and she said quietly, "I killed them, I killed them both and I am glad I did it." She began sobbing again and pressed her face against Walther's shoulder and neck. He did not know what to do. He continued to hold her tightly. He rather enjoyed it. When the sobbing stopped again, Walther led her to the red convertible and listened to her pour out what had happened inside. Once she became calm, he seated her in the convertible and told her to wait while he went inside and looked around. He removed the key from the ignition. She did not need to be driving in her condition. She nodded agreement and said, "I will wait, but I killed them both. I did and I am not sorry. There is nothing you can do." Walther was not sure.

Walther found more than he expected in the upstairs bedroom. A black woman lay on her back, naked, with blood leaking from three tiny bullet holes between her huge breasts. The man, also naked and gripping his genitals with both hands, lay in a fetal position. Blood oozed from four small holes scattered over the upper half of his body. He may not be dead, Walther thought, but did not check to see. Instead, he picked him up and tossed him onto the bed, then lifted the black woman and tossed her onto the bed also. As he picked up various items of clothing from chairs and the floor,

Walther noticed a bare foot under the bed. He tossed the clothes onto the bodies on the bed and lifted the chair near the foot and threw it across the bed onto a bedside table. The chair, lamp, ashtray and whatever else was on the table all crashed to the floor. The bare foot scooted closer to Walther. He grasped it in his huge hand and jerked. A Hispanic girl, also naked, slid screaming from the safety of her hiding place beneath the bed. Walther lifted her to her feet and asked her to stop screaming.

"The blonde bitch shot them, she shot them both," she said.

"Why did she shoot them?"

"She was mad when she found Brookings in bed with Auntie Monica and me. Brookings said she was a frigid bitch. She went wild and shot them."

. Suddenly she saw Brookings and Auntie Monica on the bed and began screaming again. The screaming, Walther knew, would upset the blonde in the convertible and certainly she already was upset enough. He did not ask the Hispanic girl again to stop screaming. With a twist of his powerful hands he broke her neck. He tossed her body onto the pair on the bed. Not wanting the woman in the convertible to become upset because he was away too long, Walther went outside to speak with her. He found her calm, almost serene, sitting as he had left her. She smiled when she saw him.

"Is everything OK inside," she asked?

Surprised at the change in her, Walther assured her everything inside was well. There were no problems to worry her. "You just sit tight for a few minutes and I will be back. I need to clean up a few things yet. Will you be all right?"

She smiled at him and said, "I'll be fine. You just hurry so we can get back before too late. I have some things I want us to do. OK?"

Again surprised at the woman, Walther gulped and then nodded his head, feeling as if he had missed part of the conversation. He took the black briefcase from the rear seat of the Belair and a coil of yellow nylon rope from the trunk. He smiled and waved to his new friend.

She blew him a kiss. Walther vaguely sensed a warning click in the back of his brain, but ignored it. The lady had created a problem for herself with no knowledge of how to clean it up. Walther would do it for her because she was his friend. Strange, he thought, how things could change in a few days. He had always been a professional killer, a "contractor." He had not been a cleaner until yesterday when he became a cleaner for Thad. Today he became a cleaner for a beautiful blonde and did not know her name. Perhaps he just answered when opportunity knocked, and from this point forward his occupation would be cleaner. That did not worry Walther.

Back in the bedroom, Walther dropped the nylon rope on the floor and opened the briefcase. An unused package from the night before rested in its indention in the foam liner. Walther gingerly lifted it out and reset the timer for forty-five minutes. He placed it on the bed between the black woman and the man the Hispanic whore called Brookings. He placed the Hispanic girl on top of the others, covering the package. Walther walked out into the hall and opened the door to the room directly across the hall. It was a duplicate of the room he had just left. He removed the mattress from the bed and carried it to the other room. Carefully he placed the mattress on top of the bodies in the bed, then tightly lashed the mattress to the bed with the yellow nylon rope. Not satisfied with the sandwich he had made, he lifted the chest of drawers and placed it on top of the mattress. It was not perfect, but time was short. He needed to be back at the Caravelle Hotel within thirty minutes or so with the blonde woman. He made a mental note to ask her name.

Walther stashed the now-empty briefcase in the back of the Belair before approaching the convertible. The blonde woman was waiting and smiling. "We need to get back to the hotel quickly. You feel up to driving?" he asked.

"Sure. I told you there was something I want to do as soon as we get back. I will drive and you follow. OK? Is everything in order in the house?"

"Yes to both questions. Lead on please."

The drive to the hotel was both quick and uneventful. They saw no one and met no other vehicles for the first eight or ten miles. No one would ever know they had been to East Point other than the three on the bed in the old Victorian house. Walther felt sure they would keep silent. The woman in the convertible acted very differently now from the woman who had run sobbing and screaming out of Auntie Monica's Inn. The sudden difference disturbed Walther somewhat. He thought perhaps his lack of knowledge of beautiful women was the problem. After parking the Belair in its proper space, he rode with Maddie. She told him her name, appearing somewhat surprised he asked. At Island Rental, she remained, at his suggestion, outside while he turned in the car. The blonde rental lady greeted him with her best customer smile. He gave her his credit card and picked up the one Maddie had left and all the papers prepared for Maddie. After signing the card printout, Walther gave the girl a fifty-dollar bill and told her to have a nice dinner at the Top Hat. She almost kissed him. Walther was pleased. This was his lucky day with blondes. Outside, Maddie grabbed his arm and hung on as they walked to the Caravelle. Walther was so pleased he almost skipped.

He secured the most prominent and obvious table in the Caravelle bar. He made sure everyone would remember him and Maddie by asking for frequent service from every server whose attention he could attract, and generously tipping each. The males, he was sure, would never forget Maddie. She washed her face in the ladies' room, renewed her makeup, and applied fresh lipstick to hide all traces of damage to her lip. She mussed her hair enough to provide a wind-blown look and pulled the tee shirt down tighter to accentuate her breasts. She hoped they would give people something to look at other than her face where the bruises lay hidden under a light film of makeup. Sipping her spritzer, Maddie leaned across the table smiling her magnificent smile and asked, "Will you go shopping with me? I didn't bring any clothes and I want to look pretty for you when we go to dinner tonight. You have my credit card from the rental place and I have two or three others so money is not a problem. I even have some of the bank's cards." She giggled.

"I will be delighted to go shopping with you and it is not necessary to worry about credit cards," Walther said. "I have cash and will be delighted to lend you all the money you need, if you wish. It would be my pleasure to buy whatever clothes you might need. However I know it to be improper to make such a suggestion to a lady."

"Oh, I don't see anything improper about it. It might be fun." Maddie giggled again. "Do you know how to buy panties and bras or do you prefer no bras?"

Another giggle. Walther became concerned. He glanced around the room and found his table to be the bar's entertainment for the afternoon. This was not good. He wanted them to be accounted for when Auntie Monica's inn burned, as it was no doubt doing now, but enough was enough. Perhaps he should change the subject, but in his limited experience with women he did not know how. His planned and programmed days contained no plan for such as Maddie. As he floundered for an escape, Maddie jumped up and, grabbing his hand, said, "Let's go. I want new clothes. Lots of new clothes." Walther left the bar practically being dragged by what he thought must be the most beautiful woman in the world.

The clothes buying stopped only after three hours, and an exuberant Maddie led a box and bag-laden Walther into the lobby of the Caravelle Hotel. She asked him for his room key. It was in Walther's pants pocket. With all the packages and bags, it was quite impossible for Walther to reach it. With another of her girlish giggles, Maddie slid her hand into the pocket and brought out the key. A self-conscious Walther glanced about the lobby to spot any observers. There were several. Walther felt the need to sit down and re-plan. His earlier plans no longer existed and he was confused. How he had become involved now seemed confusing. Maddie's change in person-

ality confused him. Shopping with a woman confused him. A confused Walther reacted very much like a wounded animal. He must
withdraw, hide somewhere and think. Thinking appeared an impossibility in her presence, yet he had to calm himself by working out a
plan for the next few hours at least.

The small elevator barely accommodated the clothes-laden
Walther and Maddie. But it gave Walther partial seclusion, and he
kept his eyes closed and meditated as best he could during the brief
ride up. A feeling of peace crept over him, easing the tension of the
hours since he had found Maddie running from the whorehouse. In
the room, Walther dumped the boxes, bags, and plastic-covered
clothes on the bed and began to shake out wrinkles and smooth
dresses before carefully placing them in neat stacks. Two boxes of
shoes he tossed on the pillows, followed by belts and bits of costume
jewelry. Walther liked neatness and order and, though unfamiliar
with the clothing items, he found the work soothing. A loud noise
nearby startled Walther and he spun around to see one of Maddie's
boots bouncing across the tile floor. Maddie tugged at the other boot
while hopping on one foot to maintain her balance. The T-shirt and
the bra hung over the back of a chair. Loosened jeans slid further and
further down her perfect thighs with every hop. When the boot came
off and bounced on the tile, the jeans fell around her ankles. She
stepped out of them. She wore only a wisp of the panties Brookings
had torn back at the whorehouse. The nearly nude Maddie smiled
her beautiful smile for Walther.

Later that evening, the manager of the Top Hat drew a line
through Mr. Walther's booking and wondered why he was a no-
show.

❧   ❧   ❧

August 25, 1970, 4:08 p.m., GMT–4. Sombrero Inn, St. Croix

Casale kicked the chair, waking the sleeping Cosgrove and setting off another round of complaints and accusations. Cosgrove continued to maintain everything was Casale's fault and none of his own, contributing to Casale's growing irritation. His irritation also stemmed from his treatment by the damn Sicilian Thad had sent to meet him at the seaplane ramp. When this was over, he would not forget the Sicilian and would set matters straight with him. No way could he hide from Casale on an island this small. "Shut the hell up, Cosgrove. Go find a phone and call Whitestar. We need to talk to him, 'toot sweet'. What a dump this is. Damn Sicilian put us in this pig sty on his own. Thad would at least give us a room with a TV. No phone, no TV, and no pictures on the walls. What a dump. Now get going, find a pay phone and call Whitestar."

"Where the hell am I gonna find a pay phone? It's only four of five miles to the cabin. We can drive there while I am looking for a phone. I can't use the one in the office with that fat, nosy bitch listening to every word. Come on, Franco. Might as well get this over with and get our ass out of here if we can."

"Damn!" Cosgrove grunted as he jerked his hands off the car's steering wheel. "Did you have to roll the windows up, Franco? This is not New-fucking-Jersey, no body gonna steal a car here. Where the hell they take it? This is an island, and a small one at that. Damn, it's like an oven in here. Damn!"

"Shut up and drive, Cosgrove, and turn on the air conditioning."

"What air conditioning? There is no air conditioning on this car. Didn't you look at it when you rented it? It is older than you."

Cosgrove eased out of the parking lot and crossed the main highway into the unpaved road leading up toward Blue Mountain. The old blue sedan with a standard shift resisted Cosgrove's attempts to find third gear for a full minute, allowing the forward speed to drop so low he had to shift back to second. Having regained his speed, he was preparing to try third gear again when he heard the sirens. A glance in the rear view mirror revealed two police cars, two ambulances, and a fire truck skidding and sliding off the highway onto the unpaved road they were on. "What the hell is that?" asked Franco, squirming around in the seat to see out the back window.

"I don't know but I am getting out of the road. They will run us over if I don't." Cosgrove managed to wheel the old sedan into a shallow ditch at almost the last moment as the caravan roared by with bells, sirens, and horns blaring. He looked at Franco, whose eyes questioned him. Cosgrove knew, and told Franco, very little existed along this road other than a few cabins, including the two he had arranged for Whitestar. They had to decide to trail the emergency vehicles or turn back and get as far away as possible. It seemed possible that the Latinos had been discovered and the police were on their way to get them. But in that event, would they be coming with sirens blaring and bells ringing? Why would they bring a fire engine and two ambulances? More likely there would only be police vehicles traveling quietly. Franco decided this group was headed to the scene of a fire and not to arrest shooters.

"Follow them until we see where they are going and stay back out of the dust," he said. Three miles later, Cosgrove and Casale stopped to decide whether to follow the police, who went to the left, or abandon the chase and turn right toward the cabin with the telephone. Whitestar would be there and perhaps they could meet with him and not be involved in whatever brought the police and firemen. Neither Cosgrove not Casale noticed they were driving through one of the most beautiful spots on St. Croix. Police vehicles were on their minds. Cosgrove wished for his hovel in Miami and for a sister who was a nun and not married to a gangster. Casale silently rued the day he met Cosgrove's sister. If only he had met Cosgrove first, he would have known not to marry her. "Damn it, Cosgrove, why are the police here?" Casale asked. "Where is the damned cabin? What are we going to do?"

"The cabin is just around the next curve. I have no answer for the other questions. You are the answer man; I am just a Saturday night pusher. You have told me that often enough. You have all the brains. You figure it out."

Cosgrove turned the old blue sedan into the cabin's driveway and stopped. The cabin appeared deserted. To Cosgrove, that was a bad omen and interfered with his simple plan. He would tell Whitestar to finish the job and give him the balance of his money. Then Cosgrove would catch the next plane to Miami. Casale's plan was more complicated and needed to be explained to Whitestar in detail in private. It included Cosgrove in the uncompleted work. Casale would keep the payment owed Whitestar until the contract was fulfilled. And Whitestar must understand fully that Casale should not be required to finish the job himself. That would be unfortunate for all concerned.

"Where does this road go, Cosgrove?"

"A mile or so around this hill to the other cabin, then back to where it split. It loops the hill. Whitestar may be at the other cabin with all his people. Want to take a look?"

"Did you forget about the police? Where are they? If this road only circles the top of the hill, they can't be far from here. What if they are at the other cabin?"

"We haven't done anything for the police to be interested in us. We only arrived today and are driving around to look at the island. Nothing wrong with that."

Casale thought about Cosgrove's suggestion while walking across the yard after making an inspection of the cabin to be certain it was vacant. If the police knew about the Latinos' hideout on the hill, he needed to know as soon as possible. Discovery of Whitestar and his group could happen quite by accident with the police so near the cabins. Better to find out what brought the police to the mountain and warn Whitestar of their presence than have him stumble into a serious problem. Driving around the hill to locate the police was a good idea with minimal risk to himself. He slid into the car next to Cosgrove and told him to drive toward the second cabin slowly.

"The other cabin is just a few hundred yards on the left after we clear this curve," Cosgrove said. "Jesus, I hope no one is there. The police can't be far away and we don't need for them to get a look at Whitestar and his gang. Everybody on this island has gotta know six Latinos did the shooting and if they find six of them in this cabin, all hell will break loose."

The old blue car nosed past the edge of the curve and onto a long straight section as Cosgrove increased speed. "The cabin is on the left past that clump of trees and bushes. I'll drive past, then if every-thing looks OK, we'll come back and check out the cabin. They have a couple of old station wagons I rented for them in Frederiksted. If they…Holy shit! Look at that! The fucking cabin is demolished and there is a police car and an ambulance. Holy shit! Here come the cops waiving us to stop. What do I do?"

"You stop, ass hole, and stop quick. We haven't done nothing. They can't do nothing to us."

Cosgrove braked and rolled to a stop beside the policeman. "What is it, officer/"

"Sir, the road is closed this way. You must turn back and go the other way. Big mess here and further on, the fire truck has the road blocked. You must go back."

"No problem, officer, no problem at all. But what happened? That house looks like it exploded. Hey is that a body they are bringing out?"

"Please sir, I am not supposed to discuss a crime scene with civil-ians but it did blow up or someone blew it up. I tell you, mon, it a mess inside. Two people killed when roof fell on them and one when somebody shot him in the head. Then down the road is a car, station wagon, I think, burned up with three more people dead from burning. Big mess, but I am not permitted to discuss, so you turn around and go back the way you come. What you doing up here anyhow? Just driving around or were you coming to this cabin by any chance?" Cosgrove became nervous when the policeman began asking questions. Knowing careful answers must be given made him even more nervous. A suspicious policeman was not needed. "No, no, we decided to take a drive and look at some of the island and this hill provides a good view, so we drove up here. We don't know anything about any cabin or anything. We only driving around." Cosgrove shifted into reverse and began backing up to make a turn. "Thanks, officer, we'll be getting on our way." Casale who had said nothing, noticed two more bodies coming out of the house. It looked as if all six of the Latinos were dead. Who did it? How, and why were they killed? It was only yesterday afternoon they shot up the people at the Buccaneer Bar. The situation did not look good to Casale.

Nervous and scared, Cosgrove backed the car into the ditch. Casale said, "Oh shit, Cosgrove! Don't get the damn thing stuck. That cop was beginning to wonder about us. If you get us stalled in a ditch, he really will wonder." He breathed a sigh of relief as the tires caught firm ground and clawed back onto the road. Cosgrove sped away a little too quickly, causing the policeman to stare after them. "What the hell has happened, Cosgrove? Whitestar and his group are dead? Who? My God, all the questions I can think of. Who did this? Why did they do it? What are we going to do?"

Cosgrove managed to get them safely back to the Sombrero Inn and into his room. He quickly grabbed a half-filled bottle of bourbon in his bag. Sipping the straight bourbon from a cheap plastic cup, Cosgrove turned to Casale for answers. Casale only had more questions neither could answer. According to the policeman, six people were dead; three at the house and three in a vehicle a few hundred feet down the road. Logic told Cosgrove and Casale six bodies, one of which was shot execution style, meant the end of Whitestar and his Latinos. Casale, upon reflection, saw the hand of Thad removing the cord connecting himself to any of the mess in St. Croix. Casale did not dismiss that idea, although it seemed impossible for Thad to get anyone to the island in such a short time. What to do about the other three targets missed at the bar became his immediate concern. He and Thad had not discussed him having to pick up the job and take care of the other three men.

Casale pondered the help, or lack of it, that he could expect from Cosgrove if Thad told him to take care of O'Rielly, Alasdair, and St. John. Cosgrove, a Saturday night pusher with no experience in hits other than cocaine, would only mess things up. Casale himself only dealt with such matters as produce companies who missed or were late on protection payments. This was his first big job. Perhaps Thad needed to be advised of the situation, but then Thad may already know about the Latinos. Perhaps Thad arranged the incident at the cabin, a thought that chilled Casale. The Sicilian who met the seaplane when they came from San Juan might be Thad's connection in St. Croix. If so, the possibility existed that he handled the six people at the cabin to show Casale Thad's displeasure with people who failed to complete a paid contract. If that was the message, it came through clearly enough for him to understand: finish the job in a few days or expect a visit from someone with a decidedly nasty disposition.

An hour passed before Casale heard the ambulances and fire truck at the intersection as they wheeled out into the main road with no lights flashing and no sirens, indicating no survivors to be rushed to the hospital. This confirmed for Casale the demise of all the Latinos. He watched the ambulances and the fire truck fade from sight with a sick feeling deep inside. His future rode in those ambulances and faded away with them. His time was no longer his own, it belonged to Thad. He could feel Thad counting the few minutes remaining to him. They flew by at double time.

"I can't stand this piece of shit room any longer, Cosgrove. Where is this Frederiksted you speak of? I want to go there or somewhere to get this shit off my mind and make a plan. You know our situation? I'll tell you. If we don't take out those three, Thad will have his man do it and take us out with them. We have no choice. We have to act. Are you ready? Can you shoot a man at a funeral? You better decide because that is your only choice."

"I didn't get into this to kill anybody. That is your business, not mine, and if that is what you want me to do, forget it. I am not into that sort of stuff. I am getting out of here and going back to Miami. All I signed on to do, I did. I furnished you the Latinos who did their job and did it well. I don't know Thad and don't give a shit about him nor any of his hit men, and they better leave me alone in Miami. I have friends there just as bad as any bum he can send to Miami to look for me."

Casale rolled his eyes skyward and beseeched the Virgin Mary for a good word on his behalf as he tried to deal with his idiot brother-in-law. Didn't he ever understand anything? "I am the bum, Cosgrove. It is me. I have to hit you if we don't get this contract finished and finished soon. You must understand your situation, and when you have to act, you better be willing and ready to act. You got that Cosgrove? If you fuck up again, I gotta take you out. Either you help me get these guys or I take you out. You got that, Cosgrove? I'm gonna shoot my wife's kid brother, the idiot one. Is that clear, or shall I draw a picture?"

"You're shittin' me, Franco, aren't you? This is crazy. I am your wife's brother. You talking about doing me in, killing me, blowing my ass away? Is that it, Franco? You're shittin' me, right?"

"No, Cosgrove, I am serious, totally serious. Get yourself together and make up your mind to help me, or I don't need you and can't afford you. Now get your ass in the car and drive me to Frederiksted "

A dejected and nervous Cosgrove struggled to rise under the weight of knowing his brother-in-law intended to kill him unless he helped in the assassination of three men he neither knew nor wanted to know. His introduction to the big time missed his expectations by a wide margin. The big time, he was finding out, is serious business for all the players. Mistakes are frowned upon and rarely forgiven. And when the frown starts at the top, someone at the bottom gets shot. Cosgrove realized he was the bottom.

The restaurant and bar sat back of a large unpaved parking area, well off the road on the edge of Frederiksted. It gave every appearance of a favorite hangout for locals if an overrun parking lot meant anything. Only Casale's yells and threats made Cosgrove nose into the lot, where he searched without success for a space to put the old blue auto. Finally, to stop the complaints from Casale, he drove over an inches-high barrier into the long-forgotten remnants of a flower-bed.

"Son of a bitch, Cosgrove. This is no way to park. Damn, I have to get out on top of a fucking wall. How you gonna get the damn piece of shit out of here?"

"Shut up, Franco. You yelled and screamed to park here like there is no other place to get a drink on the damn island. You threatened to kill me and now you bitch about where I park. From now on you can drive the damn thing yourself. I am not a driver, I am just a Saturday night pusher, you ass hole. You didn't rent no limo and no chauffeur. You rented this old blue clunker with no air, so stop acting like some 'primer donner' or something. Get out and get in the damn place and see if they got any of that Jack-fucking-Daniel's you bitched about all day."

Inside, the bar reeked of stale tobacco smoke, soured beer, body odor, and cheap pine-scented air freshener. There were no vacant tables and the bar stood three deep with working men and, apparently, working women. One of the women spotted Casale in his black silk suit and white shirt. She bore down on him like a street person going after a wrecked beer truck. "Silly ass Wop," Cosgrove muttered as he elbowed close enough to the bartender to order Coke and Jack and Coke and rum. He waved a ten-spot to show the seriousness of his request. While waiting, Cosgrove turned to see how Casale was dealing with the working woman, but onrushing knuckles on a huge fist suddenly blocked his view an instant before it landed underneath his right eye. Only the mass of people at the bar prevented Cosgrove from smashing into the bar. Instead they held the sagging and limp Cosgrove up, giving his attacker a flabby stomach for his next blow which came with speed and force. Mercifully, the crowd allowed him to slide gently to the floor keeping him out of reach of his assailant and avoiding permanent injury. As for the assailant, he turned his attention to a startled Casale, still nursing his thirst and shoving off the woman seeking his attention. To his surprise, the Latino found the black silk suit accustomed to bar room brawls. Before his two cohorts could interfere, he joined Cosgrove on the floor. He never saw the two quick jabs, a left followed by a right that placed him in a seated position next to the prostrate Cosgrove.

The Latino's associates made motions indicating no desire to take up the cudgel, but leaving no doubt they would if the black silk suit approached their fallen comrade. Casale turned his attention to Cosgrove, who appeared dead, so complete was his unconsciousness. The bartender sent Casale his Jack and Coke along with a pitcher of water to splash on Cosgrove. One of the patrons near the prostrate Cosgrove dumped the water, without ceremony or kindness, in Gosgrove's face, provoking some movement and a weak cough. Acquilla, a big-breasted barfly, noticed the ten-spot still clasped in Cosgrove's fingers, swooped it up and shoved it into the powdered cleavage between her black breasts. She was not fast enough to escape Casale's eye. He shoved his hand in between the breasts and removed the ten spot. Several other bills of various denominations came out with his hand and fluttered to the floor, much to the amusement of the crowd. The customers roared with laughter as Acquilla and two of her friends crawled about on hands and knees searching for her money while loudly cursing Casale. The bartender sent him another Jack and Coke.

Excitement over, the patrons returned to their drinking and conversations, ignoring the two Latinos and Casale ministering to their gladiators. From the floor, Cosgrove gazed at Casale through film-covered eyes that questioned but did not see. Casale had no answer, no clue as to why the man crouched next to him had attacked Cosgrove. The two Latinos tried unsuccessfully to get their comrade to his feet. However, he preferred to hold his belly with both hands as he wheezed loudly in the vain hope his breath would suddenly return. Casale's right fist was extremely effective, honed in bars and streets all over New Jersey. It would, when properly delivered, incapacitate a man for fifteen minutes. Casale, upset with his problems and his anger at Cosgrove, grateful for an opportunity to strike out at something, delivered a very proper right. What to do now began to occupy his mind.

The bartender, ever mindful of his tenuous relationship with the police, came to Casale's aid. He and two West Indian toughs cleared a route to the back door, then approached Casale and the Latinos. With a hand on Casale's shoulder, the bartender spoke quietly. "The police be here before long to check us out and I don't want no trouble with them. You and them two Spics follow your buddies out the back door and straighten out your mess back there. You may think you do but you don't want to have no trouble with our police, no matter what that Spic did to your pal. Things a little crazy on the island right now. If you want to fight when you get outside, then fight. If you want to talk, I'll send you some drinks, but you gotta get out of my place and stay out until you over this. OK?"

Each of the men with the bartender grabbed Cosgrove and the Latino by their shirt collar, dragged them through the back door, and then left them on the litter-strewn walk near the garbage cans. Casale and the two Latinos followed. The crowd filled the space and all traces of the disturbance vanished.

"We got to talk, mon." It was Estavo, one of the Latinos. "This really bad Mon. That is Whitestar and he pissed, mon, and so are we. I don't know who you are but that Cosgrove there is a bastard. I think Whitestar gonna kill him. That's what he gonna do and I gonna help him. You betta get your ass out of here before Whitestar starts breathing again."

A befuddled Casale blurted out without thinking, "Whitestar, I thought he was dead, blown up or burned in the wagon. How the hell this be Whitestar?"

Estavo and his friend pounced on Casale with intent to maim. However they failed to recognize an accomplished street fighter, an enforcer for loan sharks, because, perhaps, he wore a black silk suit. Whatever the reason, they soon joined Whitestar and Cosgrove in the trash.

Cosgrove, having managed to get to his feet, leaned against a garbage dumpster and stared at the three men scattered in the trash near his feet. Recognition flooded his eyes, then his brain, or maybe the reverse. "That is Whitestar," he yelled, pointing, "and Estavo and Furillo. How can it be? We saw them hauled off this afternoon. How can they be here?"

"I don't know, Cosgrove, but they are pissed at you, and now me because I know you. We've got to keep them under control until we can speak with them calmly. They think we tried to blow them up."

"Us? We didn't have anything to do with that. We only just got here. What's the matter with them? Why would they think we would do that?"

"Money and evidence, you ass hole, that is what they think. Keep the other twenty grand and blow up the evidence. Do away with the people who did the shooting, end the link. They don't know we just got here this morning. How could they? They been hiding to keep from getting blown up like the others. Who the hell do you suppose the other three were? Who the fuck blew them up?"

"Women, the other three were women," Whitestar muttered. He was still having trouble breathing and could not stand, but his ears worked and, between gasps, he could talk. "They got women and they got blowed up. We thought it was Cosgrove's work, that's why I hit him, I thought he here celebrating blowing up our ass. But if you didn't do it, who did and why they do it? Them women probable just whores what nobody give a shit about, least not enough to blow somebody up. We in trouble, mon, bad trouble. Somebody trying to kill us and if it ain't you, who is it?"

❦   ❦   ❦

August 25, 1970, Airport, St. Thomas, USVI, 3:48 GMT–4

"Hell's going on, Stephen?" Alasdair demanded when met at the airport by Stephen O'Rielly. "Four of our people shot dead in St. Croix, St. John missing, Maddie all steamed up and gone, leaving the bank in a snit. And I just learned somebody stole a bunch of files out of my Atlanta office. What the hell is this all about? Have you located St. John?"

"We are not out of the airport yet, Jim. Wait 'till we get in the car and we'll talk. But no, I haven't located Brookings. I don't know what's going on. I don't know what Maddie is doing, but the bank is fine. Now, here's the car, get in and light one of those big cigars and I will tell you everything I have learned since I spoke with you three or four hours ago. Not a hell of a lot in such a short time, but I will tell you everything."

"Don't patronize me, O'Rielly. I'm just concerned. You know that."

"Sure I know that and you know I'm concerned also, so give me a break. I been trying to sort this mess out same as you. I think it is just luck we are alive. If you didn't hate golf so much we probably would've played with them and been dead also. This was no random shooting, Jim, this was a deliberate attempt to kill all of us. Someone knew we all were listed with tee times at the Buccaneer Club and deliberately set us up. It was no secret we were playing golf, at least had tee times. I'm telling you somebody set us up. Why, I don't know, but they were not after one of us, they were after all of us. Hell, they left a witness, I hear. They didn't shoot the bartender, they didn't shoot the cook. According to the bullet hole, they shot two feet over his head when he ran into the bar. It's us, us, all of us they were after. Know what that means? They ain't finished. We are still alive and some son of a bitch is waiting for a chance to get us. There is the bank. We'll go in and use Brookings' office."

Alasdair puffed on the cigar while staring at O'Rielly with unbelief. "Hell's the matter with you, Stephen? None of us done anything to get shot over, especially those guys who got shot. Not you, not Brookings that I know of. Me? Maybe, but why would anybody take their anger at me out on you guys? It don't make sense."

"So it don't make sense but it happened and the chief or police in Christiansted agrees with me. Get out and come on in and see what's with the bank. The branch manager probably needs some soothing and that's your job. They all know you and Brookings run everything and when he's not here you have to take over the soothing chores. I know you are a pain in the ass and know damn little about soothing, but they worried as hell, so soothe them."

All the employees and customers stopped what they were doing and watched as O'Rielly and Alasdair strode through Maddie's office and into St. John's. O'Rielly picked up the phone and dialed Inman's number. Max Inman, a forty-year-old West Indian born somewhere near Red Hook, clawed his way through all the St. Thomas schools and finally was graduated from the island's university. His first job was in the mailroom of a bank in Charlotte Amalie, and he had been in banking since. Brookings hired him and made him manager of the main office and in charge of all branch banking, reporting to Maddie Willis.

"Max, come into Brookings' office a minute. Alasdair needs to talk to you." O'Rielly dropped the receiver on the cradle and motioned to Alasdair, "He's all yours."

"Hell's the matter with you? What do I tell him after all that drivel you just dumped on me?" Max was all business and professionalism as he trotted into the office.

"Yes sir."

"Relax, Max. We've got to tell these people something about what has happened and is going to happen. You want to do it, Max, or you want me?"

"You, sir. I am not sure what to say. They are pretty upset and concerned. You know, in spite of his badgering and pushing, everyone loves Brookings and, to some extent, Maddie. We didn't really know the other gentlemen that well, but we are all concerned. No one has heard from Brookings and several people think he has been abducted and a big robbery is coming. Maddie thinks, at least we think she does, that Brookings was shot with the others but not killed, and is in the hospital unable to identify himself and is probably unknown to the hospital staff. We think she is at the hospital now."

"Son of a bitch!" Alasdair said. "If it's up to me, go get them all together on the banking floor, employees and customers, and I will talk to them. Not much to tell, but I'll try to ease their minds on some things."

Inman gathered the twenty-two employees and eight or ten customers in a cluster near the vault door. Alasdair explained to them the terrible attack on the people at the Buccaneer Club was a random drug-crazed happening and not part of any other future action. Brookings was still missing and probably had gone to Jamaica to meet a prospective customer. Maddie, understandably upset, thought Brookings might have been shot and sent to a hospital where he was unidentified. So she went to St. Croix to check the hospitals. He felt she would be back the next day when she learned Brookings was not injured and not hospitalized. Meanwhile, Inman could handle any problems. In fact, he already did most of the supervisory and managerial work, so it would be banking business as usual. The employees shuffled back to work and the customers drifted out the doors. Few appeared soothed.

Alasdair seated himself in Brookings' chair. After pouring three fingers of scotch from the bottle Brookings kept in the credenza, he blew a haze of blue cigar smoke into the air, and said, "O'Rielly, what is this crap the police chief and you talking about and why?"

"The chief rang me last night and talked for an hour about the shooting. His feeling is we were all targeted and you, Brookings, and I survived only because we had other things more pressing than golf. There was one customer in the bar, according to the bartender, a tough looking guy drinking beer by the window. One of the shooters fired in his direction, hitting the beer mug, ashtray, and the peanut bowl on his table. It is obvious he did not intend to kill the guy when he hit everything on the table but missed a large man. The bartender was completely ignored and the cook scared by a blast well over his head. All of our people were hit with several shots capable of being fatal. Does that sound like random violence? I don't think so."

"But who would want to do this? Do you think they are after me for something and, if they are, why those, Reynolds and the rest? Their only connection with me is through the bank and insurance business. Peace Bank is pissed off at Brookings but I doubt they know me or you and certainly not the directors. Do you think the Peace Bank would kill us because of a few deposits?"

"Hell, who knows what they do up there in gangster land where Peace Bank is."

"For Christ's sake, Stephen. They are Quakers, non-violent Christians, peaceniks and that kind of people. They don't even want to harm a fly."

"The Latinos were pretty damn violent it seems to me."

"Shit, Stephen, there is no reason to think of any connection between the people you call Latinos and the Peace Bank. Probably don't know Peace Bank exists and, by the way, why we taking off on the Peace Bank? We don't know them; we don't know anyone with the damn bank except a couple of guys that work in their branch here. This is a ridiculous conversation."

"You'll think ridiculous when somebody shoots your ass."

The intercom phone on Brookings' desk buzzed, ending the deteriorating conversation. When Alasdair made no move toward the phone, O'Rielly leaned across the desk and picked it up. The bank operator told him that line one was for him and it was one of the ladies in his insurance office. He thanked her and answered line one.

"O'Rielly here." O'Rielly stiffened as he listened and grunted once, then twice. "OK, Mercedes, we will be there in five minutes." He stared at Alasdair with a questioning and confused expression. "The police chief from St. Croix is in the office looking for me and guess what, he wants to talk to you. He was elated, Mercedes said, when he learned you were here. Wave at Max and head for the car. I want to know what brought him to St. Thomas tonight. I would have thought he knew I have to be back on St. Croix tomorrow to meet with the coroner to get bodies released. No big deal over cause of death with them full of bullet holes."

Leaving the car at a parking meter, they hurried down Palm Passage to the office of King and O'Rielly Insurance, Ltd. Inside, Alasdair could not control a startled expression upon his first glimpse of Chief Constantine Halfpenny seated on the old leather sofa. The two patrolmen with him immediately leaped to their feet and, with a hand under each of his arms, lifted and pulled the chief to his feet. Fully erect, Alasdair judged him to be six feet, nine or ten inches tall and weighing at least 350 pounds. His uniform, solid white with several yards of gold braid and tassels attached to the epaulets on his shoulders, sported a red sash extending from his left shoulder across his chest and enormous belly to his right hip. There it sneaked under the black belt and up his backside to the top of his left shoulder where it was clamped to the epaulet and the other end of the sash with a huge gold medallion. Alasdair did not want to hazard a guess at his boot size, but ventured a thought about his entire presence: a grand marshal at the Barnum and Bailey circus. He wondered where the chief parked his elephant. The man was a joke, surely.

O'Rielly shook hands with the giant and bowed slightly, enough for the chief to see but, he hoped in vain, not enough for Alasdair to notice. He introduced Alasdair to the chief solemnly and seriously, making every effort to avoid eye contact until they were seated in the small conference room. Again, aided by the two patrolmen, the chief was made comfortable in a leather chair not large enough for such a man.

When Halfpenny spoke to Alasdair, his voice was deep and sur-prisingly melodic. "I come with information of importance to both of us. I felt it necessary to make this short trip from Christiansted to speak with Stephen and have him put me in contact with you. It is fortunate you are here. I think you need my help and I know I need yours. Yesterday and today have been very trying and vexing for the police department and me. St. Croix is normally very quiet and law abiding. It is indeed troubling, these events of yesterday and today. First, let me express my condolences on behalf of the department in the tragic death of your friends and associates. That aside, I must go on to the other events.

"This afternoon we received a call reporting a burning car and a cabin that appeared to have exploded. Both were and are located on the unpaved scenic road that circles Blue Mountain. I dispatched police, medical, and fire equipment to the scene at once and this is what we found: an old station wagon, still smoldering and melting on the side of the road a few miles from the highway, containing three bodies burned beyond recognition, burned so badly we are unable to determine their sex. Two hundred meters further, we found a cabin with the backside collapsed inward, apparently from an explosion from the outside. Inside, we found three more bodies, two men and a woman. The explosion and the roof collapsing on them killed one of the men and the woman. A large caliber bullet at the base of his skull pierced his spinal cord and his carotid artery and killed the other man, not the injuries he sustained from the blast. Either an extremely lucky shot or an extremely professional one. Both men were Latinos, probably South Americans or Central Americans, part Indian and only God knows what else. In the cabin, we found rifles of the type used at the Buccaneer Club, as well as clothing very similar to those described by the bartender and cook as being worn by the shooters." Here Constantine Halfpenny paused to take a few breaths.

Alasdair and O'Rielly stared at him with open mouths, unable to comment for a moment. "Are you saying that the six shooters are dead, killed by someone last night? Is that possible?" Alasdair asked.

"At first we thought that, Mr. Alasdair, until we looked at the woman. She is a local prostitute well known to the police, without any possibility of being involved in the shooting. You see, we released her from jail while the bodies at the Buccaneer were being moved to hospital. Getting back in business quickly after release is her trademark, but the fact remains she was in jail when the shooting occurred. It is my opinion two of the passengers in the station wagon are two of her female friends. I do believe the three men are without a doubt three of the shooters. Now the question I ask myself is who did this and where are the other three? Stephen, my friend, do you have something cool and refreshing for this old copper? I have heard that you, Mr. Alasdair, are quite a connoisseur of good single-malt Scotch as well as blends. Before I continue I suggest you might be well-advised to have a double."

The chief was not the fool Alasdair took him to be on first impression. What could he possibly have to report that would top what he already had said? O'Rielly summoned Mercedes, who had her ear glued to the door, and sent her to the bar next door for a cocktail waitress. Drinks for all except the two patrolmen were ordered. The chief did not approve drinks for them. Alasdair offered the chief a cigar. The chief declined. However, Alasdair began his cigar ritual and soon smoke rings floated up. The chief, now with a quart of Cruzan tea in his hand, continued.

"This afternoon, after hearing the report from the officers returning from Blue Mountain, I was interrupted by a report from a visiting fisherman near East Point. It seems he came around the point at a good clip, heading to what he hoped was a more favorable fishing spot, when he saw a really pretty house set back off the road and away from the beach, but clearly visible. He throttled back to get a good view and maybe make a picture if he could find his camera. While looking, he heard what he described as a muffled pop. He continued looking for the camera but had left it in the motel. He spent maybe three or four minutes looking at the house before continuing on to a shady spot near a line of trees that looked favorable. After ten or fifteen minutes he gives up fishing and heads back the way he came. When he passed the house, it was fully involved, as firemen say, in flames. There was nothing he could do other than call for help, which he did at a little bait shop about a mile away."

"Our investigation shows evidence of an explosion and an accelerant similar to the one used on the station wagon. I did mention the station wagon was torched, didn't I?"

"No, Con," Stephen said. "you didn't mention an accelerant and you didn't mention it deliberately, didn't you?"

"We all have our ways of telling stories Stephen. Need a bit of suspense. Now for the last bit of this story. This beautiful house that attracted the fisherman's attention is, or was, a very well-known establishment on East Point. It was called Auntie Monica's Inn."

"Oh shit, son of a bitch, Stephen," Alasdair said. "You don't suppose? Damn, damn, what…a mess There was a body or two in it, right?"

"It can't be, it can't be, Jim. Tell me Brookings didn't miss golf to go see Auntie Monica and that damn Spic girl of hers. Say no bodies were found, chief."

"I am sorry, gentlemen, I cannot say that. However, neither can I say how many bodies were in the house. You see, at first blush it seems the body or bodies were damn near holding the bomb, or whatever it was that exploded. It may be weeks before we know anything. A damn mess it is. I would call off any hunt for Brookings St. John were I you, and look at my own situation, which I suggest is tenuous to say the least. I am sure that by now my boys have located a taxi driver that delivered Mr. St. John to Auntie Monica's Inn."

"Son of a bitch, Stephen," Alasdair said. "Did Maddie know that was one of his haunts? You don't suppose she went there? Could she be one of the bodies?" Turning to the chief, he asked, "And what are you saying about Stephen and me? You think there is a mad bomber after us?"

"Don't you, Mr. Alasdair? It is past seven o'clock and I have one other bit of information to share with you, but I am fatigued and hungry. It has been a long and trying two days. At four o'clock on the 24th four people were killed in the Buccaneer Bar. Some time between 10:00 p.m. on that same day and 2 :00 a.m. on the 25th six people were killed on Blue Mountain. After lunch, sometime in the afternoon of the 25th before 4:30 p.m., one or more people perished by explosion and fire. That is a total of 11 minimum to 13 maximum. In one period of 24 hours, I have my quota of murder and mayhem for an entire year and, moreover, all these events are connected together by a thread that I have not quite figured out. The shooters shot the bankers but only got four, someone bombed the shooters but only got three. Then somebody bombed the whorehouse and got another banker. The way I see it, there are three shooters left to get the last two bankers, you two, and then the bomber gets the remaining three shooters. The link is broken to the man who hired the shooters because the bomber does not work for him and does not know him or the victims. It is all well planned. Now will you summon that cocktail lady and a waitress and order us food and drink. We will include my patrolmen on this round and let them eat in the restaurant with Mercedes. I am afraid she is going to injure her ear on the door if she stays in the office. While you are setting things up, I will stroll over to the bar and use their rest room facilities. They have facilities for the handicapped and they work very well for a man of my build."

While the chief was gone, Alasdair told Stephen, "When I first saw the man I thought he was a joke. I was wrong. Smart and cagey that man is, doesn't miss a thing. Brilliant analytical mind for police work with an understanding of the criminal mind set totally unexpected of a policeman on a quiet island such as St. Croix. Also I think he is right about what happened. Some bastard hired six dope heads to shoot some people, maybe us, and sent a cleaner to clean up the dope heads. We screwed up the plan by not playing golf and they only got four of us. Then the cleaner got half the dope heads, either before he learned of the screw-up or they were told to finish the job. Then he blew up poor old Brookings. But that is the flaw in the reasoning. The cleaner should not have known who the targets were. That is the protection for the bastard who set this up. The chief is probably right about it being the same bomber. But how did the bomber know? There is a missing link."

"Are you admitting someone may be after us, Jim?"

"Maybe. What the hell is he holding back to tell us after we eat? I can't imagine anything more that can happen in this mess. If he is right about us, Stephen, we have no protection here. I don't worry about the damn Latinos, but what about the cleaner? Who is he? Where is he? Probably on St. Croix, but we gotta be there tomorrow. Damn!"

The employees of the restaurant next door, The Squire's Table, busied themselves setting three places around the conference table. They gave the chief one long side of the table and Stephen instructed them to bring the chief some of everything, along with a gallon of Cruzan tea. Meanwhile, Alasdair walked around the office, mumbling, "Son of a bitch," and, "I don't need this shit".

Squeezing himself into one of the leather chairs, Chief Halfpenny surveyed the table layout and expressed his approval. "Mighty nice, gentlemen. I have taken the liberty of granting permission for each of you to go armed throughout the islands. That approval came directly from the damn Republican governor in spite of his knowledge of Cyril King's intention to beat his ass for governor in the election. It is coming up sometime in the future. I frankly do not remember when. Also, believing you to be peaceful and law abiding citizens, my boys have a Beretta 9mm automatic pistol and a supply of ammunition for each of you. I am right, aren't I, you are unarmed?"

"I have a Colt .357 Magnum revolver with a six inch barrel and a box of dum dums for it in my suitcase at the Windward Passage Hotel. Too big to carry under a T-shirt. Don't worry; I know how to use it. Got lots of practice on Koreans."

"Ah yes, as I expected. Respectful of our gun laws. It makes no difference to me for, as of noon tomorrow, I will no longer have any authority over this series of unfortunate occurrences. Tomorrow, some time after noon, four FBI agents will arrive at Alexander Hamilton airport to take over all investigating of the shootings, bombings, and so forth. I will be able to sit on my ass and watch four idiots fuck up everything to do with this case."

"Hell's the matter with these people? Why we need the F-fucking-BI?"

"I will tell you what I was told, Mr. Alasdair. One of the people shot at the Buccaneer Bar was an employee of the FBI."

"What? What the hell are you saying? One of our directors was a FBI agent? Who? Which one? Son of a bitch! What next? Hell's this about, Stephen?"

"Shit, Jim, I'm in the dark as much as you are. This is not real, Con. I know those people and none of them ever had anything to do with the FBI. It can't be true. Did they give you a name?"

"Yes, they gave me a name. They also told me there is an ongoing grand jury investigation that he was involved in and that you, Mr. Alasdair, are the target of that investigation. They are on their way to explain that to you."

"Me? What the hell you talking about? Who the hell's investigating me? About what? What the hell I ever done except work? Some son of a bitch gonna get his tit in a ringer fucking with me. I am not gonna to stand for this kind of shit. Who is the bastard working for me and the FBI? I'd kill his ass hadn't somebody already done it for me. Who is the son of a bitch?"

"Please, Mr. Alasdair, relax. The FBI wants to explain to you. And I think all this shooting and bombing is getting you out of the investigation. Or maybe it was about over before this started. Maybe that's the reason for all this. The FBI says somebody pissed off at you big time. The man working for FBI here was Rico Ronrico and—"

"A fucking lawyer, I should have known. No lawyer worth a shit. Fucking Spic! Quit looking at me, O'Rielly. Sure I went to law school but I ain't a lawyer. Nobody calls me a bloodsucker. Damn Ronrico. What the hell he tell the FBI? We sold insurance to friggin jewelry stores or to fishing boat operators? Maybe we got a deposit in the bank from some friend of mine in Tennessee? Tell them I call my office in Nashville or Atlanta or maybe in London? What a load of crap. Well, say something, Stephen. The bastard was your friend. Maybe he reported you for taking a bottle of rum home with you that was bought with company money. Hell,I bet you been stealing number two lead pencils. Big black market in lead pencils. "

"OK, Jim, I know you are pissed, but whatta you think he was supposed to find out. He never came around except for the meetings and never asked any questions or pried into anything. They could find out more about us reading our ads in the newspaper. You never discussed any of your other businesses at our board meetings. If he learned everything about our insurance agency, that wouldn't be much. And the bank has to report everything, so there are no secrets in that area. You never have any meetings here other than bank and insurance. Only woman you ever brought with you is your wife. You're a perfect citizen in the Virgins. He must have written dull reports if all he covered was you. Brookings, now, is a different story, most likely a case for National Inquirer because of having sex with mama and daughter at the same time. FBI really interested in that, I'll bet."

"Very well, gentlemen," the chief said, "I shall continue if you please. They will, as I said, be here tomorrow. You never asked where they're coming from, but I'll tell you, Philadelphia, Pennsylvania, home of the Peace Bank you fellows have drawn and quartered right here in the good old U.S. Virgin Islands. Tore a hole in their ass big enough to drive a semi through. All the business they got left is two penny-ante drug pushers and a street vendor. Are they pissed off at you? Probably not. Tired of banking in the Caribbean, I suppose, and you just helped them out by closing them up."

Alasdair and O'Rielly looked at each other but said nothing. Halfpenny pushed himself back from the table and wondered if he might have another quart of Cruzan tea. Alasdair lit a new cigar and refilled the Scotch glass while O'Rielly scouted around for the waiter. The clock on the wall advertising King & O'Rielly Insurance Ltd. showed the time to be 10:18 in Charlotte Amalie, St. Thomas, USVI.

"When do the FBI types arrive, chief, and where do they expect to meet with me?"

"Sometime in the afternoon would be my guess for arrival, and my office is what they suggested for the meeting. That is up to you, in my humble opinion, for I do not believe they will find you in awe of the FBI. Personally, I would let the bastards come to me, were I you. I do not have that privilege and must sit idle and allow them to take over my investigations and my office. All of this because one of the victims was a Fed informer or some shit like that. No doubt every effort will be made to humiliate and embarrass me in front of my men and the officials of the islands. I detest the sanctimonious bastards. However, I am, unlike you, in their clutches. You can make them meet you at Mountain Top and watch you consume one of their famous banana daiquiris. Better yet, make them have lunch with you at the Hotel 1829. You cannot buy them lunch because that is against their rules, but lunch at the 1829 will bust their ass for a week's per diem. I'd love to see that."

"Ah, here's Stephen with Cruzan tea and our waiter. Anything more for you, Chief, or shall they clear the table?"

"Clear the table. We all need to get some rest tonight, if such a thing is possible, after a day like today. I am staying at the Windward Passage and suggest, since you are also there, Mr. Alasdair, we have breakfast about 8 o'clock and see what tomorrow looks like."

CHAPTER 5

August 25, 1970, 10:00 p.m. GMT–4, Sombrero Inn, St. Croix

Whitestar drove the old station wagon to the Sombrero Inn, staying a safe distance behind the blue sedan extracted from its perch in the flower bed. He drove through the inn's parking area all the way to the end, then parked behind the building out of sight of any highway traffic. Furillo was uneasy with the peace they had made with Cosgrove and Casale because he was not sure Cosgrove's hands were clean in the bombing and shooting at the cabin he had rented for them. Who else knew where they were, and being in Miami did not keep him from sending the bomber. But Estavo reasoned that if Cosgrove had sent the bomber, he would not have turned up in St. Croix. Estavo and Furillo both agreed finally that neither Cosgrove nor Casale had set up the bombing. All three were in agreement that they were never going back to the cabin. Wisely they had left nothing there. Whitestar remained uneasy about what to do next. There were jobs waiting for six men and now they were only three, but they needed the cover a job offered. There was no way they could leave the island for a month, at least not by regular transport. The police knew there were six of them involved in the shootings and now they knew there were three left. They decided during the ride back to Cosgrove's motel to quit worrying about leaving the island and show up for work as planned. When asked about the other three, they would shrug their shoulders and say, "Who knows? Not our job, keep up wit dem."

Cosgrove waited for them at the door to his room that connected with Casale's room. Inside, he gave them keys to three rooms he had rented from the fat bitch while they were parking the station wagon. She agreed to wait until morning for the men to come in and give their names and other information she needed. He paid her for seven days' rent on each room. She was happy. Casale had a short speech worked out for the Latinos, then he wanted to go to bed and try to sleep. He doubted he could sleep, but he wanted to try.

"Here is the situation," he began. "You did a good job at the Buccaneer Bar, but only half of the targets were there. You still need to get the other three. I know it is not your fault they were no-shows, but neither is it mine. You are being paid for six, so you need to get six. We owe you twenty thousand dollars of the original money, and I am going to give you twelve thousand now, or four thousand each. That is more than you would have received if you had connected the first time because then there were six to split the money, and now only three. After you get the other three, I will give you the remaining eight thousand. I hope you understand that I expect you to do the entire job regardless of screw-ups that are not your fault or mine."

"That is not de kind of deal we signed on for, Casale," Whitestar said. "We only have to hit the golfers that come in de bar after the last round of de two o'clock tee off. We did that. If they'd been seven, we would have got seven. There was only four, so we got four. We never agreed to anybody other than de golfers in de bar. You some kind of bad ass somewhere, but we done killed three senators and some other official, and our ass up the bayou if we gets caught. We can't leave cause de damn police looking for Latinos like us. We got to work until they get lax, then we leave. If you want us to get the other three, we want three thousand each more. That's our final words. What you gonna do, turn us in an say these mens we hired to shoot yo senators fucked up and only got four and won't get de other three, so put them in the jail? I fucking doubt you be doing that. So get de extra money and we go to work and take out de other three."

"It doesn't work that way, Whitestar. The way it works is if you take a job you complete it or someone does it for you. Well, Cosgrove and I are the someone who has been selected to finish the work if you don't. It's my job to tell you that and make you the payment offer I just did. If you do not accept the offer, then I finish your job and keep the money and go on about my business, and you go about yours. Then my contract is fulfilled, but Cosgrove is in the shit because he hired you and you failed to keep your word. So he has to pay. Again, that is his problem which he can help by helping me finish your contract. I advise you to go to your rooms and sleep on this and we get together for breakfast at 7:30 in the morning and talk it over again. Goodnight. I am tired and have a busy day tomorrow." Casale walked through the door to the adjoining room and closed it behind him. The three Latinos looked at Cosgrove. He shrugged his shoulders and turned toward the bathroom. The Latinos wandered out the door.

Cosgrove stared at his reflection in the bathroom mirror and noticed the swelling starting under and over his eye. Tomorrow it would be swelled closed and sore. "The bastard had no reason to hit me that way and I will remember him. Fat lot of good it will do me in this mess. If I get a chance I will slip away from Casale and get my ass back to Miami. I have the keys to the car. If I decide to go I can. Casale threatened to kill me, me, his brother-in-law, so why do I owe him anything?" This conversation, conducted between Cosgrove and his image in the mirror, began to take over his thinking and the thoughts became his only way out. He began to wonder whether the water taxis were still running to St. Thomas or the seaplanes to Puerto Rico. The phone! He could call, but then he remembered there was no phone in the room. Pack a bag and go. What did he have to pack that he needed? Nothing except the twenty thousand dollars. It was still in his bag. The idea had become too strong to resist when he noticed a car parked at the far edge of the lot, near the highway, with its lights on. Maybe that offered escape. He grabbed the money from his bag and stuffed it into his pockets, front and rear. Twenty thousand dollars in various denominations of bills made a sizable stack. He locked the door between rooms and eased out through his room's outside door, locking it after him.

Not only were the car's lights on, its engine was running with no sign of the owner anywhere. Cosgrove didn't give it a second thought but opened the driver's side door. To his surprise, the driver was slumped across the seat, asleep or passed out drunk, which, from the strong scent of alcohol, seemed more likely. Cosgrove shoved him over and slipped the lever into drive, being careful not to attract attention as he pointed the car toward Christiansted. His passenger did not stir and showed no signs or reviving during the entire drive, causing Cosgrove to smile as he thought of the surprise in store for the drunk when he awakened. He parked the car in a dark space near the rear of the Caravelle Hotel, being sure to turn off the lights and the ignition switch. He locked the door to protect his benefactor from robbers and thieves before setting off to walk to the dock where water taxis and seaplanes were based. Cosgrove was lucky, the midnight taxi, the last water taxi of the day to St. Thomas, had failed to start and the repairs had delayed it for thirty minutes.

❧　　　❧　　　❧

August 25, 1970, Midnight GMT–4, Caravelle Hotel, Christiansted, St. Croix

Walther glanced at his watch again. It was midnight, but he could not sleep. He felt relaxed and contented, but questions gnawed at him. He pulled the sheet over the nude Maddie, sleeping beside him and looking like an angel. But she was, as Walther knew, no angel. The major questions that disturbed his mind were who and what she was. Walther knew the limitations to his understanding of women, especially beautiful women, but he understood enough to know women usually did not behave as she did. She came out of Auntie Monica's Inn acting as if she had known him for years and felt comfortable telling him she had just shot two people. She made the irrational assumption that he would go inside and take care of everything for her, and even insisted he do it quickly because she had things to do with him. Maddie had seen him only once before, when she arrived from St. Thomas on the water taxi. He remembered her friendly smile as she walked past him on the ramp, but that was only a polite gesture.

. Walther slipped out of bed, pulled on his pants, and walked quietly out onto the tiny balcony. He could see the dock and noticed the activity as the water taxi prepared to leave on the last trip of the day. Maddie had arrived on a water taxi from St. Thomas before noon, but showed no indication of going back to wherever she lived or worked. In fact, she gave every indication that she believed her place was with him, and appeared to have forgotten any life prior to leaving Auntie Monica's Inn except for one brief mention of a bank and having some of their credit cards. Perhaps she worked for a bank and, if so, they would be searching for her today. Walther had planning to do before anyone turned up looking for her. Walther could not live without a plan, even if it only covered a short period of hours or days.

Normally, Walther would twist her neck as he had the Spic girl and toss her into the garbage somewhere. Unfortunately, he himself removed that option when he made sure they were seen in the hotel and when he agreed to the shopping spree. Too many people saw them together for her to be found in the garbage. He wrestled with another problem, a new problem for him. He felt sure he loved her and could not hurt her, or let anyone hurt her as that Brookings person undoubtedly did. Who, he wondered, was that Brookings person and what was he to her?

Walther pressed his back against the building wall, closed his eyes, and allowed the events of the past day to spin crazily, kaleidoscope style, until they settled into some order. Once the spinning stopped, the feeling of peace Walther needed rolled over him like the incoming tide. He relaxed and saw the plan he needed for the next few days unfold and spread itself before the eye of his mind. It was clear, and he accepted it and waited until it took control of his being. Renewed, rewound, and reprogrammed, Walther went back to bed and instantly fell asleep.

❧   ❧   ❧

Wednesday, August 26, 1970, 5:02 a.m. GMT–4, Windward Passage Hotel

Incessant, unrelenting telephone ringing will eventually wake the most dedicated sleeper. Alasdair was no exception. He awoke on the tenth ring in less than a good humor. During the last forty-eight hours, he had flown from St. Thomas to Nashville, Tenn., and from Nashville back to St. Thomas, enduring a long layover in Miami with little opportunity for rest or sleep. The meetings he attended at the insurance office with O'Rielly and Chief Halfpenny were long and stressful, not at all conducive to deep sleep. As he reached for the phone, he noticed the clock on the bedside table glowed 5:02 a.m., causing him to flinch. He had expected another two hours, having left a wake-up call for 7:00 a.m. He mumbled into the phone but was instantly awake when he recognized Sue's voice and anticipated another problem.

"Sir, you must speak with Mr. Carlotta. He's in Belize, at the office, and wants you to call. He took the jet and planned to ring you but the damn phone on the plane wouldn't work. So when he got to the office he rang me. He left hurriedly and left everything in Atlanta because of the problem in Belize. You have…"

"Sue, shut up a second. What is the problem in Belize?"

"I do not know, sir, but he said only it was bad and he had to go. The police in Belize called right after he had spoken with the project manager for the cannery. He was quite upset when he spoke with me."

"Dammit, Sue, why didn't you find out the problem?"

"Sir, he hung up the phone and when I called back he was gone to the airport and no one in the office knew what was up. I did the best I could and tried to get him in the jet but, as I said, the damn phone wouldn't work."

"OK, Sue, I will call him. Damn! How many problems can I handle? The FBI is coming to see me today about some damned investigation on top of the shootings here, and now this. It can't be a simple problem or Carlotta would have handled it from Atlanta. What did you say? The police called him? Why the police?"

"I do not know, sir. Some of the men are in trouble, I guess."

"What else can happen? This is getting to be unbelievable."

"Well, there is one more thing, Ted called from London and left a message on the machine for you to ring him ASAP. Something about an IRA car bomb on Mount Street in London…"

"Hell's going on? Mount Street is where our London office is located. Where is Ted, did he leave a number, or is he home?"

"He is at the Naval Club waiting for you to call. He said he and Leslie were knocking back a few, whatever that means."

"Oh, shit. Thanks, Sue. Call Carlotta and patch me through to him. The operator here is still in bed where I had hoped to be for another couple of hours."

It never occurred to Alasdair that it was only 4:08 a.m. in Nashville and Sue was probably at home and not in the office. Nonetheless, she soon had Carlotta on the phone and agreed to get Ted as soon as Carlotta hung up.

"This is a real problem, Mr. Alasdair, a real problem. But I will tell you your man from Idaho is some kind of a man. He really is. He may be half nuts but he sure knows how to handle trouble. We've got a folk hero on our hands, a real man of the people. These people will write songs about him. A fucking failure as a guard, but who is perfect? Our man, Fontana, he is..."

"Forget Fontana and tell me what happened to get you down there."

"I'm sorry. Yesterday morning about ten o'clock, the men working on the clearing for the bean field took their mid-morning break. Fontana was sitting in the tractor listening to his country music tapes when he needed to take a leak. He noticed the men huddling around the water cooler as he got out. Modesty, I suppose, caused him to walk behind the tractor, out of view of the men. That very minute, sixteen wild-ass Mexicans with machetes stormed out of the woods and attacked the workers. Our workers had no weapons, even the axes and chain saws they had were left where they were working. In a matter of seconds, the Mexicans had hacked and slashed eighteen or twenty of them into a pile of blood and flesh. Fontana heard the yells and screams and went to the front of the tractor and grabbed his gun while the Mexicans were hacking the other four or six workers and prodding the ones chopped up during the first charge.

"Fontana goes berserk and charges the Mexicans screaming like a demon from the deep somewhere. Remember, there are sixteen Mexicans and the AR 180 only has a thirty round clip, a fact Fontana remembered also. That son of a bitch shot all the Mexicans at least once, then shoved in a new clip and shot them again. The second round the bastard gut shot them so they would die in agony, except three of them wanted a little more, so he cut their throats with one of the machetes he found lying on the ground. That son of a bitch killed all sixteen of them, and if he hadn't needed to take a pee when he did he probably would have saved half the workers. A mean bastard he is, and I am having trouble keeping him away from all the people who want pictures and to interview him. Hell, they are planning a parade for him, the great protector of the working people.

Bastard didn't save a single person but took damn good care of their attackers."

"Hell's going on, Carlotta? What brought this about? We haven't had any trouble with any locals. The government is happy. Why this bunch of Mexicans? Did you find anything on them to give us a clue as to why they chopped up our crew?"

"No identification, nothing indicating any sort of terrorist group, nothing of that sort. One chilling piece of evidence that will tell you more than you want to know is each man had five crisp new one hundred dollar bills in his pocket, new crisp U.S. one hundreds. Somebody hired them to do this. Somebody is after us and I am afraid this is just the beginning. Did Sue tell you our Belize folders are all missing from the file room? That burglary a while back, the files were what they were after, not the office junk. That was just to throw us off guard. I look for something else to happen."

"I am afraid it already has happened. Look at this. Four of the directors in this little operation were shot down in a bar, the guy running the bank was blown up in a local whore house, our workers killed on our job site in Belize. Now I have a call from Ted about an IRA car bomb on Mount Street where our London office is located. I don't think this is a coincidence. I think somebody is after my ass big time and I am not liking it one bit. I am getting pissed, but I don't know at who. But I will locate the bastard and take care of his ass."

"It does look bad and we need to come up with a plan. We have to have more guards. All they have to do is watch and point Fontana. That bastard is hell on wheels. Sixteen! He killed sixteen of the Mexicans, and let me tell you the rest of the story. After he finished, he climbed back in the tractor and plugged in a Dolly Parton tape and went to sleep. About 1:30 he woke up and radioed the office he had had to shoot some people and needed some backup. He switched the radio off and waited until two choppers of police arrived with no idea of what to expect, but definitely not what they found."

"Look, Carlotta, keep Fontana away from the news people as much as you can, but let him do whatever the natives want, parades, speeches, autographs, any of that crap will help us with workers and we are going to need all the help we can get to keep workers. Nobody wants to be chopped up. Sue, are you there? Have you been listening?"

"Yes, sir, I have and I have Ted on the line waiting to speak with you."

"Good show. Put him on, Carlotta might as well hear the other bad news. Is he there? Ted, can you hear me?"

"Oh, yes, Jim. I can hear you very well. I am afraid I have some most distressing news for you. Yesterday at about 6.00 p.m., a Rover was illegaly parked in front of the Italian restaurant under your office on Mount Street. The coppers noticed it and clamped it when they should have towed it away. Anyway, it was one of those IRA car bombs. It exploded a couple of minutes after six. Regular mess it made of the entire block, it did. The IRA is really a bad lot with no regard for property or life."

"Ted, Ted, what about our office? Were any of our people injured, or do you know?"

"Well, yes, Jim, that is what I am calling about. It seems your man Keaton and Mrs. Dobbins were there and apparently on their way to the Cellar Pub when the Rover exploded. They were passing it by at the time and the blast blew them into the restaurant and smashed them against the kitchen wall. Unfortunately they are both dead."

"Both dead! Both of them dead? Surely not, Ted, it just can't be. I cannot believe this. You hear that, Carlotta? Hell's going on I would like to know. Ted, do you know what has happened? Five of my people killed in the Virgin Islands, twenty-four or so in Belize, and now two in London, all in the last twenty-four hours. Son of a bitch! I can't go to funerals all over the world. Ted, the IRA didn't have anything to do with that car bomb, it was a message to me. I have now had four messages in one twenty-four-hour period. I suppose I am considered too dumb to catch on quickly. Very likely someone made a deal with an IRA bomber to do the Mount Street car. Get with the police and tell them the car blast is number four for me in one day and to look for reasons other than some Irish bastard who hates you Brits."

"Sue, where are you, at home?"

"Yes sir, its four o'clock in the morning here."

"Yeah, I forgot about the time. Listen, do not go to the office and call everyone and tell them to stay away until they hear from me. Then call Chief Joe Casey and Sheriff Fate Thomas and tell them I want guards twenty-four hours a day at the condo where I live. Tell Casey to send a good man over to the condo to see how many guards are needed and where to position them. I live on the eighth floor, so it ought to be simple. He and Fate have plenty of good men who want to work off-duty shifts, but do whatever it takes and I will pay the cost. Also, he needs to alert the office-building owner. That SOB will probably try to evict us if he gets a threat or thinks he might. And you, Sue, call my wife and tell her to keep her ass in the condo until I can ring her and talk. OK?"

"Yes, sir."

"Ted, if you and Leslie can, I will appreciate you taking a tour through the Mount Street office and evaluate the damage and let Sue know. Whatever needs to be done there you can do, if you don't mind. I don't have anyone else in London now. Carlotta has his hands full in Belize, and I have my own problems here. Can you give me a hand that way, Ted?"

"Sure, Leslie and I will take care of it. We will."

"Oh Ted, Keaton has a wife and four kids, and Dobbins has a husband. Look after them also. OK?"

"Surely, Jim, I will have Bobbie go see her. Bobbie is good in this type situation. She had her share of it when we lived in the Mid-East."

"What about you, Carlotta? You got it under control in Belize?"

"Unless we have a problem at the airport, I've got it under control."

"OK. Everybody ring off but Sue, and you fellows watch your backside. I sure as hell don't want any of you hurt. Any of you need me, call Sue. She can find me.

"Sue, hang on 'tillI order some coffee. Damn! What a way to start a day." Alasdair walked into the empty second bedroom of the suite and, using the phone there, ordered a pot of coffee. Shaking his head and mumbling to himself, he pulled on a pair of jeans and a golf shirt before going back to the phone. "Sue, I have an associate you do not know and have not heard about so far as I know. He is a loyal and trusted friend from years ago. I have no idea where he is in any specific way, but I am sure he is in the middle of some war somewhere. My wife knows him and knows how to contact him. Go over to the condo now and talk to her. Call first and tell her I asked you to come over. Bring her up to date on all the problems and that I want to see the colonel either here, in Nashville, or Atlanta, as soon as possible, which ever place he can get to the quickest. That is all she will need to know, and it is all you need to know. OK? And tell her I said keep her ass in the condo until I speak with her."

"Yes, sir."

"Very good, now hop to it." The coffee arrived as he cradled the phone. Coffee in hand, Alasdair walked over to the sliding glass doors to gaze at the sleeping harbor and the deserted street. Dawn began to lighten the sky. Soon the harbor would become a bustling center of activity in Charlotte Amalie and Alasdair wondered what else this day would bring. An enemy, presently unknown, was bearing down on him with a vengeance he seldom encountered even in the steamy heat and bitter cold of Korea. There, at least, he knew his enemy and more or less where he could be found. Now he faced an unknown enemy striking him viciously worldwide from his hidden lair somewhere, anywhere. "I will find you and I will destroy you as I would a thistle in my rose bed. No, as I would a rabid fox in my yard.

I will grind your ass in the dirt like a dung beetle. You cannot survive this attack on me and mine. Never! Never!"

❧   ❧   ❧

August 26, 1970, 7:08 a.m. GMT–4, Sombrero Inn, St. Croix

Pounding on the door finally awakened Casale from his first deep sleep in three days. His head pounded with each knock on the door, reminding him that he had consumed too much alcohol last night. Staggering and stumbling across the room, he jerked open the door. "What?" Whitestar stared at him, not understanding why he was not fully dressed and ready to go.

"Food, mon. We ready to eat. Cosgrove already gone, I think. We couldn't rouse him. Come on, mon, we need to eat and talk some more. We be at de restaurant waiting. You come on before they close. I see you in a few, mon." Whitestar wandered off toward the restaurant, leaving Casale mumbling to himself.

"Stupid fuck, we got nothing to talk about. He finishes his work or he gets no money. Simple." In the bathroom, Casale splashed cold water on his face and tried to rinse the fur off his teeth. As he struggled to push his foot through the leg of the black silk pants, he realized the need to buy some clothes. "I can't wear this damn suit forever and the shirt is beginning to smell real bad. Fucking bunch of Spics on that damn plane messed up my clothes. Stunk like a damn garbage scow, that plane did." Casale tried to twist the knob on the door to Cosgrove's adjoining room. It did not twist. "Locked. The fucking door is locked. Cosgrove, you in there? Why the hell is the door locked?" Remembering what Whitestar had said about not being able to rouse Cosgrove, he decided he had best hurry to the restaurant before Cosgrove said something foolish to the Latinos.

"Over here, mon, we got de table in de corner. Cosgrove is not here. I don't know where he at. I thought he'd be here. You find him?"

"No, I didn't. He had the damn door locked and I couldn't get in. Keep my coffee warm, and I will get a key from the fat broad and check his room. He can't be sleeping hard enough not to hear you and me knocking on the door."

The fat broad reluctantly gave Casale a spare key to Cosgrove's room. Casale walked into the empty room with the beginning of a sinking feeling deep in his stomach. He noticed Cosgrove's bag on the floor by the bed and his toilet articles in the bathroom. The sinking feeling grabbed hard at Casale's gut and he raced to the bag and scoured its contents with both hands. The money was gone. "The son of a bitch is gone, but where? Where the hell can he go? The car! He's gone in the car!" Casale rushed out into the parking lot and there sat the car. "Where is the son of bitch? Oh, shit! The station wagon!" Casale dashed around the end or the building and saw the station wagon setting where it had been left the night before. What, he wondered, would he tell Whitestar?

Three dark faces with questioning eyes met him at the corner table. Before saying anything, Casale grabbed the coffee mug and took a large gulp of the warm, thick liquid. "Damn, that coffee is awful. Cosgrove is not in his room. I do not know where the hell he is. All of his shit is there, so he must be here somewhere, taking a walk or something. I'm sure he will be back in a few minutes."

Furillo did not take the idea of Cosgrove going for a walk as an acceptable explanation for his absence. "De money, mon. Has he got de money? If de money gone, Cosgrove taking a long fucking walk, mon."

"No the money is safe. I have the money." Casale lied because it would be a very bad idea to tell them the money was missing. "He has not gone far. Hell, it was midnight when he went to bed last night and the car is here, so where could he have gone? We got no phone to call a taxi and I doubt one would have come out here that late had he been able to call. Just relax and eat a big breakfast, then we will make plans for how to deal with the other three people. By then Cosgrove will be back and we can get on with finishing up our work." Whitestar noticed that Casale's demeanor and attitude seemed less strident and self-assured than the night before. That concerned him, that concerned him very much. It meant Cosgrove was gone, and with him the rest of their money. Whitestar studied Furilo and Estavo, both of whom devoted most of their attention to the food, paying only a little attention to the conversation. As long as they remained sure the money was there and with Casale, everything will stay calm. Should they become convinced Cosgrove had left with their money, a shooting in the restaurant might be the result. Whitestar did not object to them shooting the arrogant Wop, but not in the restaurant at the Sombrero Inn.

The plotters could speak freely in the restaurant since they were the only customers and the waiter seemed to also be the cook and dishwasher. He remained in the kitchen unless summoned. His radio in the kitchen played so loudly it vibrated the dishes on their shelves. Both Whitestar and Casale made an effort to keep the conversation positive during the remainder of breakfast. Each presented scenarios for completion of their work. No plan emerged from the conversation. One after another proved unworkable or too risky to be successful. As time passed without the reappearance of Cosgrove, it became difficult to concentrate as the missing Cosgrove intruded more and more into everyone's thoughts. Casale introduced the subject directly in an effort to retain the three Latinos as partners in the contract.

"I am worried about Cosgrove. I may have pressured him too much and he became frightened. You know him and know he is not like us. When I explained that we expected him to take part in killing the other three people, he became very agitated. He has never done anything like that and the thought almost made him sick. I am afraid he is trying to get back to Miami and is walking toward Christiansted. I will take the car and try to catch him while the three of you remain here and come up with a plan."

"When we gonna get de rest of our money?" Furillo asked the question on everyone's mind.

"When we finish the work I will pay you, plus a bonus. Do not concern yourself about the money and I won't concern myself about you taking off and leaving me to finish your work alone." The stand-off held as Casale left a twenty on the table to cover breakfast and walked to the old blue car.

"Estavo, you and Furillo come to my room at ten o'clock to talk about what we gonna do. I don't know right now, but I know we got to make some big decisions. If we don't help, he call de police and tell them we done it at de bar. They won't know who he be, but they know us. By de time we tell them about him, he done be gone, leaving us in de trap. Maybe we jus' shoot him and get de hell outah here. You think it over and we talk in a couple of hours."

"Estavo and me think de best chance to get dem be at de funeral parlor, if we gonna get dem. They be there early to make sure everything OK, so Casale can go to point dem out and we shoot dem, then we shoot that Wop bastard too. I tired of that bastard and his threats and smart talk. We notice he ain't too damn smart ass since Cosgrove left his ass alone. But we think de money gone. That Cosgrove took de money with him, leaving us with nothing. We shoot these people and hope we find some money or we leave him alone to finish up de job. We didn't hire on for no special people, we hired on for whoever come in that bar and we got dem. Ain't our fault de whole island didn't show up. We did our job and I don't like no Wop telling me we done fucked up when we done what we asked to do. Estavo and I think if he don't show us no money before we go to de funeral parlor we tell him go by yourself and we be on our way. If he talk about de police, then I shoot him, then we go on our way. Right about now he be calling somebody for more money and sending some ass hole to Miami to shoot Cosgrove and get de money back. If he do, then we got some money. If he don't, we no worse off. Me and Estavo ain't shooting nobody until we see some money. It OK to be in his pocket, but if that Wop want me to shoot anybody else, he better have de money for me to look at, and that's a fact."

"I understand you, Furillo, and I almost agree with you. But if that bastard comes back and can't show us no money to shoot dem all, then that's what I say, shoot his ass on de spot and get de hell outta here. I understand, but you come to my room in about an hour and we decide what to do."

❧   ❧   ❧

August 26, 1970, 7:10 a.m. GMT–4, Caravelle Hotel, St. Croix

Walther awoke with a start, leaped out of bed, and rushed to the bath. He could hear the shower running. Unconsciously, acting on reflexes from long training, he grasped the revolver with which he slept with his right hand as his left hand reached for the knob on the bath door. He had no memory of removing the Smith and Wesson from under the pillow, but fortunately did remember Maddie an instant before charging into the bath. He spun around and glanced at the bed, suddenly realizing it must be Maddie in the shower. Walther leaned against the wall by the door to again accustom himself to his new situation of not being alone. He closed his eyes and thought of how he would have to develop a new plan for having Maddie with him. That did not upset Walther, for he considered Maddie worth the time required for him to develop a satisfactory plan.

Walther carefully placed the Smith and Wesson back under his pillow before putting on his pants. On the tiny balcony outside the room, Walther leaned against the wall and stared at the blue water of the Caribbean as it rose and fell with the rhythmic swells of the incoming tide. A feeling of peace moved throughout and over his mind and body, leaving him in the proper mood for intensive planning. His eyes closed, his mind opened as the plan painted itself before his mind's eye like an artist on a canvas. At first, the brush-

strokes were broad, flowing, without detail, applying color and tex-
ture until a background covered the canvas and prepared the way for
the delicate strokes of detail which soon danced across the canvas.
The completed plan leaped out to Walther. The soothing plan spread
over him just as the incoming tide spread over the beaches below. As
the water smoothed the sand, the plan smoothed the rough edges of
Walther's mind. After fifteen minutes, Walther re-entered the room
confident of his ability to deal with living with Maddie.

Maddie emerged from the bath, fully clothed and glowing. She
flashed her gorgeous smile at Walther, causing him to stumble over
his shoes even before he heard her beautiful, lilting voice. Surely she
was an angel sent to look after him. "Hurry, get dressed. I am hungry
and we have a big day before us that I have planned for a long time
and we need to get started." With that she kissed his reddening cheek
above the red beard and bounced out onto the balcony. Walther did
not understand blushing. He did not recall ever having that feeling
before, the heat rushing to his cheeks. It did not bother Walther.

Maddie's statement of having planned what she wanted to do for a
long while disturbed Walther only for a second before he passed it
off along with another click he heard in his mind's ear as he stepped
into the warm flood of shower water. No where in his line of work
could Walther find a niche for Maddie. He needed no assistance and
no partners. Only loners engaged in Walther's work, yet he found
himself searching for a niche for Maddie. In his latest plan he had
slid her in as if she was an insert on a map. Now, in the early morning with shower water beating down on him, he turned once again to
the Maddie incident. He replayed the tape in his mind covering his
meeting with Maddie. Love struck and awed, Walther admitted his
relationship with Maddie made no sense. There was no logic. The
woman he had observed fleeing Auntie Monica's Inn bore no resemblance to the woman he found thirty minutes later sitting in the red
convertible, or to the woman in the bedroom. It did not bother
Walther.

Maddie watched, without comment, as Walther strapped on his ankle holster, but helped him when he fumbled with the Velcro straps which held the star dagger on the underside of his left fore-arm. Walther omitted the shoulder weapon, feeling it unnecessary for breakfast in the Caravelle dining room. Maddie accepted the weapons as she would a belt or hat, neither making comment nor asking questions as if this was a normal part of her and Walther's life. She did not ask, or had she ever asked, for her .25 caliber Beretta semi-automatic Walther had placed between Brookings and Auntie Monica. Before leaving for breakfast, Walther studied himself in the full-length mirror on the bathroom door. He observed that his hair looked exceptionally well but his beard needed trimming. He would do that later in the day.

Walther selected a table in the Caravelle's open-air dining room next to the railing with a good view of the water. He needed the com-fort he gained by watching the water as he listened to Maddie explain how she planned for them to spend the day snorkeling on the reefs near Buck Island. Walther explained he had never snorkeled but would be willing to watch her as she did. Maddie explained that snorkeling was not a spectator sport but a participation sport. She said she would teach Walther and make him proficient in a few hours. Her enthusiasm was only slightly dampened when Walther explained that he considered ocean water beautiful to watch but too dirty to get into. She explained away and answered all questions and objections offered by Walther. No, it is not dirty. No, it will not ruin your hair or bleach out the red color. And, yes, you can wear a shirt to protect you from the sun.

Walther moved the conversation from snorkeling to her job at the bank. He suggested she call and explain her absence. She replied that she was never going back to the bank. She said she didn't work for the bank but worked for Brookings St. John. She said she had told him that if he deserted her for a black whore again, he would have her resignation. He had done that and now she guessed he would just have to get along at the bank without her. Perhaps his whore would be a good replacement and, no, she didn't give a damn about anyone at the bank. She told Walther to forget the bank. She was not going back. Walther heard the click in his head again. This time it bothered him more, but he chose again to ignore the warning.

❀   ❀   ❀

August 26, 1970, 8:45 a.m. GMT–4, Windward Passage Hotel, St. Thomas

A disheveled and irate Alasdair arrived late for the breakfast with O'Rielly and Chief Halfpenny on the Windward's open patio. They waited with coffee. Halfpenny had shed the gigantic white uniform for breakfast, wearing instead a shirt and jeans, both of which also were gigantic. For thirty minutes, Alasdair told them about Belize and London. "I am finished being kicked around and intend to strike back, and strike hard." They pointed out that he could only strike back when he located a target.

"There are three men left on St. Croix who shot our associates in the Buccaneer Bar. I will find them, and when I do they will tell me what they know, however little that may be. But it will be enough to lead me to another man. That man will tell me a little more, and I will work my way to the top of the chain. Then a settlement will be made. There is another man on St. Croix waiting to dispose of the remaining three Latinos. He missed them on his first try and is not anxious to miss again. He may be waiting to give them a chance to get Stephen and me. More likely the Latinos are hiding because they know he is after them. I intend to find that man and he will tell me who he is working for. Also, there is a witness who has not come forward for some reason. I intend to locate him and get an explanation as to why he has remained a silent witness. Chief, now that you have been relieved of your duties by the FBI, perhaps you can help me. Speaking of the FBI, when do they arrive?"

"Like I told you last evening, sometime in the afternoon, possibly four o'clock or thereabouts."

"Stephen, what is the time frame for releasing the bodies? Have you spoken to the coroner or the families?"

"The coroner may release the bodies this afternoon according to what he told me," Stephen said. "The coroner has to do an autopsy to determine the cause of death, even though they each have eight or ten bullet holes in their body. I told the families I would see to the paperwork and get them to the funeral parlor. The funeral director made arrangements for one big room by moving partitions in the three regular rooms in order to accommodate all four caskets. The families plan one massive funeral service for all four."

"Hell's the matter with you, Stephen? Half of St. Croix and a good part of St. Thomas will show up. Much better to stagger them out over two or three days than to try to do it all at once. Hell, three senators and the senate lawyer shot at once. A joint funeral will bring a crowd of thousands. None of my business, so you handle whatever you have to, and I'll do what I need to do to solve my world problems. Ought to throw Ronrico out in the street."

"Jim, we need to go to the bank. Chief, what is your schedule? When are you going back to St. Croix?"

"I have to be back by four o'clock to meet the feds. That is my schedule."

"Go to the bank with us, and when we finish there we can take the water taxi to Christiansted and relax on the way. Plenty room for you at the bank, lots of desks and telephones, so you can do whatever. Jim has a bunch of calls to make and I need to speak with the manager."

"Very well, I will do that. By the way, where is Cyril? He should be here for the funerals to shake hands with the people, his people. The governor will be there, you may be sure."

"The chief is right, Stephen. We better try to get him back here for this occasion. You know what they say, 'Any occasion is better than no occasion.'"

Max Inman stood in the doorway to the Island Bank, watching Alasdair and O'Rielly walk the last two blocks from the Windward Passage Hotel. No word from Maddie, no word from St. John, and the remaining two directors walking toward the bank. Perhaps they would be able to tell him something. Customers were becoming worried and employees edgy. Not unexpected, he supposed, in situations this uncertain and strange. "News, any news. Just end the uncertainty, then we can proceed with business," Inman said to the FDIC decal on the door.

"Good morning, gentlemen," he said to Alasdair and O'Rielly. "Come in, please. As you can see, we are open for business. But business seems a bit slow this morning."

"It is a good morning, Max. Come into Brookings' office and we will have a chat," O'Rielly said. "Who is your next in charge, the head teller or one of the loan officers?"

"The head teller, Ithica McGurk, and our head loan officer, T.J. Rye, are on a par, each with specific duties and responsibilities, Mr. O'Rielly."

"Ask them to join us in the conference room for few minutes, please, Max."

Inman introduced McGurk and Rye to Alasdair, and everyone seated themselves expectantly, waiting for either O'Rielly, whom they all knew, or Alasdair, whose name was more familiar than his face, to give them the news.

Alasdair spoke. "This is the scoop as we know it. This afternoon the bodies of the directors will be released to the funeral director and a massive service is planned, tentative only, for Friday. Whatever day, the bank will close. Otherwise, we will maintain our regular schedule. The police still maintain this publicly to be a random drug-crazed shooting by disgruntled veterans. That is our public stance also.

"We fear there is bad news about Mr. St. John, so far unannounced. We prefer it remain among the employees as long as possible, probably today, hopefully tomorrow. There was a house fire at East Point and at least two people burned with the house. It was Auntie Monica's Inn, which, I am sure, is familiar to all the employees. The authorities are thus far unable to identify, or even determine the sex of, the victims. They do feel, however, one of them is Brookings. This we have been asked to keep quite as long as another day or so to help them with the investigation. The initial investigation shows strong evidence of, in their words, foul play."

"As far as Maddie is concerned, she was seen at the hospital in Christiansted looking for St. John. Failing to locate him, she became, according to doctors and hospital personnel, irrational and stormed out, vowing to find and kill Brookings for reasons unknown to them but not so unknown to us. We have heard nothing of her since."

The three bank officers nervously and self-consciously adjusted their positions in the chairs, but said nothing. They did think of the snide remarks and jibes made in the past at Maddie and, perhaps, regretted some of them. The information, what there was of it, came direct and clear but no one accepted the theory of disgruntled veterans. Max Inman asked the question on everyone's mind.

"Have you any reason for the shootings and Brookings' death other than the official version? None of us believe this a random act. Is there any indication you and Mr. O'Rielly are also targets? After all, you were scheduled to play golf, and afterwards planned a dinner at the Buccaneer. Had everything gone as planned, all seven of you would have been neatly in a package when the Latinos burst into the bar."

"That is speculation, Max. I understand that. In fact, Stephen and I have been doing our share of speculation. Do it among yourselves and not to the newspaper people who will be here soon. So far, they are content to confine themselves to St. Croix. But look out, you are in for several visits. Tell them anything you know, but do not speculate."

A light rap on the conference room door interrupted the meeting, irritating Alasdair and Inman. The receptionist stepped into the room and apologized for the interruption. "Mr. Inman, that Devoe person is on the phone again, calling for Miss Willis. He has called three times already today and does not leave a message. But he says it is very important he speak with her and always asks for other numbers where he might reach her. Do you wish to speak with him?"

"Who is this Devoe person?" Alasdair asked. "Do any of you know him?"

Ithica McGurk answered, "Tamara, the teller who shares a condo with Maddie, told me he works for the Peace Bank in Philadelphia, and for the last three weeks he has been calling her at home and here also. She told Tamara he was always after her when she worked for the Peace Bank there, but had not heard from him for years until three weeks ago, when he started calling. Sometimes she would talk to him and sometimes she would just hang up."

"Just ask him to leave a number and tell him Maddie will not be in this week, which I expect is the truth."

"Yes, Mr. Inman," the receptionist replied as she eased out the door.

O'Rielly and Alasdair looked at each other quizzically. Alasdair spoke. "Max, Chief Halfpenny is probably in the lobby. If he is, please ask him to wait for me in Brookings' office. If you don't know the chief you will recognize him instantly. He will be the largest thing in the bank, including the vault." Inman left the meeting as Alasdair turned to Ithica. "I think the meeting is about over, and if you have any more questions, Mr. O'Rielly will be here to discuss them with you. Which teller is Tamara?"

"Window number three, sir."

Tamara in window number three, one of the few off-islanders Brookings had hired, was a pretty young blonde from Chicago who came to St. Thomas for a vacation and never went back. She looked up to see her customer and gulped. "Mr. Alasdair, good morning, sir."

"Tamara, I want to talk with you for a moment. Please come with me to Mr. St. John's office and do not be alarmed by the man in the office. In spite of his size, he is a very nice man from St. Croix."

Tamara was already alarmed by the man in front of her window and doubted the man in the office could add to her alarm. She was wrong. When Alasdair introduced him as the chief of police in Christiansted, she neared panic and began to shake.

"Relax, Tamara," Alasdair said, placing a comforting arm around her shoulders while directing her toward a chair. "Nothing is wrong. We want to ask you some questions about Maddie. May I get you something to drink, coffee maybe? Everything is OK."

Tamara did not feel OK. Tamara was nervous. The chief spoke to Alasdair in his deep melodious voice. "As I have told you, Mr. Alasdair, you have an overwhelming presence and scare the hell out of normal people. This beautiful girl probably thinks she is going to be fired or arrested, or both, though she knows of no reason for either. Now, Tamara, you relax, for you are in good hands, mine. I apologize for Mr. Alasdair dragging you in here with never a by-your-leave or if-you-please. Are you all right now?"

"Yes, sir, thank you. It is just that so much has happened and now Maddie is missing, or at least she has not called me. I'm scared."

"Do not be. As I said, you are now in my hands. Just answer the questions from Mr. Alasdair without any worries or concerns."

"Tamara, I am sorry we frightened you and will explain to the employees that our questions concerned Maddie, not them or you. Mr. Devoe recently began calling Maddie for some reason. Will you tell us what, if anything, you know about him or his calls?"

"Only what Maddie told me. Years ago she worked with him at the Peace Bank where he asked her for dates. Then, when she always said no, he harassed her at work and when they went to bankers' conventions, office parties, and anywhere he could. She regretted not insisting that Mr. St. John do something about him. Three weeks ago he began calling to ask how she was doing, did she still get along with St. John, questions about the bank, and such. 'Nothing calls' is how Maddie described them."

"Did she ever mention him asking any specific question about the bank? Anything you can think of, no matter how trivial it may seem."

"Once she said he seemed overly interested in the upcoming directors' meeting. You know, wanted to know where and what they did, things like that."

Chief Halfpenny raised his eyebrows and glanced at Alasdair, whose eyes said, 'Ah ha!' but gave no indication of anything to Tamara. Halfpenny eased back in the chair, focusing his eyes on the ceiling as he wondered how much Devoe would enjoy his surprise visit with Alasdair.

"Do you know if Mr. Devoe still works at the Peace Bank?"

"Yes, sir, in Philadelphia. Maddie said he was recently promoted to executive vice president in charge of all marketing and branch banking everywhere."

"Thank you, Tamara. I will tell Max to tell everyone we talked with you only because you and Maddie share an apartment."

Neither Alasdair nor Halfpenny spoke until a relieved and calmer Tamara returned to window three amid stares from other employees.

"I take it you are ready for the FBI, Mr. Alasdair."

"You're very correct, Chief Halfpenny. Shall we gather O'Rielly and be on our way?"

❧   ❧   ❧

August 26, 1970, 11:00 a.m. GMT–5, Peace Bank, Philadelphia, Penn.

"Island Bank."

"Maddie Willis, please."

"Miss Willis is not in the bank today. Would you care to leave her a message?"

"Do you have a number where I can reach her? It is rather important."

"Who is calling, please?"

"This is Mr. Devoe in Philadelphia. I worked with Maddie at the Peace Bank several years ago. I really need to speak with her."

"I am very sorry but she is not in, nor has she called. I have to assume she is in St. Croix. I can tell you no more than that because that is all I know. If you want to leave a number..."

"No, I will try again later. Thank you."

Roy Devoe leaned back in his leather executive chair, scratched his left jaw with his right hand, and studied the ceiling. He really needed to speak with her. Newspaper reports on the shootings were non-existent and TV devoted sixty-two seconds to it on the twenty-fourth and ten seconds yesterday. He was being pushed for a report and had nothing to report. The branch managers of the Peace Bank in St. Thomas and St. Croix knew nothing and didn't want to know anything. Both detested St. John and both hoped to hear soon that he was dead. Maddie was his source and the best source, but she probably was with St. John somewhere. Either dead or alive, she would be with him. Stupid bitch with her fixation on St. John, the fat, ugly bastard treats her like shit and she eats it up.

Devoe lifted the receiver of the phone on his desk and dialed a number from memory. It was answered on the third ring.

"This is Thad."

"This is Roy Devoe at the Peace Bank, sir. You need to make a deposit in the scavenger account, sir. I will be glad to come over and pick it up, if that will help you."

"Thank you, Roy. I am just leaving for the club there near your bank and will buy you lunch if you have time. It will take me about an hour and I will have a deposit for you. Thank you for calling."

Devoe replaced the receiver, folded his hands across his chest and studied the Rolex on his left wrist. In his mind the situation was nearly at the explosion level, causing both Thad and himself a problem of rather alarming portions. The man on the other end of the situation did not accept failure graciously, and Thad had failed in St. Croix. Perhaps it was not too late to do something about the unfulfilled contract if they were given a sufficient amount of time. All along Devoe counted on getting information from Maddie, who now considered him her friend. He had had no trouble with the golf tee times and the meeting afterwards in the bar. All seven agreed to attend. It was not her fault, and neither was it his, that three members elected to do other more pressing work. Thad blamed him for bad information and the man on the other end blamed them both for taking his money and not finishing the job. Roy felt himself free of blame but getting it nonetheless, often the fate of middlemen during a failed deal. He buzzed his secretary to call for a car to take him to an important meeting at the City Club.

"Thad, I am worried about the man I am representing. He has shoved nearly everything aside just to devote full time to ruining Alasdair. He is obsessing on Alasdair as if he never believed you would be able to take him out. I know he has other people working to destroy the bastard's construction projects. Why would he do that if the man is dead? What purpose will it serve. Hell, I think he has lost his mind, blown a fuse somewhere. Hell, you should hear our conversations. They make no sense, no sense at all. Threatens me, of course. He does not know you just as you do not know him, but that does not keep him from threatening to kill you. He is beginning to worry me bad."

The secluded corner table in the City Club looks out over Philadelphia from twenty-four floors above the snarling and noisy traffic of downtown. Usually Devoe found a lunch there relaxing, but not today. The call earlier in the morning not only threatened his life but his job, his security, his position in the business inner circle in Philadelphia, and his social connections. His mentor, his friend, was one of, if not the largest, stockholders in the bank. But now his friend was his enemy because of Thad's failure in St. Croix. He had screamed obscenities and threats over the phone like a man possessed. Devoe's promotion to executive vice president, which came with a hundred thousand dollar raise, was due primarily to the man's recommendation, which he now threatened to withdraw. "What I give I can take away," were his words. Today Devoe's message to Thad was, "Get it finished, it is becoming a problem for me." He must get the message across without irritating Thad too much. Thad had ways of solving problems when they became too much of an irritant. Devoe decided to call Maddie again as soon as possible. He had no other source of reliable news from the islands. Perhaps it was all over now and he had nothing to worry about. After all, Thad's people were there and working.

⁂   ⁂   ⁂

August 26, 1970, 11:50 a.m., GMT 4, Christiansted

Casale searched for two hours before admitting to himself that Cosgrove had left the island with the money, leaving him alone with a serious problem. He wondered what to tell Whitestar, a question for which Casale had no answer. In the bar at the Caravelle Hotel, he ordered two Black Jack and Cokes. He gulped the first and nursed the second. He was at home on the streets of Camden, New Jersey, or even Newark, but Casale found himself lost in St. Croix. As useless as

Cosgrove was, he knew his way around the island. Too late, Casale realized that threatening Cosgrove had led directly to his present problem. "Admit it," he said to the drink, "you always let your mouth overload your ass. Maybe I am just a street goon capable of dealing with pimps and lot lizards, and breaking legs of scumbags who don't pay the vigorish on the money they got from the sharks. Whatever my abilities, I am in a hell of a mess right now."

Casale studied his problem, searching desperately for an answer. Finding none, he began to search for possibilities. Grab the next plane to Newark? Not possible. Get the plane to Miami, find Cosgrove, and get back the money? Not possible because of time constraints. Explain to Whitestar and reason with him by promising a bigger bonus? That was a slight possibility because only a slight possibility existed that Whitestar would listen long enough for him to explain. Now he began to deal with the only option left: get away from the Latinos, find the three targets, kill them, and get off the island quickly.

Step one in the plan he began to develop called for getting rid of the black silk suit first. It made him easy to identify. It was probably the only one-button black silk suit on the island of St. Croix. Noticing his drink glass empty, Casale glanced around for the bartender, whom he spotted in back of him through the mirror behind the bar. Casale froze when he saw the beautiful blonde woman and the massive shoulders and flowing red hair of the man with her. He remembered Whitestar remarking that he did not shoot the readhead in the bar because the poor bastard was too big and too ugly to shoot. Surely the man seated with the beautiful woman was the same redhead Whitestar described. The newspaper said there was a witness who did not come forward, and so far the police had failed to locate him. Obviously the police had a low priority on finding the witness, especially this witness a blind man could find.

The bartender returned and, noticing Casale's anxiety and empty glass, delivered another Black Jack and Coke. Jack Daniel's mixed with Coke was a sad waste of good sour mash whiskey, in his opinion.

"Say, barkeep, who is that red head you just served?'

"Oh, that is Mr. Walther, a guest in the hotel. The dish is a friend of his, a really good friend. Makes me wish I were ugly."

"What is he, a tourist, or does he work here somewhere?"

"Nah, he don't work here. He's a tourist or taking a break from somewhere, New Jersey, I think. The desk guy says he gotta couple of calls from Camden. I know where that is. I used to live in Millville. God, I was glad to get outta there, whatta burg."

Casale no longer listened to the continued ramblings of the bartender. "A coincidence, that is all. Lots of people in Camden, New Jersey, and most of them would rather be in the Virgin Islands. Just a coincidence. He came here to meet a chick and what a chick," Casale thought. "Still, would it be possible to get the phone number that called him?" Casale made a mental note to try later. He devoted his attention to his pressing problem for a few seconds. Then the coincidence of Camden crowded everything else out of his mind. Once was a coincidence, but twice? That's another deal and you would do well not to ignore the second one. Once was at the bar when the shooting occurred, twice was a call from Camden. Could he be Thad's man, the cleaner who cleaned up six people on Blue Mountain? Cleaned them because he thought they did their job, then got a call to wait on the other three until they finished their work. Now just waiting with a beautiful woman. "Nah, makes no sense. Be a nut to bring a woman with you on a cleaning deal." Casale motioned for the bartender, who brought him another Jack and Coke.

"It's worth a hundred bucks if you can get the number in Camden that called the red head, or any number he called there," Casale told the bartender.

"Can't do it, sir. Be my job if I got caught doing something like that. Sorry."

❧   ❧   ❧

August 26, 1970, Noon GMT–4, Caravelle Hotel, Christiansted

Maddie's disappointment spilled out through her eyes when told there were no spaces for snorkeling until the weekend. Walther expressed no disappointment, but offered her comfort by making a reservation for a half-day trip the following Sunday morning. Snorkeling remained very low on Walther's scale of things to do with Maddie, regardless of the Sunday morning reservation. Walther knew he could, and would, plan his way out of the snorkeling training session. Other problems were occupying his mind while they waited for the bartender to bring tea, iced for Maddie, hot for himself. Today he had skipped his morning exercise for the first time in years. Maddie's presence prevented his feeling free to do the exercise, plus he had no desire to leave her alone. He realized that at some time he would have to leave her alone, but he did not want to do so until he could develop a plan. Would she, at some time in the near future, suddenly realize she did not know him and wonder how and why she came to be with him instead of at work? When she did, what would her reaction be? Would she remember killing the Brookings person and his whore?

Sooner or later, someone would recognize Maddie and ask her questions, questions that might awaken her memories. Would that be dangerous for Walther? It could be, but to Walther it was worth the risk to be near her and to bask in her glow. Walther began to think of himself as a romantic. He had no plan for being a romantic, especially since no clear definition of a romantic appeared anywhere in his mind. He did find a mental file for the man sitting at the bar, the one with the black silk suit that looked slept in. Walther remembered him from his conversation with Thad, when the man had been added to the packages to be sent home.

The tea arrived in the hands of the bartender, whose eyes never strayed from Maddie. There was not a glance at Walther. She affected all men the same way. Walther knew that and it did not worry him.

"That man over there, the one you served a second ago, who is he?"

"I don't know, but he was interested in you. Asked about you and where you are from and why. Very curious. I told him you were a guest here on vacation."

"Yes, thank you. If you get a name, let me know. He looks like someone I once met in New Jersey."

"Well, that's interesting. I think he is from New Jersey. I lived in Millville myself, and the only place I ever saw a suit like that was in Newark, usually on some hood arrested for shooting somebody."

"If you two are finished gossiping, I would like some lunch," Maddie said. "What is a poor girl to do if big strong men won't look after her? I am starving. The shrimp salad, yes, that is what I want."

Curiosity sometimes leads to problems better left undiscovered. The black silk suit would do well not to become too curious about Walther. Walther knew all he needed to know about the silk suit, and devoted his time and attention to Maddie. Later he would have time to plan and deal with the curious man at the bar. That made Walther feel relaxed and at ease.

CHAPTER 6

Wednesday, August 26, 1970, 4:00 p.m. GMT–4 St. Croix

The phone on Chief Halfpenny's desk rang incessantly as he walked down the hall to his office, making no effort to hurry, knowing urgent or important callers would ring again. It was his personal direct line and it continued to ring until he seated himself and lifted the receiver.

"Halfpenny."

"This is Special Agent Edward Edwards, FBI. We are, for reasons completely unknown to me, in Atlanta. Something about hydraulics. We'll just call you tomorrow sometime. Have you caught the shooters yet? They can't go far with the Coast Guard, customs, and your people surrounding them on an island."

"You are correct, Agent Edwards, and although we have not apprehended the perpetrators, someone, a good citizen no doubt, has thinned their ranks along with the ranks of our prostitute population. Since I last spoke with you, we have discovered, we believe, three of the perpetrators either shot, blown up, burned, or all three, along with three of our most active prostitutes. Additionally, we believe the president of the bank whose directors were shot, is the victim of an explosion and fire in a local hostel noted for prostitution, along with one, perhaps two prostitutes. We are unsure because there is very little to identify."

"Damn, Chief, St. Croix sounds exciting, not to mention violent. Any idea who the mad bomber might be?"

"Not the foggiest, not the foggiest. I will save that investigation for you. Call me tomorrow."

Halfpenny put down the phone thinking, "Bastard FBI crud."

Tilly's Funeral Parlor needed help with traffic and crowd control for the mass funeral scheduled, tentatively, for Friday, August 28. Chief Halfpenny sent one of his patrolmen over to work with Tilly in an effort to bring some order to what had every chance of being a circus. The FBI being stuck in Atlanta freed the afternoon for the chief, who had blocked out the rest of the day for them. He was thinking. "I need to do something productive rather than sit around here. I'll get a car and go to Tilly's. At least I can help the patrolman in planning traffic and crowd control, and O'Rielly with getting the bodies released to Tilly."

He did not expect to see Alasdair at the funeral parlor, especially not in Tilly's chair behind Tilly's desk.

"He took over my office the moment he arrived," Tilly moaned. "I tried to send him to the room where we meet with families to plan funerals, but no, 'You use it,' he said. What he is doing I have no idea, but he is calling people all over the world."

"Don't worry, Tilly, just add rent for your office to the funeral cost. He will be paying for at least three of them. I think he may draw the line at paying for Ronrico. He is pissed off at him even though he is dead. Keep that in mind. Go work with the patrolman I saw out in the lot looking confused and lost, while I speak with Mr. Alasdair."

Halfpenny entered the office as Alasdair finished his conversation. The chief stood in the open doorway and appeared uninterested while listening intently to every word and nuance. The incident at the Buccaneer Bar convinced Chief Halfpenny that Alasdair bore little resemblance to the normal businessman in the islands. Maybe he met the norm for businessmen in the U.S. or U.K. However, Halfpenny doubted he could find anything normal about Alasdair's activities. It always seemed strange to Halfpenny how Alasdair dropped out of thin air to finance a plaything for Stephen O'Rielly, a politically connected politician, and Cyril King, the man everyone knew would be the next governor of the U.S. Virgin Islands. He also dropped into the life of Brookings St. John and furnished the money he needed to rip apart one of, if not the largest, banking operation in the Caribbean. Even stranger was the crime wave, violent crime wave, flooding the peaceful Island of St. Croix, a crime wave thus far affecting only associates of Nigel James Alasdair. Were it not for London and Belize, Cyril King and Stephen O'Rielly might be the target of the violence, a message to Cyril not to seek the office of governor. But not now, not after the bombing in London and the massacre in Belize, plus the FBI investigation.

"Put him on the jet and fly him here to Alexander Hamilton Airport," Alasdair was saying into the telephone. "Send someone with him to serve as a guide as well as a guard. We don't want Fontana to blow up in front of a bunch of reporters. I need him here. No, don't let him bring the damn gun. I have enough problems without an armed nut to handle. OK, of course I know he is not a nut, he is a bloody folk hero. But there are no more folk for him to shoot, at least not here. Bring him to the Caravelle Hotel. That's where I'm staying. We will have a room for him. I am going to need the jet so don't look for it back for a week or so. OK, Carlotta, thanks for your help, and keep it in a row."

Alasdair turned to Chief Halfpenny. "Well, don't stand there looking innocent, sit down and we'll talk," he said. "My guard in Belize is getting so much attention he is becoming a nervous wreck. I am bringing him here, then when I go to London next week I will take him with me. After that things in Belize will be back to normal and he can go back. What is the next question?"

"You are stopping in Philadelphia, I assume," Halfpenny said, still standing at the door. I suggest you use discretion while there and, if you ask, I may be able to help you. I do have some connections that will dig out the dirt on Devoe, if you have need for such information. It might be leverage when you speak with him."

"Listen, Chief, I've got two dead people in London and twenty-four in Belize, five here, and you are worrying about me mistreating some crappy little banker in Philadelphia. Killing is too good for him, but all I'll do is ask him a couple of questions, and not until I get back from London. My number one man is in Belize with the families, O'Rielly is here, and I'll be in London. I have no time and no inclination to mess with that shitty bastard banker. If you want to take a few days off, I'll let you talk with him."

"It would be my pleasure except I have the FBI to deal with which, incidentally, are stuck in Atlanta and won't be here until tomorrow, thank God. I have had enough for one day. If you ever decide to engage a chief of security for your company, be sure to remember me, unless you have any FBI people around. Uh, oh, look at that. Here comes O'Rielly with the bodies."

"Shut the door, Chief, and get inside. I have calls to make and things to get moving. Tilly doesn't have a secretary. Can you believe that? I had to get Sue on the phone to place my calls, so whatever you do don't hang up that other line. Do you know that SOB Tilly doesn't have any whisky and told me not to smoke in the viewing rooms. Viewing rooms? Hell's a viewing room?"

Alasdair ripped the cellophane from a Macanudo, shoved it into his mouth and lit it with a gold lighter he fished from his pocket. "You got the job if you start tomorrow, double your pay," he said. He grabbed the other phone and barked into it. "You got my wife, Sue?"

"She's on the line, sir."

"You heard from the colonel?" he asked his wife.

"Thank you, dear. I am fine," she replied. "How are you? Thanks for asking about me."

"OK, OK. Fate and Joe get some guards out there? Are they doing a good job? Serious about it, I mean."

"Yes, they are here and have got every body who lives here pissed off. You sure this is needed? We won't have a friend left."

"Who gives a shit. If you are dead, rooms full of friends don't offer much in the way of comfort. What about the colonel?"

"On his way to Atlanta, he thinks. He's in Mozambique, Palma, he said. Way up north somewhere. Says he'll get a boat to Zanzibar, then to Dar es Salaam, then a plane from there to somewhere. Wherever he ends up, he will get to Atlanta over the weekend and will call me. I told him I would meet him at the Ritz Carlton and we would wait for you. You know I like the Ritz Carlton, and I haven't been there in a while."

"You keep your ass on the eighth floor at home. These people have killed almost forty people in the last three days and show no sign of letting up. You are no good to me dead, just as I am not worth much to you dead. When the colonel calls, tell him to come to St. Croix any way possible. I need him here and not in Atlanta. I will have the jet here tomorrow and can send it for him wherever he gets in the U.S. Explain to him I need him here. OK. Hey, I am just thinking. I have to go to London Saturday, Sunday the latest, to see Keaton's and Dobbins' families. If you want to go with me I will come by and get you, but I need Konrad down here for a day or so. Do you know where he is now?"

"No, he said he would call from Dar. It's only a day from Dar to where you are. BCAL or British Air has flights from London to the Caribbean every day. Surely he can make it to somewhere you can pick him up. I'll talk to him when he calls, if he calls."

"Good deal. Thanks. I'll be in touch tomorrow."

Then he spoke with his secretary again. "Pack it in, Sue. I'll talk to you tomorrow. It's getting to be a long day for both of us."

Alasdair rose and began dusting the cigar ashes off Tilly's desk, mumbling that a man who has a funeral for four people in one joint service certainly needs a secretary, or maid, or something. The inability to get a glass of Scotch whisky in a funeral parlor made no sense to him. Suddenly O'Rielly burst in without knocking. "Chief, I gotta have some help from you, and from you, Jim. I got at least a hundred family members out there fighting over everything, like where is the most important position in the line of coffins. Is the center the position of prominence, or are the ends? Or maybe the two on the preacher's right are more important than the two on his left. With four coffins, they don't understand there is no middle. God, I wish we had enough of Brookings so I could put him in the middle. Damn, what a mess."

Halfpenny rose to his full height, flexed his muscles, and cast a sad glance at O'Rielly before speaking. "You are on your own, Stephen. I just quit this job, but I will call and have some help sent over before I slide my resignation under the boss' door."

Stephen's jaw dropped.

❦   ❦   ❦

August 26, 1970, 2:30 p.m. GMT–4, Danish Manor Hotel, St. Croix

Casale left the bar in the Caravelle Hotel and wandered aimlessly about downtown Christiansted for an hour, stopping briefly at bars for more Black Jack and Coke, until he stumbled into the Danish Manor Hotel. On the verge of complete intoxication, he rented a room from a hesitant clerk torn between the rent money and an obvious drunk. He reasoned the suit, though wrinkled and rumpled, probably cost five hundred dollars no more than a month or so ago. That fact, along with the gold wristwatch that had diamonds for numbers, swayed the desk clerk in favor of the money. Obviously a businessman fallen victim to the cheap booze in the Caribbean. In a land where rum is ninety-nine cents a fifth and Coke is one dollar for a six ounce bottle, there is little likelihood of finding much Coke in a rum and Coke. That is the demon that traps tourists and traveling businessmen such as Mr. Casale, just now heading for his room.

"I have to call Thad and talk with him about Cosgrove," Casale was thinking, "but first I'm gonna take a nap. I'll talk to him after a nap."

Something struck the door to Casale's room with enough force to rattle the hinges and awaken him. Casale sat bolt upright, shook his head and yawned. Damn, what was that racket? In the bathroom, he splashed cold water on his face, then toweled it off in the bedroom while looking for his pants. He found them neatly folded over a hangar underneath the suit coat. "I don't remember hanging the suit in the closet," he thought. He leaned against the wall for support while getting into his pants so he could check the door.

"Damn, all that racket made by a newspaper thrown against the door? Kid must be mad at somebody to throw a newspaper that hard."

Somewhere between drunk and sober, Casale sat in the chair by the window to read the paper, a special edition. The entire issue, other than the advertisements, was devoted to the murders and their investigation. On the front page were pictures of the dead bank directors, including St. John, with an article about the fire and explosion destroying Auntie Monica's Inn. Casale grinned as he read of St. John's death and noted he owed the damn bomber for cutting his list of targets down to two. On page two, he found almost life-sized pictures of O'Rielly and Alasdair, for which he gave thanks. Now he could identify the two men he previously knew only by name. He began to feel better about matters and his ability to handle those two, as well as the Latinos.

Hell, I won't have to worry about Whitestar and company after I get rid of Alasdair and O'Rielly, the damn bomber will do that for me. All I got to do, then, is get my ass outta here so he don't blow me up. I can do that, you bet your sweet ass I can.

As a feeling of euphoria swept over him, Casale rang room service for two Black Jack and Cokes, then gave the operator Thad's number. He sipped the Jack while waiting for Thad to get on the line. The conversation went better than he had expected. Thad promised to take care of Cosgrove and get the money back. He said that the confusion at a mortuary would make it a good time to strike. "No doubt the two johns will be there, sorting out relatives and undertakers, not to mention reporters for newspapers and television. Newspaper reporters will leave to get their story in so they can have a drink, and the TV people got to be ready for the news at either ten or eleven. You go in about nine-thirty and you probably get to shake hands with them. Now is the time, Franco. Go do it and, man, I give you all the twenty-two thousand Cosgrove took. Fuck the Latinos. You don't need them."

In his office in Camden, Thad smiled and then laughed after hanging up the telephone. "No, Franco, you don't need to worry about the Latinos. Walther will blow their asses sky high and then he will stick dynamite up your ass, too." Lou put down his magazine and looked at Thad.

In the Danish Manor Hotel, Casale entered the shower with a new feeling of confidence and power. He knew Thad was right. Now is the time to get them, when they are busy and off guard. Clean, refreshed, and freshly shaven, he ordered two more Jack and Cokes from room service while he brushed and shook out the wrinkles in his suit. Rereading the paper and studying the pictures Casale finished the two drinks, then set out on the short walk to his car near the Caravelle Hotel.

From the box in the trunk of the old blue car, he removed his 9mm pistol built on a Colt .45 frame and three nine-round clips of hollow point cartridges. He shoved one clip into place, chambered one round, and carefully lowered the hammer. He stuffed the weapon into the waist of his pants and buttoned the coat to make sure it was concealed. Then he walked to the Caravelle Bar where a bartender different from the one during lunch served him two more Black Jack and Cokes. From time to time he readjusted the pistol, trying to find a comfortable position. Unlike in the movies, it gouged him painfully in the groin. At 9:00 p.m., Franco Casale walked outside to find a taxi.

⁂   ⁂   ⁂

August 26, 1970, 9:00 p.m. GMT–4, Tilly's Funeral Parlor, Christiansted

"Isn't it amazing how dragging out a coffin for St. John and putting it in the middle solved all the squabbling between the relatives," Chief Halfpenny said. "Also, if I say so myself, the lady I sent over to replace O'Rielly did a great job of getting all the families organized. Thank God all the coffin-shuffling involved empty coffins. I assume everyone knew the bodies were downstairs in the embalming room." Halfpenny paused to take another bite of the pizza slice in his right hand while, with his left, carefully guarding the pizza in the box in his lap. O'Rielly, much relieved to be free of the crowd outside the office door, leaned back in his chair, sipped his beer, and was grateful to Halfpenny for getting him out of the funeral hassle. Alasdair toyed with his pizza while on the telephone agreeing to Carlotta in Belize that the company would pay for the twenty-four workers' funerals, but not a dime for the Mexican attackers shot by Fontana.

"If Belize has no provision for burying terrorists, then they should keep them out of the country. No money. No money, Carlotta. I don't give a shit if they leave them in the field where Fontana shot them. Hell's the matter with those people to think we owe them something. You tell them, Carlotta, and if they don't like it, tell them to call me here at this funeral home where I am burying more of our people."

"Hell's the matter with people?" Alasdair shouted, slamming the receiver onto the hook. "My guard killed fourteen or fifteen murderers and these pricks in Belize want me to pay for their burial. They have no money for that purpose. Well, tough shit. I'll be happy to have my men dig a hole and push dirt over them, but that's it. I don't want to talk about it. Too damn ridiculous to contemplate." He devoted full attention to his portion of the pizza.

"It's a real zoo out there now, Chief," O'Rielly said. "That policewoman of yours has everyone lined up for interviews with newspapers, TV, radio, and who knows what else. Every two-bit politician is out there grinning, crying, talking about what a good friend he was to the senators. Whatever the interviewer wants to hear is what he is getting. Enough to make me ill. I swear, half the people never met any of the dead folks and the relatives are just as bad. A reporter asked one fellow how he was related to old Balboa and the bastard didn't know. You oughta been out there, Jim. It was, and I guess still is, a circus."

"Circus? In here has been a circus. I still can't believe the government in Belize wants me to pay the funeral expenses of that bunch of killers. Gad! As for out there, I heard enough through the door. You are good at that stuff, Stephen. You oughta be a consultant, a funeral consultant. Cut down on expenses, bury them all at once, save money, twenty-five percent off with the special Tilly group discount. OK, enough of that. You heard anything from all those tests on the 'krispy kritters' at Auntie Monica's, Chief?"

"Only enough to know there were two, maybe three women and one man."

"Is it possible one of the women is Maddie? No one has heard from her since ten o'clock Monday. She is the best looking woman on this island, so if she were out running around someone would have spotted her. Is she one of them, Chief?"

"No she is not a victim, I am almost sure of that. The second person is Monica's daughter by some Puerto Rican. That was, as you may recall, Brookings' favorite pastime, having sex with the two of them. We located a taxi driver who took Brookings out there and we are unable to locate anyone who brought him back. As to Maddie, I don't have anyone looking for her. We do not consider her missing, just pissed off. The hospital personnel said she threatened to kill whomever she was looking for because he was not in the hospital. But somehow I doubt she blew his ass up along with two whores,"

The office door opened and the tall, slender, distinguished, graying Purdy Tilly entered quietly. Discretely closing the door behind him, he announced that a friend of Mr. St. John was waiting in the lobby and asking to see Mr. Alasdair. "I am terribly afraid he has been drinking rather too much alcohol. What shall I tell him?" No answer came because the door suddenly burst open, striking Tilly's back a violent blow and knocking him aside and onto O'Rielly, seated to the left of the door. Franco Casale charged into the room tugging at the large pistol that seemed entangled in the tail of his white silk shirt. He stopped abruptly at the sight of the massive chief of police a few feet from him. He pointed the pistol first at the chief, then Alasdair, and was momentarily distracted when O'Rielly jumped up, allowing Tilly to fall to the floor. Casale fired twice in the general direction of Alasdair, the loud shots vibrating the walls of the small office. Those two shots were followed by three thunderous explosions as Alasdair pumped three hollow point .357 magnum slugs from the big Colt revolver into Casale's chest. The force of the three bullets drove Casale backward through the door. He crumpled to the hallway floor. Mr. Purdy Tilly, a dealer in death, fainted, causing both O'Rielly and Halfpenny to go to his aid in the mistaken impression that the shots had struck him. Alasdair returned his weapon to the holster under his shirt.

Franco Casale expired on the hallway floor, spread-eagled, eyes open, five or six feet from his pistol, and just outside Mr. Tilly's office. His final moment came under the gaze of at least fifteen reporters of one kind or another. For a moment, and only a moment, there was absolute silence in the hallway and lobby. Then flashbulbs snapped, TV cameras whirred, and voices all yelled together. Inside the office, Chief Halfpenny closed the door and placed his bulk against it, allowing the occupants time to recover.

O'Rielly placed the awakening Tilly in a chair and held him in place until the fainting passed, then assured him no bullet had touched him and, yes, it was normal for his ears to ring. Loud noises in small spaces caused that, and it would go away soon.

Alasdair's new chief of security looked at his boss with a certain amount of awe before saying anything. He had not seen the big Colt appear and neither did he see it disappear. Obviously it had a place somewhere on Alasdair's person, but not a visible place. He did not know if the hammer snagging on Casale's shirttail gave Alasdair the edge he needed, or if he needed an edge. He did believe the shirttail snag kept himself from being shot.

"Didn't you think he might have shed light on the shootings if you had left him alive for a few minutes, Mr. Alasdair?"

"No, that thought didn't cross my mind. I did think he might shoot you. He didn't expect you and that confused him. I don't need any information from him. The banker in Philadelphia will tell me all I need to know. Go deal with the press."

"Yes, massa, I git rat out dare."

"Pissoff, Chief," Alasdair said. "Stephen, how is Mr. Tilly? He didn't get hurt did he?"

"No, he's fine. He just had his breath knocked out of him when that bastard kicked the door into him. He said that guy was drunk. If that is true, why the hell would anybody send a drunk to kill us? It doesn't make sense to me."

"Maybe he wasn't drunk when somebody sent him. Maybe nobody sent him. Maybe killing us was his job. If so, why did he get drunk? Courage. Courage, Stephen. It takes courage to kill someone and he had to get his out of a bottle. Illogical, but often true. Mr. Tilly, I see a door in the other office, where your secretary would be if you had one. What's behind it?"

"The room where employees take their breaks and wait when not needed in the viewing rooms or elsewhere. It has TV, couches, and recliners for use if they have to stay the night."

"Does it have an outside door to get away from the crowd out front?"

"Oh, my, yes. It opens near where we bring bodies in for embalming and preparation. There is an elevator to the basement and to my living quarters upstairs. If you would like to leave unnoticed, you can go that way. I am sure Chief Halfpenny has the people outside under control. A good organizer he is, yes indeed. No problem for you to leave either way, but I need to go outside and help in whatever way I can."

"OK, Mr. Tilly, but you stay in here until Stephen and I have time to get outside. I do not feel up to talking to a bunch of reporters and agitated family members. Come on, Stephen, we need to get out of here."

Once outside and unnoticed, O'Rielly and Alasdair walked behind St. John's Anglican Church to Company Cross Street, then over to Kings Street, and past the police station to Kings Cross Street. They then walked toward Caravelle Arcade and the Caravelle Hotel. The moon was bright in contrast to the dark brooding undercurrents rife on the beautiful island. Alasdair, suffering mood swings from elation to depression brought on by his taking of a human life, talked continuously, rehashing his opinion of the immediate past as well the immediate future. Later he would wonder how he so accurately worked out a theory on the series of events which started at the Buccaneer Hotel and culminated at Tilly's.

"I don't want to bore you with my analysis of the situation we are in, but here goes. Someone wanting to ruin or kill me made a deal with the middleman banker in Philadelphia to get someone he knew in the business of murder to arrange for us to be shot in the Buccaneer Bar. That man used the goon I shot tonight to arrange for the Latinos to be the shooters. They were on time and did their job as well as I have ever seen. It wasn't their fault we didn't play golf. This big man, probably in New Jersey, sent a cleaner to St. Croix to take out the six Latinos as soon as they finished their work, to end the paper trail, as it's called in bookkeeping. That man was efficient and took out three of them and three unfortunate whores within hours of the shooting. Quick action, action he was able to accomplish because he knew where to locate the shooters. When he reported that he got three of them and would finish the other three the next day, he was called off because the Latinos missed three of us. The big man then sent the goon who hired them to make sure the Latinos finished their contract. That is the man I shot tonight, trying to do the job himself and keep the unpaid portion of the Latinos' money.

"He knew himself to be safe from the Latinos because they would be as good as dead the instant the cleaner heard of our deaths. I haven't figured out the Brookings incident satisfactorily, but neither did the bastard at the funeral parlor. It merely reduced the number of people he needed to kill to keep the money and get the hell off St. Croix.

"Hell's the matter with me, Stephen? Last time I shot somebody it was a fucking Korean in what I thought was a war. It didn't bother me then and hasn't since. I sort of feel good about shooting the bastard a few minutes ago. I want a cigar and a glass of Scotch whisky. Is that normal? Who gives a shit? I'm gonna shoot some more bastards before this mess is cleared up. I'm anxious to speak with Devoe. That bastard is gonna tell me everything he knows."

Inside the Caravelle, Alasdair looked for the bar. "Lets get a drink. I need one. Cyril. What about Cyril?"

"Cyril is on his way back, or will be tomorrow. His trip was only one day or he wouldn't have left. Hey! Look, getting in the elevator. It's that red headed dude again."

Alasdair caught a quick glance of the man getting into the elevator behind a woman with a shock of beautiful blonde hair. It contrasted wildly with his flaming red. Is that the elusive witness, Alasdair wondered, and if it is, why hasn't he come forward?

❧   ❧   ❧

August 26, 1970, 11:00 p.m. GMT–5, The Sombrero Inn, St. Croix

"Whitestar, Furillo and Estavo sat at the bar in the same sleazy club where they had first met Casale with Cosgrove. Estavo drank beer and complained about how Whitestar had allowed them to be cheated out of the money they had earned. He reminded Whitestar of the number of hours since Casale had left to find Cosgrove. "That Casale, he ain't coming back, and I don't believe he got no money cause I believe Cosgrove screwed over him and took de money and left. Casale, he can't call nobody and ask for more money because they be pissed off at him already, and they won't give him no more money but tell him he better get de work done. He can't come back here because he thinks, and he may be right, that Furillo and me, we shoot him. That's de way it is, Whitestar."

`"OK, Estavo. That's enough. You done said all that before and I agree with you, so you can just shut up about it and figure out what we do next. Hey! Look at that TV, the news is coming on and something is happening. They all at the funeral parlor. They all milling around in de lobby and hallway. Listen! You hear that? That mon said Brookings St. John is dead. That's one we were supposed to get, de one Casale said was important along with that Alasdair. Son of a bitch he done been blowed up in a whore house. That bomber one busy son of a bitch."

"Hey! Here come that big police chief and he gonna say something. You suppose something happen there? Why all this going on at the funeral parlor? They had a shoot out in de funeral parlor. Hee hee, that's funny, mon. Somebody took a couple shots at that Alasdair in de office of the funeral establishment with the police chief in there too. Hey! Look at that on de floor, that's de mon what did de shooting and somebody shot him. Look at him, Estavo, you too,

Furillo. Don't he look familiar with that black suit. Hell, that's Casale."

"Shut up, Whitestar, so we can hear. Listen to de chief."

"About an hour ago, Mr. Alasdair, Mr. O'Rielly, and myself were in Mr. Tilly's office discussing the upcoming funerals and the matters leading up to them. Mr. Tilly came in to tell us a gentleman was in the lobby asking to see Mr. Alasdair. He claimed to be a friend of Mr. St. John. Suddenly, he burst into the office shooting at Mr. Alasdair and myself. Due to recent events leading us to believe Mr. Alasdair might possibly be in danger, the FBI investigators and myself authorized him to carry a weapon for protection. Mr. Alasdair had the weapon, whereas neither Mr. O'Rielly nor myself was armed. Mr. Alasdair shot the man three times in or near the heart, killing him almost instantly. The identity of…"

"You hear that? That Alasdair, who is some kinda banker, done shot poor old Casale in the heart three times. That some kind of shooting for a banker. Son of a bitch. Hey, Whitestar, you and Estavo can have the banker. Mon, I don't want nothing to do with no son of a bitch can shoot you three times in the heart while you shooting at him. Hell no!"

"I think we done swapped one problem for two. That Alasdair one tough son of a bitch, I believe. That bomber, a mean son of a bitch also. He after us to keep anyone from finding out who hired us. We don't know who the money man is but we know Cosgrove and that be enough for that Alasdair. He make Cosgrove tell everything he knows. Hell, he probably don't know nothing either. Casale knew everything and he's dead."

"Hey, Whitestar, why you think Casale didn't shoot anybody in that little office? Shit, mon, he know how to shoot that gun and he shot two times before Alasdair shot him. How come he miss? Dat's what I wants to know. How the hell he miss that cop? He big as an elephant. Nobody could miss him. Shit, you hit him without aiming, just shoot anywhere cause he so big he everywhere."

"I ain't worrying about Casale, Estavo, I worrying about us. I bet they think Casale be to blame for a bunch of the shootings and ease off on checking so much on people leaving this island. We must keep an eye on the water taxis to see how close they being checked. If they let up on watching the taxis we can go one at a time to St. Thomas, then we can get to San Juan the same way. When we get there we can go home with no problem. As I see it, we do that or we go to work where we got a job and stay until it all over. I don't think the bomber can find us there cause he won't be looking for people working. He think we be doing nothing but laying on our asses spending our money."

"I made up my mind when I saw that TV news. I going to that rum place and go to work and stay away from anything for a month or so, den I sneak off dis island some way. You and Estavo do what you want to do, Whitestar, but old Furillo going to work and keep low profile. I don't want no bomb under, over, or in my ass, so I'm going into hiding out in the open, so to speak. I going to work at the rum factory."

Shortly thereafter Whitestar drove them back to the Sombrero Inn and the rooms Casale and Cosgrove had rented for them. Tomorrow they would leave early before the police found where Casale lived and noticed three Latinos living in rooms paid for by the dead man. Early the next day, the three Latinos left for Frederiksted only thirty minutes before Alasdair, Halfpenny, and a squad of police investigators arrived.

Thursday, August 27, 1970, 7:00 a.m. GMT–4, Sombrero Inn, St. Croix,

Victoria, the manager of the Sombrero Inn, sat on a stool. At least a third of her sat on the stool. The other two-thirds hung over the edges all around. The stool behind the counter facing the window, gave her a view of the entire parking area and a wide expanse of the highway. Long before the three police vehicles traveling from the direction of Christiansted reached the entrance to the Inn, Victoria knew their destination, the rooms of the supposed buyers of fishing boats. One look at them had convinced Victoria that neither knew a fishing boat from a cruise ship. She only hoped that whatever their troubles might be they would not involve her and the motel. As Chief Halfpenny extricated himself from the lead automobile, she wondered how long it took him to get into that ridiculous white uniform. The Sombrero Inn's location put it within the Christiansted jurisdiction by only a few hundred feet, much to Victoria's regret. Halfpenny was too smart for her liking. She preferred the Frederiksted law enforcement authorities, mostly because she believed them barely capable of even finding their way home.

Halfpenny and the white man with him were in room No.18 before the patrolman reached the office to explain that a dead man in Christiansted had the key to No.18 in his pocket at the time of death. A search of the body turned up no identification of any sort, unusual but not illegal, thus requiring the trip to the motel in hopes of some identification left in the room. He explained to Victoria the chief's order for him to check the register for any information to help them find a name and home address. Without hesitation Victoria spun the Lazy Susan holding the registration book to face the patrolman.

"His name, as you can see, is Smith, a representative of some company interested in buying a fishing boat. Mr. Jones in No.17 came with Mr. Smith to look at a boat or boats. Neither Mr. Smith nor Mr. Jones was in for breakfast. I suppose that explains Mr. Smith's absence, but I have no idea about Jones."

In room 18, Alasdair and Halfpenny watched as the detectives took the room apart. They found no luggage, no clothes, only a small bag containing a plastic insert from a billfold with a driver's license, a Social Security card, three credit cards, all with different names, insurance cards, and a couple of pictures. The driver's license, Social

Security card, insurance cards, and one credit card were in the name of Franco M. Casale of Camden, N.J. In the bathroom they found only toothbrush, toothpaste, razor and shaving cream, all purchased, according to the tags, from the Sombrero Inn. Mr. Casale they adjudged to be traveling light for a boat buyer.

The door to the adjoining room stood open, allowing free access to room 17, which received a thorough search, revealing another light traveler with only an empty bag and a few toiletries. One item had a tag from the San. Juan airport gift shop.

Chief Halfpenny walked to the office to chat with the manager and thank her for her assistance, which was minimal since she never left her stool. Having properly completed that task and determined that her information was exhausted, he bowed, said goodbye, and turned to leave. Victoria spoke up. "Don't you want to look at rooms 19, 20, and 21?"

Nigel James Alasdair leaned his lanky frame against the police vehicle and puffed lazily on his Macanudo cigar, waiting for Halfpenny to emerge from the office. Emerge he did, a smile on his face and a handful of keys in his hand. He moved so fast small dust puffs from the dry and dusty parking lot arose around his large feet. "Ah, Mr. Alasdair, I think we have stumbled onto the mother lode. Come with me and I will tell you what I mean."

Inside room 19, they found it hot and steamy from the early morning sun. Obviously its former occupant cared little for air-conditioning. Alasdair, however, did and flipped on the switch. Saying nothing and asking no questions, Alasdair joined Halfpenny in a casual search of the room before turning it over to the professionals to take apart. They found nothing and did not expect the professionals to do any better. Room 20 presented a much better site for conversation. The air-conditioner operated at about half speed and kept the room cool. The chief seated himself on the bed and invited Alasdair to take the only chair.

"These rooms, Mr. Alasdair, were rented by the person accompanying Casale for two weeks, to be used by three Spics, the manager's word, who are working for the rum company, or soon will be working there. They arrived here, on the island I mean, last Friday and have not yet gone to work. They need one more day of recreation before starting to work to get over a very trying experience. The men are, according to the manager, brown skinned, not Negroid, maybe Mexican, Puerto Rican, Colombian or other South American, or a mixture of some or all. They are not from this area. They have had a very trying experience and they are what we sometimes refer to as Latinos. What does that tell you, Mr. Alasdair? Look up that road across the street. If it had a sign it might well say Blue Mountain road. That is where we found the six bodies, three men and three women."

"Son of a bitch, Chief, it's them. They were all together here in a group and we missed them by how much this morning?'

"The manager says thirty minutes or maybe an hour, and she does not believe they will come back, ever. She is very likely correct."

"Where did they go, Chief? What do you supposed happened between them that sent Casale off drunk to kill you and me? Something is wrong, Chief, very wrong. Who was the man in room 17 and where is he?"

"His name is Cosgrove, Mr. Alasdair. Where he is I can't say. I hope he is still in the islands somewhere, preferably St. Thomas. I had…"

"Cosgrove? You know his name? How did you find his name?"

"As you people from Tennessee like to say, 'We didn't just fall off a turnip truck today,' Mr. Alasdair. We checked the land ownership records and located the owner of the cabin to give him the news about his property. Incidentally, he also owns another cabin near the crime scene, and he told us he rented both cabins to a man named Cosgrove. One cabin for him and the other for his brother-in-law, whose name the owner didn't know. The owner turned out to be some right wing religious nut and blew a fuse when he heard whores were in his house. He thought Cosgrove's family and his sister's family were there."

"This morning when we found the rooms for Smith and Jones, I had one of the detectives put out an APB for Cosgrove, using the description from the cabin owner and the large lady manager up front. Unless he got away last night or very early this morning, we will have him either here or on St. Thomas. We were unable to get a phone number for Casale, but have the Camden Police breaking the news to Gosgrove's sister, who is Casale's wife. We may have a report when we get back to the station."

"I am impressed, Chief. Why the hell we need the FBI? You got this thing under control."

"Oh, sure, Mr. Alasdair, unless you get killed or the bomber cuts our search down to one perpetrator, himself. Our search is narrowing, but we have had damn little to do with it. I think perhaps we—"

Patrolman Roberts came in excitedly and grabbed the chief's arm. "Chief, Chief, look at this, the only thing we found in any of the rooms. Matchbooks from the Copia Club, that junky place close to Frederiksted. I'll bet they been hanging out there. It's a real piece of work and I mean a real piece of work. They probably be there tonight, maybe this afternoon."

Alasdair was quickly on his feet and speaking to the chief as he headed toward the door. "What are we waiting for? Lets go."

"Please, Mr. Alasdair, please. The Copia is in the Fredericksted jurisdiction, I have no say there and neither do my men. We barely are in the Christiansted jurisdiction here. No, we have to speak to the chief in Frederiksted before we go plunging into his territory."

"I can go. Let me have a car and I'll go see if I can spot them there. You can send a driver with me just to drive. That won't mess with your jurisdiction. OK?"

"Wait, just hold on. I will radio the chief and tell him our suspicions and he will meet you, or us, or send a detective that may know the owner. I can't have you busting in and killing somebody else. We need someone to question, not another body. Tilly has more than he can handle now."

Alasdair unwrapped a cigar and sat back in the chair. "Work it out, Chief, work it out. Then tell me what to do. I am in your hands."

♣   ♣   ♣

Thursday, August 27, 1970, 7:30 a.m. GMT–4, Caravelle Hotel, St. Croix

Exercise completed, a freshly showered, neatly trimmed and fully dressed Walther gazed down on the sleeping Maddie. How beautiful she looked to Walther. How much he loved her he was not able to express. What to do with her he could not imagine. Walther was bothered. Walther had watched the television news and saw a rerun of Chief Halfpenny at the funeral parlor. Thad had told him he was sending someone to clean up the mess in St. Croix but failed to tell him he had sent an idiot. Walther did not know the cleaner's name and had no wish to as he looked at him spread out on the funeral parlor floor, bleeding on his white silk shirt and black silk suit. "What an idiot. He certainly underestimated the Alasdair character. Three bullets in the heart while being shot at." Walther whispered those words to himself as he eased out through the door.

He ordered his regular breakfast with tea. While waiting, he began formulating his plan for the day with possibilities for two more days. Alasdair, he now knew, was chairman of the board of the bank where Maddie worked, or had worked. He knows her and he is staying in the Caravelle Hotel also. O'Rielly is at the funeral parlor most of the time, according to the paper and television, and also knows Maddie. Both are wondering about her, where she is, why she is not at the bank, why she has not called to show her concern for St. John. It would only be a matter of time before he and Maddie ran into them in the lobby, restaurant, or hallway. Walther worried about Maddie's reaction to such a meeting. It bothered him. Walther did not like to be worried. He ordered more tea.

Nowhere in Walther's contract with Thad did Alasdair and O'Rielly appear. He owed no responsibility to Thad for them and wanted nothing to do with the mess the black suit and the Latinos had made of their contract. Walther's plan began to take shape. It rolled before his mind's eyes like the unfolding of a map, a section at a time. Section one laid out a simple plan, easy to follow and without risk. It presented only one problem, fortunately a solvable problem, Maddie. Would she object to moving to Frederiksted? Walther hoped not. Work of the sort Walther usually did required him to plan for contingencies because the unexpected always occurred. Walther prepared himself by always having an alternate plan. When he had first arrived on St. Croix, he had scouted Frederiksted and located two excellent places there catering to tourists. Not even Murphy's Law would bring either Alasdair or O'Rielly to "On the Beach" or "Cottages by the Sea." That part of the plan began to roll over Walther, giving him a secure and safe feeling. He and Maddie would move to On the Beach. Walther preferred it to Cottages by the Sea.

Section two slid into place, filling his body with confidence and certainty. Walther knew the three remaining Latinos would surely come to Frederiksted. No way would they go to Christiansted because it was a hotbed of anger and suspicion. No way would they go back to the cabin, or near it, for the police surely had it staked out. Only Frederiksted was left, the west end of the island. No chance they would go to the east end because he had blown up the other banker there. He had the Latinos in his trap and he would spring it today or tomorrow. They could not hide from him, and when he found them he would send them home. That out of the way, he would have only to fear a chance meeting between Alasdair and Maddie.

Walther was beginning section three of his plan when Maddie joined him, breaking his trance-like concentration. Walther did not like to be bothered while planning. Before expressing anger at being disturbed, he noticed it was Maddie and smiled. An interruption by Maddie could not bother Walther.

"Good morning, Walther. Let me order some breakfast, then I want to talk with you about something I want to do."

Walther heard the click in the back of his mind, but once again he chose to ignore the warning. Whatever Maddie wanted to talk about or do was OK with him.

"Bacon, eggs, and a lot of coffee."

"You care for some fruit? We have nice ripe homegrown pineapples today."

"No thanks." Reluctantly the waiter left. "Walther, aren't you tired of this place? I am."

Walther choked briefly on his non-greasy hamburger patty. "I was thinking just a moment ago I would like to move to Frederiksted. There…"

"Oh, great. That is where I want to go. A place called On the Beach is nice and the food is great, too. We can play in the water by the beach. I'll teach you to snorkel."

The waiter interrupted. "Your food, madam. Anything else? I brought a chunk of pineapple, on the house. It is really good. Try it for me."

"Thank you, waiter, that was very nice," Walther said. "Now, Maddie, how did you think of or find out about that place? I was thinking of the same place or Cottages by the Sea."

"The book by the bed. They have an ad in it. It looks nice. What made you think of it?"

"I have some business to complete in Frederiksted."

Section three of the planning map slid into place. Maddie would be safe in Frederiksted until he could find the three Latinos and send them home. At that point the island would be cleaned of all of Walther's responsibilities, leaving him ready to take Maddie and go back to his own land. So far as he could tell Maddie had no relatives closer than Philadelphia, no ties in the islands since she had quit her job, and no reason to stay. Walther knew he would have his work finished by Sunday. His ties with Thad would be severed. He really had no ties to Thad other than an occasional contract, no personal relationship, no friendship, only a straight business relationship. He no longer needed money. He and Maddie would live and put down roots in Gaborone, Botswana, where he already owned a nice house and several acres or land.

He mentally folded the map carefully and filed it in his mind. Again the feeling of peace rolled over him and smoothed and soothed him as the tide smoothed the hot sand on the beach.

⚜   ⚜   ⚜

August 27, 1970, 2:00 p.m. GMT–4 Frederiksted Hotel, St. Croix

Waiting for the detective assigned to him gave Alasdair little comfort, but he had to accept the deal Halfpenny had made with the chief of Frederiksted or stay in Christiansted. Halfpenny promised to throw the white uniform away as soon as he finished with the FBI agents, and Alasdair agreed to a meeting with them after the Friday circus ended. The authorities, whatever the phrase meant, asked Halfpenny to remain as chief until the investigation of the Buccaneer Club murders was cleared up, or at least in the final stages. For Alasdair, that meant finding the remaining three Latinos, hopefully over the weekend. He no longer believed them to be a threat to O'Rielly or himself, especially after the Casale fiasco. The Latinos, he reasoned, were melting themselves into the fringe of the laboring class in Frederiksted, losing themselves in the raucous workers' night life. Shades of color and nuances of language go unnoticed in dark busy bars at night but stand out during the daylight.

Alasdair felt the net tightening about the three Latinos. First, they had lost their cabins, paid a month in advance by Cosgrove, and then lost their rooms at the Sombrero Inn, paid a week in advance by Casale. Now they were on their own and confined to Frederiksted. It is a small town with limited facilities, catering to locals. Halfpenny rated the police in Frederiksted competent and dedicated, with one or two tenacious detectives who were seldom discouraged once on a case. One such detective was to meet Alasdair at the bar in Frederiksted where he waited.

Stripping the cellophane from a Macanudo Prince Phillip Café, Alasdair began his cigar lighting ritual while looking for a server. He located the server near the lobby door in confrontation with a man seeking entry. One could reasonably assume the problem stemmed from his appearance, unkept, untidy, and possibly unwashed. The waiter lost the battle but followed closely as the man made straight for Alasdair's table. "Sorry I'm late but I have been most of the night and morning in the alleys and trash heaps of Frederiksted. I am Detective Foley. A pleasure to meet you, Mr. Alasdair."

"I'm sorry, Detective, but you look like you live in a refrigerator box," the waiter said.

"Sure, waiter, forget it, and bring me some food and a beer. Beer first. Any food will do. So, Mr. Alasdair, shot any New Jerseyites today?"

"The old woman's fish be OK?" asked the waiter.

"No, but I'm looking to shoot three Latinos if I can find them," said Alasdair.

"Old woman's fish is fine" the detective said to the waiter. "You eating, Mr. Alasdair? I'm starving. Surprising, since I dug in garbage all night. Old woman's fish is good."

"Hell's old woman's fish?"

"That's what the West Indian laborer or idler eats for dinner, old woman's fish. Whatever fish the old woman caught today. Usually it's that bigheaded fish because it's easy to catch. Big head, no brains."

"OK. Bring it on. Any news for me, Detective?"

"A little. One of our guys ran into a foreman at the rum ware-house bitching about how hard it is to get help. Said he hired six Mexicans from an agency in Puerto Rico. They never showed up. Nobody wants to work, he said."

"Well, well. Only three left to show up and they are likely to do just that. Somebody be waiting on them, right?"

"Right."

"Excuse me, sir, watch the plate, it's hot."

"Thank you," Alasdair said. "Bring me a bottle of water and him another beer. You back on duty tonight, Foley?"

"Yeah. Ten o'clock. I'll pick you up here. Chief said take you on patrol with me. You got any crappy clothes? Probably not. Go to a used clothing store, I'll tell you where, and get an outfit. Get stuff that's too big for you and don't forget some shoes. Those damn Churchills won't get it done. Sunglasses, you need sunglasses because you face was all over the TV after shooting that Wop. Who you think this son of a bitch bomber is? He got one of our whores and two of Halfpenny's when he blew up the first three Mexs. I bet he's still after them. Called off until they got you. Now he will get them cause things got screwed up when you shot Casale. What the hell was that about? Son of a bitch crazy or drunk or both? Can't shoot people in a funeral home. Too many people. With Casale out of the picture, the bomber will turn his attention to you, or he may say screw it and leave. That's what I would do."

"You know, Foley, everything makes sense except the St. John bombing. The bomber's job was never to kill any of my people, only get the shooters to end the trail. So why the St. John bombing? I don't know what that was about, but I don't think it had anything to do with St. John. I can't figure it out."

"Confusing."

"That it is."

"You bringing that big-ass gun with you tonight?"

"I planned on it."

"Well don't use it unless there is no other way. Chief have my ass you shoot them and we don't get to ask no questions."

"My word on that, Detective Foley."

Detective Foley intended to get three or four hours sleep before he and Alasdair started the rounds for the night. Alasdair, meanwhile, had nothing to do and no desire to sleep. The clerk at the desk had no car available for either loan or rent. He did have motorcycles, Indians. Not huge Harley hogs, but small Indians suitable for in-town use by tourists, but not, he pleaded, in the lobby, bar, and halls like the last group from Tennessee. Unruly sort, money but no class, was his description. The only exception was the Smith man, Boy Smith was his name, the clerk thought. He offered to pay for the damage. However, the owner suggested they leave and he would forget the damage, just get out. They left.

For the next three hours Alasdair rode the Indian over every street and alley in Frederiksted before extending his tour over a wider area. He headed south along the Shore Road all the way to Westend Salt Pond before turning back the way he came. Passing the On the Beach resort, he saw a couple in the distance walking along the beach. All he saw of the woman was her shock of blonde hair billowing in the breeze, her body hidden by the broad shoulders of the slightly shorter man walking, plodding, beside and slightly behind her. A flash of sunlight reflected off the man's red hair, giving Alasdair a shock almost electrical. Once again the redhead turned up near, but seemingly uninvolved, in Alasdair's life. He thought of turning the Indian onto the beach and overtaking the couple but better judgment convinced him such a course could be both foolish and embarrassing. He headed for the used clothing store.

When he spoke with Mrs. Alasdair later in the evening, she was adamant in her belief that everyone where they lived was now her enemy. On her balcony, Nashville's most obtuse cop sat smoking and talking into his irritatingly noisy radio to someone known as Tojo who lurked among the cars parked in the covered parking lot. Both talked to Marcellus, hiding in a van near the entrance to the property. All three of these were employees of Sheriff Fate Thomas. In the lobby with the creepy old doorman were two of Chief Joe Casey's uniformed men and another by the elevators on the eighth floor.

"I'm the only one here that people know. You are not ever here. If you show up during the time normal people are up and about, you have on your bastard face. No one wants to speak to you when you glare at them as if they were a piece of shit."

"Hell's the matter with you, woman. I am not a freak of some sort. Fate and Joe are looking after you like I asked them to do."

"Yeah? Well the people here think the place is staked out to arrest you if you ever come home. No one knows what you do, me included, but they're sure you are a crook of some kind."

"Who gives a shit what the fuckers think. Have—"

"I give a shit, you bastard, and, yes, I heard from the colonel and also from little Miss Goodie Goodie Two Shoes. Little bitch is trying to tell me what to do. If you have something to tell me, don't pass it through the front desk slut or Miss Goodie Goodie. Tell me yourself."

"Hell's the matter with you? I'll tell Fate to send somebody and take you to get your hair fixed. That's gotta be your problem. Tell him to take you in a fucking Wells Fargo truck, I will. Damn, I got more problems than to listen to all this shit when I am trying to keep you alive. God knows why."

"You bastard. The colonel is still in Dar. The plane from Zambia crashed when landing. Nose wheel collapsed. He said it'd be the middle of next week before another plane comes in. Do you think it helped your reputation to shoot some ass hole in the funeral home? All over the local news here. Local man makes good, shoots a mourner at a funeral."

"Hell you talking about? The son of a bitch shot at me twice before I shot him, and I'm afraid there's one looking for you. What am I, a fucking embarrassment to you because I didn't get killed? Son of a bitch, I'm really glad I called to check on you."

"You didn't call to check on me. You called to see about the colonel. Need him to help you shoot some more people. What the hell you doing I don't know about? Shit, I forgot. I'm a woman. Not supposed to know nothing. Can't you see I'm worried about you, you bastard? Say something nice to me before I cry."

"Tell the colonel to stay where he is. I can handle this and I'll see you Sunday. Bye."

"Ass hole." Click.

❧   ❧   ❧

August 27, 1970, 4:00 p.m. GMT–4, Police Station, Christiansted, St. Croix

Resplendent in his white uniform, red sash, and gold braid, Chief Constantine Halfpenny was determined to hold court one last time. No FBI agent could intimidate him ever again. Seated in the chairs he carefully arranged before the agents arrived, the three men from Philadelphia seemed anything but intimidating. Edward Edwards sat in the center chair with Robert Roberts on his left and McKinley Jones on his right. Not even the most heartless mother could bring herself to name a son 'Jones Jones,' Halfpenny surmised with a smile.

"Gentlemen, I am turning this investigation over to you with pleasure. I am glad to be rid of it."

"Chief, earlier when I spoke with you I had the impression you resented our presence."

"Before people started shooting at me in funeral parlors, Mr. Edwards."

"In funeral parlors?"

"Yep, that's what happened. Didn't you see the news?"

"We didn't see anything. Been on a plane for a week it seems. Supposed to go from Philly to Miami. Instead stopped in Atlanta, hydraulic problem. Unload plane, wait, reload plane, wait, unload plane, wait. Never took off."

"A mess, Chief. New plane went to Orlando, then to Miami. Change planes, then to Puerto Rico. Change planes to St. Thomas, then on a seaplane here. Edwards about to have a fit."

"Damn sure. Five hours turned into twenty-four. You got anything to drink?"

"Coffee and Jack Daniel's."

"Bring on the Jack."

"Where is Alasdair? When we gonna talk to him? Jones has got a big folder for him. Somebody is after his ass big time."

"I think that has sunk into his thick head, Agent Edwards. He is in Frederiksted. All those funerals tomorrow. But he will meet with you after they're over. Afterwards he's got to go to London to bring bodies and families back home."

"How is your investigation going, Chief?"

"I will explain it to you, Mr. Roberts. It is drawing to an end. The participants are killing each other off. I think if I just sit here, the suspects will narrow down to only one, if Alasdair doesn't kill him. Pissed, Alasdair is. Refused to pay for your man's funeral. Told Tilly no money for him, not one fucking cent. Ronrico a real disappointment for Alasdair."

"Disappointment for us, also. All we got was Alasdair's itinerary. Useless investigation. It's over now and he is cleared. I'll tell him and get my ass chewed out like I had something to do with it."

"Man's got a lot of problems. He's pissed to the gills and dumps on everybody. Won't be bad. He took most of it out on Ronrico's corpse and the Wop, Casale. Who the hell is he, or was he? You know?

"Camden is my area," Roberts said. "Edward and McKinley are book types. I am the shit stirrer. Casale was shit. Small time enforcer for loan sharking and bookmakers. No visible reason for him to be here. Probably connected, remotely, to the Thad Rosamiro family.

Rosamiro is way too smart to use him for anything more than breaking a welcher's leg. Rosamiro is getting old, but not that old. He'd
have to be crazy to send Casale here.

"Let's get out of here, Chief. Drink some Jack in a bar instead of a
police station. Eat something. Then I want to go to bed and sleep. If
the bomber don't blow up everybody tonight, we get to work tomorrow while you go to funerals."

CHAPTER 7

August 27, 1970, 7:30 p.m. GMT–4, On the Beach Resort, St. Croix

Walther suspected Maddie Willis could not cook long before their stay at On the Beach proved him right. Maddie's knowledge of cooking ended at the kitchen door. She could make good coffee, but not tea. Maddie was not embarrassed by this lack of ability and it did not bother Walther. He devised a plan to see them through the problem. They would eat out or get their food to go. That was simple, straightforward, and totally acceptable to Walther. He lived alone and knew how to cook when he wanted to. Tonight they would go out, maybe to Le St. Tropez or, perhaps, to the Frederiksted Hotel. Both places were good. That probably would eliminate the problem of Maddie inadvertently meeting Alasdair or O'Rielly and remembering too much. Walther turned to thoughts of the three Latinos.

He decided to begin his prowl of the sleazy bars and clubs at ten o'clock, after making Maddie comfortable. With a little luck he would find all three. Maddie relaxed on the small patio while Walther set about re-arming his briefcase. His watch read 8:30 p.m. as he placed the briefcase in the car prior to helping Maddie, in his gentlemanly way, with her door. Ten minutes later the hostess seated Walther and Maddie at a table for four in the far corner of the dining room at the Frederiksted Hotel.

In his room upstairs, two floors above the dining room, Jim Alasdair studied himself in the full-length mirror on the back of the bathroom door. Well-worn and outrageously large clothes and a five o'clock shadow substantially altered his appearance. He barely recognized himself. Glancing at his watch, he decided to make a few calls before meeting Foley. He located Sue and she soon had him in contact with Carlotta in Belize while Ted, in London, waited.

"What about Fontana? Is he on the way?"

"Yeah, I've got him set up to get there tomorrow afternoon. Smitty is coming with him and they've got a reservation at the Caravelle Hotel. You can find them there after the funeral. I guess the pilots will be there also. You know how they are. May sleep under the plane."

"Is Fontana OK? What happened to the Mexicans he killed?"

"Ah, who knows? The authorities did something with them after they were sure you weren't gonna pay them anything. Fontana is OK, a little crazy but OK. He'll be no problem to you. He might be of help, keep you from having to shoot any more of us good Italians."

"Oh bullshit, Carlotta, you are no Italian, probably some kind of Slovak or worse. You staying there awhile or going back to Georgia?"

"I'm staying on. When you finish with the plane, send it back and I'll go to Atlanta. I need to look over the airport work here. They sort of drag-assing around."

"OK. Sue, put Ted on. Hey, Ted, I'm not coming to London. Keaton and Deana, uh, their bodies are being flown home this weekend with the families. We all appreciate you and Bobbie and Leslie."

"You there, Sue?"

"Yes, sir. Do you want me to get Mrs. Alasdair for you?" She knew the answer but asked nonetheless.

"No, I spoke with her earlier. She thinks we are ruining her life, so you and Jean leave her be. I'll be there Sunday. Make sure I've got a car at the hangar. Fontana is coming with me, so get him a…No, that's OK. I'll put him in the guest quarters out where I live. Get my…"

"Ooh, I want to meet Fontana. I never saw anybody who killed sixteen people."

"And you won't see this one. Neither will Jean. Fontana is a pretty literal person. One of her cute little suggestions and before she can blink she'll be in a pile. And don't you say anything. And stay away from the office unless I am with you. And keep everyone else away, OK?"

Alasdair walked over to the mirror on the back of the bathroom door and looked at himself again. "God, I feel awful. Think about what I have done to people this week, and there is no use to sugar coat it. I have done this to these people. Five people here, twenty-four in Belize, two in London, five whores caught up and killed in the spill-over, families messed up. And for what? For knowing me or people I know. My wife, I understand her with all that yelling and protesting. She's worried about me. There's Sue and Jean having to hide out at home because they know me. And what am I thinking about? A joke, a frigging joke. Henny Youngman's, I think, or maybe that guy Cohen's. Remember, the beautiful woman relaxing in the first class section of a 747, hands folded in her lap, ten-carat diamond sparkling on her finger. Man sitting next to her keeps shifting his eyes from the woman's face to the diamond. Stewardess comes by and asks, 'Can I get you anything, Mrs. Kloppman?' 'No, thank you.' Finally he says, 'That is a beautiful diamond.' 'Thank you,' she says, 'it is the Kloppman diamond, you know. It has a curse.' He says, 'A curse? What is the curse?' She says, 'Kloppman.'

"I am Kloppman," Alasdair said to the mirror. "I am their Kloppman." The mirror did not reply.

A few minutes before ten o'clock, Alasdair rushed through the lobby with the hope he would be unnoticed, and outside into Foley's waiting car.

Walther, between bites of steak, saw for an instant a shabbily dressed man dash through the lobby. Except for the clothes he would have sworn it was Alasdair. Since he heard no click in the back of his mind, he returned to his steak.

❧   ❧   ❧

August 27, 1970, 11:15 p.m. GMT–6, Brookmont Terrace, Nashville

The hill behind the tennis courts at Wessex Towers is steep, heavily wooded, and filled with underbrush. Two men climbed, crawled, and struggled to the top and to the fence surrounding the Wessex property and tennis courts. With heavy-duty wire cutters they sniped a hole large enough to squeeze through and lug their equipment onto the asphalt court. The night was not as dark as they would have preferred and the parking area was well lit. However, the lights were out on the tennis courts. Fortunately, most of the residents were asleep, judging by the many dark windows. Working quietly and quickly, they sat up their equipment while maintaining a lookout for any activity. Regardless of the assurances they received, not all the old people who lived there were in bed by 10:30 p.m.

"Look up there on the balcony. Someone is out there, smoking. See the cigarette end glowing when he puffs. Which floor is that?"

"I count nine. We want eight. Do you think he sees us?"

"Hell, I don't know. If he does, what can he do? Get that launcher together and put it on my shoulder. I am gonna send a rocket right under his ass. He will help my aim."

On the balcony outside Unit 812, Grogan used his thumb and forefinger to flip the cigarette butt twenty feet into the darkness. He watched as it fell into the grass nine stories below, just outside the basement door. He looked out toward the Ford glass plant and the Riverbend prison complex, both well lit and glowing. Grogan turned to his left and glanced at the tennis courts. "What the fuck?." He pressed the button on his two-way radio. "Tojo, Tojo. There are two men on the tennis court doing something. Get up there quick."

Grogan saw a flash of light on the tennis court an instant before he heard the swoosh of the rocket as it passed under his feet through the glass doors into Unit 712. It exploded with a loud thud. He heard shotguns blazing away on the tennis court as light flashed again from the rocket launcher. He watched the second rocket scream overhead and slam into the penthouse. Suddenly the tennis courts lights came on and he saw Tojo and Marcellus bending over two bodies, prodding them with shotgun barrels.

Pandemonium broke loose in the high-rise building.

❧   ❧   ❧

August 27, 1970, 10:30 p.m. GMT–4, The Copia Club, Frederiksted, St. Croix

"Shit, man, if you gonna smoke that damn thing we got to do something about the size of it. Cut it in half with that steak knife. Nobody here ever saw a cigar that long."

"Gritting his teeth, Alasdair cut the cigar and then lit the longer part. The table Foley chose gave them a good view of the L-shaped room. Foley had a view of the long side of the L and the front and rear doors. Alasdair could watch the base of the L and the side door. The bar was busy, with most of the patrons standing two or three deep as near to the long side of the bar as possible. A few people occupied the booths along the wall, while virtually all the tables were vacant on Foley's side. The base of the bar served as the hangout for the prostitutes and a couple of bar flies. Three men occupied a round table for five in the dark corner near the side door. They alternated between drinking beer and discouraging two pushy whores. The working women at the base of the L-shaped bar pointed at and whispered about Foley and Alasdair. Cops. They could tell. However, they pursued their profession with undiminished vigor.

Alasdair watched the three men at the corner table and knew he had found the shooters. How did he know? He wondered. They appeared little different from the three men in the booth across from Foley, or from any three of the men at the bar. Yet he knew, in his bones he knew. "Puffing on a piece of a cigar, peering through sunglasses in a dark bar, drinking warm beer, is this an undercover cop's life?" he asked Foley.

"Yeah, ain't it great.? Pays good, too."

"Yeah, I'll bet. Say, you notice the three in the corner?" Alasdair whispered.

"Yeah. I wondered if you did. Don't whisper, just talk low and don't look at anything but old big tits at the bar. Not much crowd, but they can't hear you. Get suspicious if you whisper."

"What do we do?"

"We wait, and then we wait."

☙   ☙   ☙

Walther said goodnight to Maddie after explaining that his work required him to be away for a couple of hours. She seemed to understand and offered no objections. She told him to be careful and come back as soon as possible. Walther liked that, but he did not like leaving her alone. If the plan worked tonight, his work was over. Earlier, while driving through Frederiksted, Walther had spotted a likely dive, the type the Latinos might choose. Off the beaten track, Copia appeared unlikely to be a hangout for undercover cops. A middle-grade dive, it was not bad enough for the real underbelly type criminals and not good enough for the top-drawer crooks, but just right for the has-been and the never-were. It was a good place not to be noticed. He drove the old rental car just below the speed limit, being careful to observe all the rules. A traffic stop was not in his plan.

There were plenty of empty spaces in the parking lot. It apparently was a slow Thursday night. Unconsciously, Walther surveyed the lot and was amazed at what he saw parked under the only light in the lot. There sat the other station wagon, Whitestar's old station wagon. The idiot still had it, still drove the old wagon, and even parked it in the bright light. Walther left his old car near the street, picked up his briefcase, and walked toward the station wagon.

Stopping at the rear of the wagon, he paused briefly, shook his head in disbelief at the sheer stupidity of some people, and then knelt beside the rear wheel. He removed the gas cap, opened the briefcase, and lifted the bottle of dark liquid from the foam liner. Carefully he poured the liquid into the gas tank and replaced the cap. From its place in the briefcase Walther gingerly removed a small oblong package. It had a small but powerful magnet firmly attached to it with duct tape. Reaching under the wagon on the passenger side, he placed the package, magnet side up, against the floor pan under the front passenger seat. Hearing the click when it touched the metal floor, he knew it to be secure. He pulled taut a thin wire attached to the package and ran it underneath the frame into the wheel well. He attached it to the base of the radio antenna with a "roach" clip of the type pot heads used to smoke their dope. Satisfied, he dusted himself off and returned the brief case to his car. Then he walked on toward the side door of the Copia.

Inside the Copia someone turned up the volume on the jukebox until the boring reggae beat pounded Alasdair's brain, preventing him from any semblance of intelligent thought. The cigar stub had lost its fire and had a bitter taste. The Jack Daniel's sour mash he found only marginally better than the hot beer. The mixture of odors, sour beer, bad pine scent, body odor, and cheap perfume, assailed Alasdair's nostrils with a vengeance. "I think I am going to puke," he told Foley, who chuckled and said no one would notice. Foley appeared to be enjoying himself completely.

Watching the person referred to by Foley as 'big tits' gave Alasdair an opportunity to scan the entire room as she circulated in search of a customer with money. The three men at the table near the side door approached being pleasantly drunk but showed no interest in any of the women who stopped at their table. Foley also gave the appearance of a man with a buzz. However, Alasdair observed, he actually drank very little. The prostitutes bothered neither him nor Foley due, he surmised, to them knowing a cop when they saw one. For that he was glad.

"We can't just sit here, Foley. We've got to do something. I'll go over and talk to those guys or accuse them or something. This is not getting us anywhere."

"True, but we have no proof, not even a hint, they were involved. They are the right color and the right number, but so are the three in the booth and the three at the far end of the bar. We wait. Something will happen."

"Hell's the matter with you, Foley. Nothing gonna happen unless we make it happen. Shit, man, I have to do something other than just sit here. I'll go over…"

"Sit! Wait. That is what we do. Something will happen. Relax and drink that sour mash."

Foley was proven right the next minute. Something did happen. Alasdair tried to relax. He threw the stub of the cigar away, and lit the other portion he had kept. Which end to light took his mind off matters for a second. Tired of having trouble seeing through the dark lenses, he stuffed the sunglasses into his shirt pocket and searched for the woman he had been told to watch in order not to appear too interested in any particular customer. The side door opened and what he saw surprised him. The short, broad, redhead from Christiansted stood in the doorway looking at the three men in the corner. He glared at the larger one in the center of the group, then walked over to the table. He spoke, but Alasdair could not hear the exchange.

"You should have shot me. You, in the middle, I am speaking to you. Your cap with the white star I remember as well as my bowl of peanuts. I paid for them and for the beer. You owe me, Whitestar, and I intend to collect tonight."

Startled and rattled, Whitestar fumbled for words. "What de hell you talking about, mon? I don't know who you are but you better get away from me or I have a chunk of your ass."

"I doubt that, Mr. Whitestar, but remember what I said. You made a mistake by not shooting me." Walther smiled inwardly. His plan was working. Upset them and they will leave. He plodded his way toward the bar, giving no indication he saw or recognized Alasdair. He ordered a draft beer and sipped it while staring at Whitestar, who huddled with his two friends. The staring made him nervous but Whitestar had no desire to start a fight with the redhead weirdo. Furillo proposed leaving. Whitestar voted to stay, as did Estavo.

"That really is the weirdo," Whitestar said, "the one I didn't shoot because he so fucking ugly. Now he here threatening us. Bullshit. I shoot him now he fuck with me. Holy shit, look at that!"

"What, mon, what you talking about looking at?"

"That table over there. See de guy what just took off his cheaters. You know who that is? It be one of them bankers, the big daddy, Alasdair. Right here dressed like a bum. Hell, he looking for us."

"Hey, Whitestar, you think he got that big gun what he shot that Wop with," Estavo asked?

"You don't want to know, Estavo, but I know we got a problem. Look at him. Now he staring at that weirdo. I think he knows him and he knows us, and he trying to put it together."

"We got to do something, Whitestar. We better get the fuck out of here."

"Why you say that, Furillo? We ain't done nothing. They can't prove anything unless the weirdo says something, then it just him against us."

"Uh, oh. Look up. Here he come again. What the matter with that ass hole? You and Furillo better think of something, Whitestar, or I shoot that ass hole right here and now."

"No, Estavo, no. Just sit still and keep you mouth shut."

"Look around you, Whitestar," Walther said. "You see the out-of-place gentleman at the table with the cop. That is Mr. Alasdair, the man that Wop tried to shoot. Look back by the back door. You see that man staring at you from that back booth? I'll tell you something for your health. That man is an explosive expert. I think he is the one who blew up your friends. Things closing in on you?"

"The fuck you talking about, mon? We never see you before and don't want to see you no more. Just leave us alone."

"Very well." Walther felt good because he knew his plan was working. To cinch it, he turned and walked straight to Alasdair's table. Alasdair leaned over and spoke with Foley. It did not escape Walther's notice.

"Good evening, Mr. Alasdair. My name is Walther and I am the man from the Buccaneer Bar when your friends were shot, the witness I am sure you have heard about."

Alasdair and Foley stared at him as he turned and pointed a stubby finger at the three men just leaving the corner table. "There are three of the men who did the shooting. I recognized them as I came in only an instant before I recognized you." Foley leaped to his feet intent on stopping the men at the side door. Walther blocked his way briefly, but long enough to allow the Latinos a momentary head start.

"Watch it, man. Get out of the way. I'll get them."

Walther grasped Alasdair's arm as he attempted to join Foley in the chase. "Wait, Mr. Alasdair, the cop will get them. You and I need to talk." Alasdair pushed Walther aside and dashed to the door behind Foley in time to see the station wagon roar across the lot and into the street. Foley was in his car with the motor running when Alasdair leaped into the rear seat barely before it shot out into the road. Walther shook his head, removed a small black plastic box from his pocket, extended the antenna, pointed it in the general direction of the fleeing station wagon, and pressed the small red button. The explosion was not particularly loud but the wagon flipped over and the ball of flames was large. Walther walked to the back of the bar to the booth just vacated by the man he had pointed out to Whitestar, tossed the little box onto the booth seat, and then went out to the parking lot. As the crowd rushed into the street to see the gruesome remains of the station wagon and its passengers, he removed the briefcase from his car and tossed it into the high weeds along the drainage ditch. He then joined the crowd. Walther was pleased. He would wait for Alasdair and begin the second phase of his plan.

Foley and Alasdair stood behind their vehicle well back from the roaring inferno that was once the station wagon. "Nothing can burn like that." Foley said. "It is unbelievable. There will be nothing left to identify. They'll be burned to a crisp just like the other three. Same ass hole got these. Determined bastard, I would say."

His brain spinning, Alasdair spun around to face the crowd of onlookers pushing closer. In the middle of the rear of the crowd he saw the man who gave his name as Walther. "You handle this, Foley. I am going to talk to that red-headed bastard who walked up to our table just before this mess started. I am sure half the cops in Frederiksted will be here in a few minutes. At least he didn't run, so I'll talk to him. Damn little good it will do now."

When there are too many coincidences they are not coincidences. That old axiom Alasdair believed to be true here. The redhead turned up too many times and waited too long to come forward as a witness, waited, it seemed, until the need for a witness had passed. The interview needed to be carefully conducted, private but with plenty of people close by. At the moment, being alone with Walther did not seem wise. The redhead not only wanted to talk, he seemed anxious, walking to meet Alasdair half way. Together they went back to the Copia.

"I want to know what the hell kept you from coming forward before now as a witness. I don't understand why you didn't run to the cops with your story. Surely you knew the people behind all this wouldn't want a witness left."

"If those creeps intended to kill me they would have done it in the bar. They didn't bother me so why should I bother them? We do need to talk, Mr. Alasdair, but not about the Latinos. They are no longer of any concern to you or me. It is other things we need to discuss."

"What could that possibly be, Mr. Walther?"

"Unresolved matters, unresolved problems we both have. You don't know who is after you or why. I cannot help you with the why, but I may be able to help you with the who. Is that of interest to you, Mr. Alasdair?"

"Hell's the matter with you? I will turn you over to the police and get whatever information you have that way. Of course that is of interest to me, but what the hell could you know, unless…That's it, isn't it? You are the bomber. You blew their asses up. By God, the police will make you tell them a hell of a lot!"

"I doubt it, Mr. Alasdair. They have little interest in me. They have their shooters. The matter is settled. Why not close the books?"

"The matter of Brookings St. John. The Latinos had nothing to do with his murder. The police are interested in that matter. You do remember how he was blown up and burned?"

"Indeed, I have heard of that, Mr. Alasdair. Also, I have heard the remains are unidentified. So until they are, this Brookings person is just missing. On a trip, perhaps. Got married and went on a honeymoon. Stranger things have happened. Could be he decided not to sit around and wait for someone to shoot his ass like you and O'Rielly are doing. Or perhaps the other missing person did it, the one no one admits is missing. Miss Willis, isn't it?"

"You son of a bitch, what do you know about her? It is not the police you have to worry about with her, it's me. Tell me what you are talking about or, by God, you will have a problem here and now."

"Perhaps we should try to avoid that. I do not underestimate you and I do not believe you underestimate me. A confrontation would serve neither of us well. I told you I have a problem far removed from the Latinos or St. John but close to you and me, and it does not need to be aired in the Copia Bar. Outside I have a vehicle and on the Shore Road a cottage at On the Beach. We need to go there and talk, quietly and seriously. We can solve both our problems."

"You have some information I want and I can get it through the police, and we do not have a common problem, Mr. Walther."

"You are mistaken, Mr. Alasdair. We do have a common problem and its name is Maddie Willis. Sit down now, Mr. Alasdair. Any undue attention to the two of us will be very detrimental to Miss Willis."

Rage tore through Alasdair like a storm at sea. The look in Walther's eyes caused him to control the storm and talk. Later he would shoot Walther as he would a mad dog. Now he would talk.

"OK, you son of a bitch. What do you want?"

"I want you to go with me to see Maddie and to listen to my proposition."

"To see Maddie! You know where Maddie is?"

"Yes, Mr. Alasdair. She is living with me…"

"You lying son of a bitch! Living with you? Bullshit. If she is with you it is because you have kidnapped her. You are not helping yourself with this kind of crap."

"In spite of your anger and disbelief, she is living with me and intends to continue living with me, and I will kill anyone who tries to make a problem for her, be that you or the entire island police. No one is going to hurt that lady. Am I clear?"

Alasdair stared into Walther's blue eyes and, with an extreme effort, put his anger on hold. The man was a dichotomy, torn between great violence and gentleness, an outlandish, almost repulsive person, yet strangely fascinating. "Yes, you are clear. But I have no knowledge of anyone trying to cause her a problem. Who might that be, if not you?"

"Go with me to see her and I will explain. Walk outside with me and I will show you why you should go with me. Please, I need your help. Maddie needs your help. I have avenged the death of your friends. I will lead you to the person who is after you. But first you must help Maddie and me."

Outside, Alasdair began to have fewer second thoughts about the wisdom of accompanying the redhead. Walther had been almost pleading before stepping outside. His words no longer seemed menacing. Thinking back over what Walther had said, he could find few threatening statements. Alasdair believed the redhead and walked toward the car. Walther opened the trunk. "Mr. Alasdair, I have an ankle holster with a revolver. Do not be alarmed. I am going to put it in the trunk." Carefully he pulled up the pants leg and removed the revolver and tossed it into the trunk. "Under my left arm inside my shirt is another. I will place it in the trunk also." He did so. "Now one more. Strapped to my left forearm is a dagger which I will now consign to the trunk. Feel free to pat me down if you want to be sure I have no other weapons. The briefcase that contained the explosives is in the drainage ditch for your police friend to use for evidence. You may keep the large weapon you have concealed inside those baggy pants as your security. I am risking my safety to you, no questions asked." Walther breathed a sigh of relief as Alasdair slammed the trunk lid and slid into the passenger seat.

His plan was working and Walther could feel it renewing his confidence and restoring his peace. A feeling of warmth flowed over his body as he closed his eyes for a brief moment. He knew he and Maddie would be safe. That made Walther happy.

As he drove carefully and cautiously along Shore Road, both men retreated into their private thoughts, saying nothing. Alasdair glanced at his watch when Walther turned the vehicle into the driveway of On the Beach. The dial blinked midnight. The cottage, the last one on the property, showed no sign of life. No lights burned. Maddie waited in the darkness until she saw Walther approaching. Amazed, Alasdair watched as she ran to Walther and embraced him possessively, kissing his beard before taking his arm, before turning to face Alasdair.

"I brought Mr. Alasdair to talk with us, Maddie."

"I am glad you are with Walther, Mr. Alasdair. I worry about him when he goes away even for a short time. Come inside and I will make some coffee."

"Maddie makes very good coffee, Mr. Alasdair. It is her best domestic ability, for which I am enormously thankful."

"Thank you, Walther," Maddie said. "Isn't he nice to me, Mr. Alasdair?"

"Indeed he is. May I smoke?" Stripping the cellophane from the Macanudo without waiting for a reply, Alasdair felt he was in a commune of idiots. Here he was, making coffee at midnight with a mass murderer and a beautiful bank employee, both of whom acted as if it were as normal as sunrise, their conversation inane and bubbling as if he were a long-lost friend come to rescue them from the great unknown. Only when the coffee was made and they were seated around the tiny table did any semblance of normal interaction between rational people occur, and then only for a few seconds.

"Did someone steal your clothes, Mr. Alasdair?" Maddie said. "Did Walther tell you I killed Brookings, that bastard, and the black whore with the big tits?"

Alasdair leaped to his feet, brushing the ashes and fire from his lap where he had dropped the cigar. Then he stooped to retrieve it from under the table. After the few seconds necessary to regain what little composure he had left, he looked at Maddie's beautiful, innocent, questioning face before answering. "No, no, by God, Maddie, he overlooked that."

"Well I did. I killed him and that black bitch both. Walther happened by and was nice enough to go in and clean up the mess. I really do appreciate him doing that. Walther is always nice to me."

Stunned again but not unprepared, Alasdair held on to his cigar this time. "Happened by, cleaned up the mess?" he said. "Damn, Maddie, he blew Brookings' ass all over the east end of the island and burned the pieces. Cleaned up the mess? Hell, I reckon he did. How did you kill Brookings and how do you know you killed him?"

"I shot him, Jim. May I call you Jim?"

"Hell, call me whatever you like. You shot him?"

"I did. I shot him four times and I shot the whore three times. I kicked the sorry bastard in his bare balls, too, I did. I left them on the floor. I ran out because I didn't know what to do and there was Walther just parking in the drive. He knew what to do. He came to help me, he did. I knew it when I saw him."

"Maddie, Maddie…" Alasdair looked Walther in the eyes and found them guileless. "What the hell am I to do with this story? The police think three people were killed, including the black whore's daughter. Was she there?"

"Yes," Walther said. "She was there and she saw Maddie shoot her mother. She may have been under the bed when Brookings was shot, but she knew Maddie did it. I added her to the pile because she could identify Maddie."

"You added her to the pile? To the pile? Son of a bitch! How long had you known Maddie when this happened?"

"I had never met her until she ran out of the house."

"I knew him," Maddie said. "He was sent to me and I knew him.".

"Sent, Maddie? Sent by who?"

"By God. God sent him to rescue me, and he did."

"Somehow, Maddie, I do not believe God involved himself in this mess."

"Oh, but he did, Mr. Alasdair," Walther said. "I believe he sent me because he planned for me to have Maddie and for Maddie to have me."

"Is there anything to drink in this fucking insane asylum beside coffee? Sent by God to shoot poor old Brookings, then blow his ass to hell and back, then live happily ever after? Not the God I know."

"I have some wine," Maddie said. "I like spritzers. In fact I wouldn't mind having a spritzer now. I will fix us both one. Walther only drinks beer."

"Sure, just what I need, a spritzer made by Lizzie Borden, or whomever. Damn, a spritzer! Walther, what kind of shit do you expect me to believe? You believe God sent you? Get ten or twenty pounds of plastic explosive and go blow up Brookings St. John and I will give you Maddie Willis. God said that? Is that what you believe and want me to believe?"

"Yes."

"Son of a bitch! Where the hell is the wine? God sent you Maddie and only provided me with a spritzer? Where the hell is my spritzer, Maddie?"

Two hours later, after stories were told and retold, Alasdair extracted himself from the embrace of Maddie. Walther drove him to the hotel.

❧　　　❧　　　❧

August 28, 1970, 2:30 a.m. GMT–4, Frederiksted Hotel, St. Croix

In the lobby, the night clerk greeted Alasdair with a hand full of messages. Tired and confused, he accepted them and trudged to his room. He thumbed through the messages to pick out the important ones. The attempt was useless. All were equally important. One from Sheriff Fate Thomas he moved to the top, above those from his wife and Sue, his secretary. It was 2:30 a.m. in St. Croix.

Fate answered the phone. "Hey, my man, fucking war out at your place. Couple foreign dudes set up a rocket launcher on the tennis court and attacked your building. Made a mess, man. Didn't involve you. Rocket went into seventh floor and killed an old Jewish couple, and one went into the penthouse and blew that Arab or Albanian, or whatever he was, all the way over to Highway 70. You are in the clear. Since they scraping that Arab out of the trees and off the street, Casey didn't discourage the reporters. They think that guy was the target. I think they missed your floor cause Tojo shot their ass with a shotgun. Killed them both. Tojo seemed to think we didn't need no foreign dudes to mess with. Courts too busy now."

"Wait, wait! Slow down, Fate. What happened at my house?"

"Couple of ass holes declared war on it. Used some kinda big bazooka or something to blow it up. Missed your place cause Tojo shot their ass with a shotgun."

"Nobody hurt except the ones you mentioned?"

"Yeah, that's right. Your wife still pissed off. Cause she didn't get hit, I reckon. I don't understand women. Talk to her and tell her to cool it. It's over."

"Who were they, Fate?"

"Hell, I don't know. Didn't have no ID pinned on their shirt. None in their pockets neither. Hell, who cares who they were? Tojo took care of them."

"I care, Fate. I'd like to know who sent them, who is trying to wreck me and kill everyone I know. I care, Fate."

"Yeah, I know. They probably didn't know who hired them. Just some middleman with no trail and who probably didn't know either. Forget it. We'll find him another way."

"Yeah, I'll do that. Thanks, Fate, and tell Joe thanks also."

"OK."

Next he rang Mrs. Alasdair. Steeled for her onslaught, he found himself unprepared and surprised when she began talking. "Well, you were right. Someone wanted to kill me and might have if Fate's men hadn't been alert. I will never say anything bad about Grogan or Tojo again. Casey indicated the target was the Serb, or whatever, in the penthouse. Fate says shut up and let the reporters talk about him because he is scattered all over the streets and roads. Tojo took care of the rocketeers, so there is no one to talk except me. I'll shut up. The rocket came in his window and took him out the window on the other side and exploded over the highway, is what they think. Big mess. You were right to look after me, and I appreciate it more than I indicated the last time we spoke."

"I know," Alasdair replied, "and I am coming to Nashville as soon as the plane gets here. Screw the funerals. I have too many problems. I'm bringing a planeload of nuts and I don't want them where we live. Rent the big suite at whatever that motel is at the airport, Silver Wings. Or is that the restaurant? Rent five other rooms near it if possible. Get your stuff together and check in. I'll call you when we get close. I don't know where the plane is now but I'll call you back. Oh, shit, I forgot the FBI. I have to meet with the FBI tomorrow after the funeral. It will be Saturday before I can get away from here. Get the rooms anyway and get everything set up. I'm sorry."

"Tell the FBI to get lost. Somebody is shooting rockets at your wife. Come home."

"I'll do my best."

"Bullshit."

Alasdair tried unsuccessfully to visualize anything Sue could add to what his wife and Sheriff Thomas had told him. He put her message aside and lit a cigar. He slid the big overstuffed chair across the floor so he could sit with his feet propped up on the bed. August 27 exceeded all his expectations for an eventful day. Neither he nor Foley expected to locate the Latinos. They only hoped for a clue. Finding them and becoming witnesses to their murder by explosion and fire certainly never crossed their minds. Alasdair wondered if he needed to try to contact Foley, but quickly dismissed the thought. Tomorrow would be soon enough, and by then he needed to have some explanation, a good explanation, for disappearing in the midst of the excitement.

What to do with Maddie and Walther required his attention. Turning them over to the authorities was not an option because Maddie would go to jail and Walther would have to be killed before he permitted Maddie to be taken away. If he protected Maddie, Alasdair knew Walther's strange sense of loyalty, loyalty that required him to complete his Latino contract, would extend to him. Could he use Walther? Did he want Walther in his employ? What about Devoe, the banker who used Maddie for information leading to the shooting at the Buccaneer Bar? What about the man who hired Walther to kill the Latinos? His thoughts drifted to the person, the yet unknown person, responsible for the attacks on him and his associates. The banker knows his name. Alasdair had no doubt of Devoe's willingness to divulge the name when asked a properly phrased question. Properly phrasing the question led to hiring Chief Halfpenny for his obvious talent in that direction. Then there was the colonel. With the colonel, very few people would fail to answer questions truthfully and eagerly. Now Halfpenny had to deal with the funerals, the murders, the FBI, and could not leave St. Croix until those tasks were completed. The colonel seemed to be stuck in Tanzania without hope of leaving for several days. Walther could replace Halfpenny, and Fontana might replace the colonel. Regardless, Alasdair intended to ask the Philadelphia banker some questions on Monday.

"Where the hell is the Sabreliner?" Alasdair spoke to the empty room, a plan beginning to materialize. "If it were here, I would load another homicidal maniac or two inside with Fontana, fly them to Philadelphia, and put them to work. Sheesh, what a mess!"

The Saberliner, with its plush configuration, accommodated ten passengers easily. Its range included either Nashville or Philadelphia. Alasdair decided, if everything went well, Maddie and Walther should never return to the islands. Halfpenny easily could leak the idea that she had died in the fire with St. John. They would fly on the

Sabreliner to Belize, and from there take a commercial flight to Botswana via the southern route through Rio de Janeiro. There they would be free to live happily ever after, or whatever fate had in store for them. "What a passenger list? Poor Smitty. Can he feel comfortable with us? Between the four of us we have, this week, killed twenty-nine people and I only got one. Even Maddie did better than me. I suppose Smitty is along because he can control Fontana. Maddie can control Walther and I can control Maddie and Smitty, at least until we get to Philadelphia. Oh, hell, the phone. Must be Sue."

"What is it?"

"You weren't going to call me, were you? Its just Sue. She doesn't know anything. I understand. Well, I do so know something you don't. The plane is in San Juan. Airport on St. Croix closed at 10:30 but the plane will be there at six this morning. You want to come to Nashville, they'll be ready. OK, now I'll leave you alone."

"I'm sorry, Sue. Its been a helluva day. I know you do your job above and beyond, as they say. I'll see you tomorrow."

. "Yeah, tomorrow, after you see everyone else. I'm always last, aren't I? It'll never be me, will it? Always that hard-hearted bitch at home. Always her, never me."

"Sue, Sue…Oh, shit! Dial tone. Might as well use it."

"Hello," Walther answered.

"You and Maddie get your shit together and meet me at the airport. Six o'clock. That's about three hours. Get everything you want because neither of you is ever coming back here. Whatever is in Maddie's condo, I will ship to you wherever you end up. OK?"

"Yes, sir. That is definitely OK."

❦   ❦   ❦

August 28, 1970, 6:40 a.m. GMT–4, Alexander Hamilton Airport, St. Croix

Engines screaming at full power shot the Sabreliner into the clear blue sky above the dark blue Caribbean at twenty minutes before 7:00 a.m. Rusty Lawrence made the turn required to put him on the flight plan he had filed thirty minutes earlier. In six hours the Sabreliner would coast to a stop at Nashville's Berry Field. Having reached the scheduled altitude, Lawrence throttled back the engines, leveled off, and engaged the autopilot. He relaxed. Wallace Locke, the pilot in the second seat, finished his duties and buzzed the stewardess for coffee before hanging his clipboard on the hook by his window. The weather was great all the way to Nashville, making for an easy, uneventful flight.

The Sabreliner, a beautiful plane with a crew of three and only five passengers, knifed through the air at thirty thousand feet, turning a ground speed of more than four hundred miles an hour. At that speed and altitude, noise was minimal. The ride was comfortable for both passengers and crew. Locke and Lawrence looked forward to the weekend in Nashville. Alasdair said they would leave early Monday morning. Locke had raised his eyebrows when Alasdair told him not to worry about a flight plan for the Monday flight because he was unsure where they were going and would decide once airborne. Alasdair had said maybe he would want to go to some small airport, he just did not know. This trip was already strange in Locke's mind and no flight plan countermanded Alasdair's standing order to not leave the ground without a detailed flight plan. He was sure it would all clear up over the weekend.

"Wally, you see that woman back there? Most beautiful woman I ever saw, and her hanging onto that red-headed weirdo. Makes no sense to me. Fontana nearly choked when he saw her. Crazy bastard never took his eyes off her."

"I noticed. Alasdair said he disarmed the whole frigging bunch. I hope he ain't lying. What a load we got back there. Smitty is the only one hasn't shot anybody this week. I'm wrong. The redhead, he didn't shoot anyone. Blew up six men and four whores plus, as I understand it, the two the blonde shot. Shit! Alasdair is a piker, only shot one. Fontana is the big-game man with sixteen."

"I'm surprised Alasdair told us about the other two he brought along. Felt he owed it to us to tell us what we are flying, I suppose. No wonder he wanted to skip the meeting with the FBI. Where we going next week, or are we going somewhere this weekend?"

"Damn if I know."

❧ ❧ ❧

August 28, 1970, 8:00 p.m. GMT–6, Airport Hilton Hotel, Nashville

Alasdair felt like a rope-walker. He was determined to reassure the Nashville office employees and maintain peace among the diverse factions from the islands and Belize, while convincing his wife he was home to look after her. That all proved difficult. The number of people invited for the weekend meeting at the Airport Hilton was large. He had a suite for himself, five rooms for the five accountants in the office and their wives, five rooms for the secretarial staff and their whatever, one room for Sue and Jean to keep them under control. Smitty and Fontana were in one room for the same reason, Walther and Maddie were in a small suite away from everyone because, in Alasdair's opinion, both were lunatics ready to blow at any minute. The pilots wanted no part of the meeting and went off on their own. Sheriff Thomas and his latest joined for dinner, bringing the total to thirty.

In his suite Alasdair, opened the curtains and stood looking out on a gigantic parking lot, asphalt and more asphalt. "What a view," he said to Mrs. Alasdair. "Sure beats having to look at the damn Caribbean and all its water. Hell's the matter with people? Nobody happy about his or her rooms. Sue and Jean both bitching. Fontana says Smitty is no fun. You don't like this place. Damn, what am I supposed to do?"

"Well you could have gone to Atlanta like I wanted," she said. "Instead I, your wife, have to put up with these, these people. Sue and Jean both want to room with you. Jean would have settled for anybody. Why can't you hire some ugly women like everybody else? You don't care about me, do you? Been happy if that rocket carried my ass across the highway instead of that fucking Armenian. Only reason you came back was to get that bunch of nuts out of St. Croix. Don't give a shit about me. I work my ass off for you, put up with all the gossip about you, stay away from the club because of talk of you hauling your girlfriends all over the world. Is that fun? I don't think so. You never take me anywhere unless it's deductible. What a life!"

"Why don't you shut the fuck up? I got problems and I don't want one of them to be the fact you are still alive. Just forget it and get your ass ready for the party. You can talk to Fate. He still talks to you."

"You bastard."

It was eleven o'clock before Alasdair was able to have a short meeting with Walther and Fontana. He was surprised to notice that neither drank much, although most of the crowd seemed pleasantly drunk. Reassured, they relaxed, probably for the first time this week. Mrs. Alasdair was the perfect hostess the entire evening, not once cutting Sue off at the ankles or denigrating Jean. She kept her distance from Walther and Maddie Willis. She privately referred to them as "the nuts." Barbara stuck close to Mrs. Alasdair while Sheriff Thomas covered the room and omitted no one from his tales and humor. Finally in the bar with Walther and Fontana, Alasdair explained his plan to leave early on the first of September for New Jersey. Whatever supplies Walther needed would be provided. It would, if everything went correctly, be a quick in and out.

Alasdair explained a slight change. "The chief financial officer of Empire Industries and his wife, along with Jean and Sue, will represent me to the families of Keaton and Dobbins. The Sabreliner will fly them to Oklahoma and California on Sunday. Our group will fly from Cornelia Fort Airport, just across the river here, in a friend's Aero Commander, either late Sunday afternoon or early Monday morning. If Maddie can work her magic, we may only stay three or four days. That we will play by ear. Maddie's magic! We are depending on Maddie to deliver Devoe quietly into our hands. Can she do it, Walther?"

"Maddie can do it. I will make a plan for her."

August 29, 1970, 3:00 p.m. GMT–4, St. Thomas

"Orlando, this is Thad. What is going on down there? I can't get any information here. The news people here don't know and don't care what goes on in your precious islands."

"What is going on here is something I want to stay as far away from as possible and I do not want you to call me anymore," Orlando replied. "I am not involved but I suspect you are. If so, you are in deep shit. That idiot in the black silk suit made a really big mistake shooting up the funeral home. Not smart. The word here is he tried to kill Senator O'Rielly, Chief Halfpenny, and that guy Alasdair, the one who shot him. Got his gun tangled up in his shirt, according to the chief. Threw off his aim. Alasdair had a gun because of threats, they said. He popped three caps at the Silk Suit. Hit him three times. Coroner said you could cover the holes with a drink coaster. Good shooting for a businessman, wouldn't you say?"

"I have no idea what ever possessed that man in the black suit to attack the funeral home, certainly not anything involving me. I sent him there for clearing up some unfinished business for me, but it had nothing to do with that senseless act. I can assure you of that. In fact, his job is still open, that is why I am…"

"Forget me, Thad. I have a job. Forget me and don't call. Just watch your ass. Better pray you find the drunken friend of Old Black Silk Suit before someone else does. FBI, Chief Halfpenny, and Alasdair all looking for him. If you involved he will lead them to your ass. Somebody will get him, probably Alasdair. If he is really looking for him, that is. His big ass private jet flew in here yesterday morning. Brought his friend from Belize, the one that just killed sixteen Mexicans in some kind of bean patch fight, and another guy my drivers at the airport couldn't find out anything about. Alasdair and two other people showed up at the airport and they all left for Nashville by way of Miami. Didn't stay for the funeral. Had something else on their mind. Been nice knowing you, Thad."

"Orlando, wait a…Hell, hung up."

Lou walked into the room as Thad cradled the phone, his face taut, his expression worried. "I couldn't find Walther," Lou said. "He checked out of the Caravelle. They don't know where he went. Three more Latinos got blown up in Frederiksted Thursday night or early Friday morning, just after Walther checked out. You owe him any money, Thad?"

"Yes, I do and I will pay him. I always pay Walther by bank transfer to some African bank. Different one nearly every time. He will let me know."

"I'm betting he shows up here for his money."

"Not possible, Lou. We never meet. I have only seen him once and that was years ago. Why do you think he will come here, Lou?"

"Because he is worried, worried about his money, worried about why this deal was so screwed up. Three bullet holes in Casale's heart. That worries Walther. Cover them with your hand, fired off while being shot at. That worries Walther. Worries me too and ought to worry you. This Alasdair is one strange banker."

"Alasdair doesn't know who we are, Lou. How could he? Walther blew up the trail to Casale and Alasdair finished off Casale. That ended it."

"Cosgrove, Thad, Cosgrove. Walther will be here before Alasdair finds Cosgrove. Cosgrove knows. We better find Cosgrove quick. Who we got working in Miami on Cosgrove?"

That is why I called Orlando. I wanted him to take care of it."

"Thad, Orlando is gone, gone. He's a businessman in the islands. He's gone. We've got to send some one to Miami today. Alasdair left yesterday. He may already be in Miami and he can find Cosgrove. We must get someone after Cosgrove, now. For your sake, Thad, send someone. I suggest Bruce."

"You are an alarmists, Lou. Cosgrove knows nothing. Casale was dumb but not dumb enough to tell him about me. We can forget about Cosgrove. Forget Alasdair. He has problems in Nashville."

Thad pushed the leather-covered chair back against the walnut credenza and lit his own cigarette as Lou stared out the eleventh floor window. His thin lips puckered tightly as he drew smoke deep into his lungs. He expelled the smoke through both nostrils in two distinct streams while smoothing his white hair with his left hand. Lou was, in his opinion, overly concerned with the St. Croix incident. He had in his seventy years dealt with far more formidable characters than this Alasdair person. Still, it might be well to send Bruce to Miami to settle the Cosgrove matter.

A more troubling thought flashed its way into his mind. The funeral, Casale's funeral, would happen soon. In a few days the police would release the body and ship it to Mrs. Casale, an attractive but witless woman, in Newark. Ostensibly, Casale was an employee of Thad's scavenger company in Newark. Would that witless woman be in touch with her brother, Cosgrove, and would she insist he come to Newark to help her with the arrangements? Thad decided to act to solve the Cosgrove problem.

"Lou, we own a funeral home down state with a competent man named Ferguson running it. We need him to take charge of the Casale funeral and all arrangements so we can keep Mrs. Casale from control as much as possible. Speak with Ferguson and have him contact Casale's wife and explain that, as an employee of Reliable Scavenger, Inc., Casale is entitled to a fully paid funeral and burial from the Garden of Prayer Funeral Home. Is that the name of it, or is that the cemetery?"

"I don't know."

"Whatever. Call the undertaker and tell him. He will know what to do and how to make arrangements. Tell him to get the right funeral home in Newark to actually handle everything. I'll get Bruce informed and underway while you do that. Remember Mrs. Casale will know where and how to contact Cosgrove, so be nice and comforting. Then get what information you can. I don't think it's necessary to worry about Alasdair, but if you are concerned then I am also."

"I'll take it from here, Thad. I think this is the right way to go."

CHAPTER 8

❀

August 29, 1970, 11:00 a.m. GMT-4, Police HQ, St. Croix

"OK, Chief, I don't blame Alasdair for getting out of here," FBI Agent Edward Edwards said. "Somebody shoot a rocket at my wife I'd go home, too. We got some good information for him but never had a chance to give it to him."

"You know, Chief, this entire investigation was started by a banker named Devoe in Philly. He works for the Peace Bank, which is owned, damn near, by a guy named Brown. Right after the investigation started the banker got a big promotion and a helluva raise. Think on that for a minute. That banker, Devoe, is one lying son of a bitch. He pumped the Justice Department full of crap, and that stupid congressman from Jersey, God, he ate it up. We had no choice but to investigate."

Edwards made himself as comfortable as possible in one of the uncomfortable chairs in Halfpenny's office. Halfpenny glanced at the faces of the other agents and knew himself to be in for a long and maybe boring story. So what? Part of the job.

"This goes back to World War II. In the late thirties and early forties football coach at Tennessee, Coach Neyland, was looking at kids from the coal and steel areas of Pennsylvania as good, strong football players. In some little hollow near Pittsburgh there was a kid named Brown, Cheshire Brown. Not much of a player in knowing how to play, but full of determination. Coach figured he could teach him the fundamentals in a year. The war in Europe got hot and during his freshman season, football season that is, the Japs bombed Pearl Harbor. Shortly thereafter his ass was drafted. Four years later he went back to Tennessee and they took him in. Put him on the team. He wanted to kick ass and take names, but so did fifty or sixty others. He got to play only a little and one Saturday scored a touchdown against Alabama.

"He went back to Pittsburgh after graduation and got a job in a bank. Greedy son of a bitch, he was. Became a loan officer. Charged customers under the table to make them a loan. Cash or stock in the company. Eventually he owned a bunch of customers and became a big stockholder in the bank. Whatever money he made on the loan deals he used to buy stock in the bank. Pretty soon he owned a big damn mattress company and all sorts of little businesses in Pennsylvania, New Jersey, and Ohio. One was a construction company. Left the bank and hit the mattress business big. Believe it or not, there was a big rush on mattresses in the fifties.

"Everything boomed until the middle sixties when Alasdair comes on the scene with his Empire Industries. Alasdair decides to do construction world wide, and he fucking knew how and where. Beat the shit out of Brown everywhere. By then Brown owns control of the bank he once worked for, the Peace Bank, and is cutting with a big knife in the Caribbean. Alasdair gets in the banking business and cut his nuts out in the Caribbean. This is bad because I think Brown was laundering all kinds of money through the Peace Bank. Then, according to the New Jersey congressman, Alasdair bribed General Noriega, the man in Panama, who by now is running Torrijos, who Brown thinks he has in his pocket. Empire contractors already beat him out on three airport jobs in Africa and a big deal in Belize: airport and cannery for beans. Also got the bean-growing concession. Then when he starts fucking with him in Panama, Brown can't stand it no more. Much to his surprise, Brown finds out he has no political friends in Tennessee and few in Pennsylvania. All he has left is Mafia-ridden New Jersey and there he comes up with a sleazy congressman friendly with somebody in the Justice Department. That is when we get called in to investigate Alasdair, who is allegedly bribing people all over the world and mistreating this poor Brown."

"Shit, Edward, give it a break," Agent Jones said. "I'm hungry. It's noon. Can we get some food, Chief?"

"Agent Jones, it will be my pleasure to feed you if Edwards will allow us go to the small private dining room at the Top Hat."

"Fine with me, if you will remember where I am in this story."

An hour later, seated at a large round table loaded with food, both Danish and Caribbean, the narrative continued, mellowed somewhat by whiskey and Coke.

"Three weeks ago we told the congressman our investigation was over and we could probably indict Brown and his companies eight or ten times, but Alasdair was clean as a coal miner's dick on his honeymoon. Didn't set too well with anybody, but facts are facts. Have to face them sometime. Alasdair's got some colonel that trails about six yards behind him, and rumor is if anyone gets out of step, they have a serious, often fatal, attack of something. Alasdair is, so far as we can find, the only person ever to walk through Africa, Central America, the Middle East, Mexico, wherever, you name it, without ever bribing a single soul. Never even thought about it, so far as we can tell.

"I never met this damn colonel and I don't want to. I interviewed dozens of people who have, and they don't want to see him again. Where is he, by the way, Chief?"

"I do not know. I never knew he existed before now."

"You must be one straight feller, Chief, or Alasdair would have run him by you."

Edwards paused for a new glass of Jack Daniel's, and Jones spoke up. "We only here for one reason, Chief, to tell Alasdair what went down and to see who killed our man Ronrico. Seems we have now done both and are through here. Relax a little and get our asses back to the States. I would strongly suggest you urge Alasdair not to respond to Brown in the U.S. We don't want to have to investigate him again. If you see the colonel, tell him we are friends for life."

"I do not know this colonel, and urging Mr. Alasdair is usually a waste of time. I do want your report to give him, however. Why don't you boys go to Nashville and meet with him there? He is anxious to talk with you."

"I doubt it, I doubt it very much. Was he really pissed about Ronrico?" Jones asked.

Chief Halfpenny, using a butter knife, stirred the fresh glass of Cruzan tea delivered by the tall, blond Danish bartender, while thinking more about the colonel than Jones' question. If the colonel existed and did the job that the agents indicated, why did Alasdair want a chief of security? "I am sorry, Agent Jones. What was your question? I was wandering about in my own thoughts."

"Ronrico. Ronrico, Chief. Was Alasdair really upset about him working for us?"

"Upset? Upset is not the word I would use. Livid is a more descriptive, a more fitting word. Alasdair paid, is paying, for all the directors' funeral and burial expenses except Ronrico. Not one penny for him. Alasdair was indifferent as to who employed Ronrico as a spy, but not to his being a spy. Disloyalty. Disloyalty is not a word acceptable to Alasdair when describing an employee or associate. Yes, he was pissed, as you put it. More than a little. Not at you so much, though your organization is not looked upon kindly. It seems our Mr. Alasdair believes in handling his own problems without the assistance of people such as you and me. He finds law enforcement people unnecessary for anything other than traffic control and such."

"The bastard is going to need a few of us before he finishes with the guy in this report," Jones said. "The bastard in this report is crazy, Chief, crazy. When he found Alasdair looking to open an operation in Panama, he flipped. Lost it big time. You ask Edwards and Roberts. They'll tell you, Alasdair is being pursued by a crazy man."

"Jones is right, Chief," Edwards said. "I was in charge of this investigation and it soon became clear to me that the man is crazy. Listen, Brown has always been a crook, living on the edge of everything. When he heard Alasdair met with Noriega he couldn't handle it. Dropped into serious paranoia. You've seen what he has done and tried to do to Alasdair in the last week. Well, if he ever gets it in his mind that Alasdair is in Mexico, the shit will really hit the fan. Crazy man with all the money in the world. Man, he can do you some serious harm."

"Serious harm? What is serious harm, mon? They killed thirty-two of his people, thirty-three if you count Ronrico. To me that is serious harm."

"Right, Chief, but the man will lose it totally if one more straw is added to the load he imagines he is carrying because of Alasdair. He is capable of being out of control, totally, if he thinks Alasdair is after him again."

"I understand, Edwards, but doesn't he have any other competitors? Hell, Alasdair does not run the entire world."

"Try telling that to Brown."

"What is the Mexico deal? Surely Brown doesn't think Alasdair has any interest in mattresses.?

"No, Chief, it is not mattresses that will trouble Brown. It's gold."

"Gold?"

"Gold, man. There is still gold in Mexico and Brown is after it big time.

The colonial types stripped the country of gold during the eighteen hundreds and early nineteen hundreds. When the gold got too difficult to mine, they left. But they still owned the mines and the land. Mexico has been angry for years over the abandoned mining operations. Finally they nationalized the mines and took them, and now they're selling mining concessions. Mines are there, geologic reports are easy now, compared to a hundred years ago. Mountains of unprocessed tailings. New equipment and methods make processing the tailings profitable. Never was before. Brown is quietly buying concessions everywhere they are available. Many, if not most, are near Monterey, where his big mattress spring facility is located. Convenient and possibly very lucrative."

Chief Halfpenny studied the agent while again stirring his Cruzan tea with the butter knife. "Why the agent felt the need to share this with me I do not understand," he thought. "Does he think Alasdair knows of Brown's interest in gold and is planning to bid against him for concessions, or is this his way of giving Alasdair a tip about a profitable venture? If so, why? Alasdair's distaste for the FBI is no secret, so why would an agent try to help him in any way. Perhaps this is not intended to help."

Halfpenny decided to ask. "Agent Edwards, I know of no interest on Mr. Alasdair's part in mining of anything, gold included. Why are you sharing this information with us?"

"It is very simple. While I have no liking for the man, neither do I have a dislike for him. I am sure, however, he will retaliate against Brown outside the normal courtroom of justice. When he does, I do not want to be the agent searching for evidence against him. After this week he needs to be left alone. Whatever he does to Brown he deserves. I am telling you he will not find Brown in Knoxville. He will be in Mexico. Please, for all our sakes, advise him to extract his brand of justice from him in Mexico. Mexico is out of my jurisdiction, don't you see? As of this moment he has no knowledge of Brown's involvement. But once he gets this report, which he is legally entitled to, and which I have been instructed to give to him, he will know. Although this report was prepared well before the Buccaneer Bar shootings and contains no hint of any illegal activities planned by Brown, or even suspected of him, Alasdair will know and will, in my opinion, go to Knoxville to see Brown."

"What are you trying to say, Agent Edwards?"

"I am saying your future boss will go to Knoxville, maybe with you or maybe with the colonel. But he will go. And if he finds Brown, when he finds Brown, Brown will be dead. Who will be suspect? Him. Who will be remembered as investigator? Me. I don't want the job. I am telling you to go to Mexico to settle this mess. Or don't give him the report. Then maybe he'll never know about Brown."

"Agent Edwards, I suspect it will be a month before Alasdair reads this report, if then. He will find the trail to this Brown person without this report. I do not think he plans to return here any time soon. I do not know when or where I will see him again. My work here, like yours, is almost complete. I agreed to remain in my position until the shootings at the Buccaneer Bar are cleared up. I believe the shooters have received justice from someone. The mysterious bomber is far away by now, and I sense no great surge of indignation on the part of either the public or the politicians, no pressure to locate him. Thus, I, as you, have a few days to rest and clear my desk before reporting to a Mr. Carlotta in Belize.

"Alasdair is in Nashville now, but indicated to me that he and his wife would probably take a few days of vacation in Atlanta. He needs to get her away from the investigation, if any. It is pretty cut and dried in Nashville. The perpetrators were caught and killed in the act. The police think they were after some poor rug dealer from Iran or somewhere. No one in Nashville gives a care about the Iranian. They are sorry about the elderly Jewish couple, but the killers are dead. The Jews died accidentally, not intentionally."

"So you plan to hang on to this report until you see Alasdair?"

"Yes, Agent Edwards. That is exactly what I plan to do."

"You will urge him to be cautious, won't you? Stay out of Knoxville. Even if he finds Brown without this report, remember it exists. I do not want to be involved in Alasdair's life again."

"I have the message and will deliver it personally."

❦   ❦   ❦

September 1, 1970, 11:30 a.m. GMT–5, Philadelphia, Peace Bank

"Roy Devoe."

"Roy, this is Maddie Willis. Are you surprised? I only have a minute, but I want to let you know I appreciated your calls and the concern you expressed for me during all this mess in St. Croix. I am just sick of it all and have come home."

"Maddie, I don't believe it!. Come home you say? Where are you?"

"You won't believe this either, but I am in an airport limousine by your door on 37th. I asked the driver to stop and let me call an old friend to see if I could say hello. I am on my way to Camden, but could not pass your building without at least calling to say how much I appreciate the concern you expressed for me. It is really a mess down there and I am happy to get out. I never knew what a bastard St. John was until the shooting at the Buccaneer Club. It was ever so sweet of you, Roy. Your concern, I mean."

"It turns out I am free today, Maddie. If you have a few minutes I will run down and say hello."

"Oh would you, Roy? That is what I hoped for. Yes, the driver says he is in no hurry. I will be waiting. I have been traveling for hours and am somewhat disheveled, but I promise I will look better the next time we meet. Hurry! I'm waiting."

Roy put down the telephone and glanced at the new Rolex Oyster watch he had purchased a few days ago. He leaned back in his leather chair, clasped his hands behind his head, and decided to let the euphoria of Maddie's call sink in, but not for long. Moments later he was out the door and down the hall to the private elevator.

Before opening the side door Devoe looked for the limousine. There it sat, just across the street with the chauffeur standing by the rear door. The passenger hidden inside the cool interior behind the heavily tinted glass was not visible to Devoe. The chauffeur showed no recognition when he saw Devoe moving through the doors, but a few spoken words and the finger gesturing from the upper fourth of the partially open window pointed him out. The chauffeur waved a hand in greeting as Devoe made his way across the three lanes of traffic. He didn't give a rip about the traffic. He aimed for the car, aimed toward Maddie.

He gave the chauffeur a quick once-over. Six feet two or three, stiff as a board, one ninety or ninety-five, probably a retired Marine or something else military. Typical airport driver these days. The chauffeur opened the rear door for Devoe, who bent to peer inside to see the glorious smile he remembered, and Maddie's beautiful face. He did not see Maddie as a huge hand grabbed his tie and collar, then yanked him into the limo just ahead of the chauffeur, who followed him inside and slammed the door. "Go," the chauffeur shouted to the driver on the other side of the glass partition. The pressure on Devoe's throat did not let up as he roughly was rolled onto his back on the floor of the limo. Devoe kicked and tried to yell, but the pressure on his neck would not let him make a sound. The chauffeur, or the person he thought to be the chauffeur, grabbed his thrashing feet and quickly lashed them together with the skill of a calf roper at a rodeo. He used duck tape to bind Devoe's hands at the wrist, then used more tape to secure his feet at the ankles. With a flick of his wrists, he removed the rope from the ankles and made a loop, which he slipped over Devoe's feet. The ends were run between Devoe's arms, above the duck tape on the wrists, and drawn up until Devoe was in a sitting position with his wrists and ankles touching and bound tightly together. He may not have noticed the acceleration as the limo roared out into the traffic.

The hand at his throat did not relax the pressure that prevented him from speaking and, very nearly, breathing. Scared beyond belief and in terrible pain, Devoe stared at the person squeezing his throat. There was nothing in the pale blue eyes under the flaming red hair that gave him any comfort. The chauffeur jerked him around and shoved him between the jump seats with a warning. "Keep your mouth shut or I will break your jaw. We want to ask you a couple of questions and we want answers without any waste of time. I am John and he is Henry, Mr. Devoe. Now that we all know each other, let me explain the program."

From the pocket on the door John withdrew what appeared to be a railroad spike and a large hammer. "This is a spike much like those used by railroads to fasten their rails to the cross ties, and this is a three-pound hammer. It will not drive the spike into the cross tie, but it is heavy enough for light work. Take a good look at these tools. The spike has nice barbs all over it, big ones. Now listen carefully to what I say. I do not intend to repeat anything, including the questions. If we keep the limo over an hour it costs an extra fifty bucks, so don't waste our time. Look closely at this spike and remember it, for you are not likely to see it again if you answer my questions. Roll him over."

Henry yanked up Devoe, shoved his head against the floor of the limo, and arranged his rear end so it pointed upward. In a voice muffled by the carpet and shrill from fright, Devoe squeaked, "What are you going to do?"

"I am going to ask you a couple of questions and if you answer truthfully, I will put the tools back in the door pocket. If you don't, Henry will drive this spike up your ass one barb at a time until you answer truthfully. You know us, we're John and Henry, the steel driving men."

John jerked Devoe's pants down and pushed them below his hips. "Leave the jockeys up, John. He will probably shit when the barbs go in." Devoe began to sob and snivel loudly. Henry suggested to Devoe that he be quiet, a suggestion ignored until John kicked him viciously in the crotch.

"Here is the first question. What is the man's name who furnished the money to pay for the execution of our friends in St. Croix, London, and Belize?"

When no answer came within ten seconds, Henry shoved the spike into position. The answer poured out before it became necessary to tap the spike.

"What is the name of the man who made the arrangements for the incident in St. Croix. Also, London and Belize?" After a ten-second period of silence, Henry struck the spike gently, but not too gently, which was immediately followed by a scream, then the name of the man.

"Here is question number three. What are the names of any other people you know to be involved with this or any other attack, planned or perpetrated, against my friend from Nashville?"

Again a torrent of answers came from the carpet, muffled but understandable.

"Question number four. Is there anything else we need to know? Now think carefully about that answer before you speak." The reply offered assurance that Devoe knew of nothing more to tell.

"Thank you, Mr. Devoe. We are finished and you will soon be able to return to the bank. In the future I suggest you give thought to whether you really want to play with the big boys. Also, I suggest you forget about this interview unless you want a return visit." John picked up the telephone and spoke to the driver. "We are finished back here." He listened for a few seconds, then replaced the phone in its holder. "Mr. Devoe, it is unfortunate, but we are not sure you know how serious we are about you not talking to anyone about this meeting before we have an opportunity to meet with the people you mentioned."

"No, no, never! I will never say anything, never! Please, God, I never will!"

"Pull him out of the floor, Henry, and sit him up. The Man is afraid he will call, write, or talk to someone, and suggests we fix him up to prevent him making the mistake of doing that. Use the hammer. I will remove the rope to make it easier."

"Wait a minute, John. Get the phone and tell the driver to pull off the road for a second. We will solve this problem quickly and without using the hammer."

The Pennsylvania interstate highways have wide shoulders for drivers with automobile problems, allowing them to get safely out of traffic. The driver slowed the limo, braked, and stopped at the furthermost edge of the shoulder. Quickly John got out on the side away from the traffic. Henry pushed Devoe's bound hands toward the door, smoothing out his fingers as he pushed. When Devoe understood what was about to happen, he began to scream and thrash about. Henry stifled the screams by placing a large foot on the back of Devoe's head and jamming it hard against the limo floor. He then continued forcing the bound hands partially outside the edge of the door. When the hands were in just the right place, John, using his entire two hundred pounds, crashed his shoulder into the door, closing it almost completely. Devoe screamed as bones were crushed, flesh was mashed, and blood vessels exploded. Opening the door proved to be difficult, but it gave in to Henry's third kick. Devoe had fainted and did not feel the additional agony when Henry broke both his jaws with the three-pound hammer.

Traffic on this particular section of highway often thinned out, and several times the driver noticed that no automobiles appeared in his rear-view mirrors. He saw a bridge ahead and maneuvered the limo onto the shoulder. He waited until he saw no traffic in his mirrors before backing to the edge of the bridge. John opened the door. Henry shoved Devoe out of the limo and rolled him down the embankment to the dried-up creek. The limo continued on its way until a crossover allowed it to be turned back toward Philadelphia. At a do-it-yourself car wash, Fontana and Walther washed and cleaned the limo until it sparkled inside and out. Alasdair watched.

☙   ☙   ☙

September 1, 1970, 3:00 p.m. GMT–5, The Wayward Wind Inn, New Jersey

The Wayward Wind Inn, somewhere south of the airport at Teterboro, boasted in its ads of a huge suite suitable for meetings, private parties, wedding dinners, or other special occasions. Outside, the Wayward Wind appeared a normal businessman's motel. Inside, it was more intimate, almost cozy. Off the lobby was a small, dark lounge, the Snug Harbor, well out of the way of any wayward wind, according to the drink menu. The Snug, as the staff called it, served a limited menu of appetizers and a sandwich or two. Otherwise, all meals were from room service and ranged from snacks to five-course dinners. A businessman from Indiana might have thought the arrangement a bit strange, but to most of the inn's guests it was perfectly normal.

Three men in serious conversation occupied the Snug's round-table for six, reserved earlier for Ranger Securities, the same group that had the suite. Mario, the bartender and Heather, the cocktail waitress, watched them with a mixture of curiosity and boredom. It was 3:00 p.m. and they were the only customers before the four o'clock regulars began to trickle in. The rush sometimes came at 5:30. It might not come today. The middle of the week usually was slow.

To Heather they were one Dewars, one Bud, and a cherry Coke. To Mario they were the Big Man, the one with the Dewars and the cigar; his bodyguard, the stiff-backed, ramrod-straight, military type with the cherry Coke, and the redhead, shorter, really broad shoulders and huge arms and hands. Mario wasn't sure about the redhead. He hoped the women in the suite would join the men soon. There were two of them, both good looking, but one was gorgeous. The other man was a guard for the women, Mario assumed. At least he stayed with them at all times, or had since they arrived on Sunday evening. The company had rented everything on the top floor, the suite with two bedrooms and a living room, a dining-meeting room, and four other single rooms. Mario assumed they did not want to be bothered with other guests on the same floor.

Alasdair busied himself with lighting the Macanudo and swirling the Scotch in his glass. Walther closed his eyes, working out a plan for the next few hours. After all, he knew Thad and had not been surprised when the banker spewed out Thad's name on the floor of the limo. Walther had been to Thad's office once, and even if he could not find the building, he remembered the layout of the offices. Now he belonged to Alasdair until he and Maddie were on the plane to Botswana. He knew the rules. "Thad must be sanctioned and you know him, so you will participate as a leader," Alasdair had explained. The feeling of warmth and peace was slow in coming due, he supposed, to mixed loyalties.

During a ten-year relationship, Thad had paid him quite a lot of money for his work. He had completed each project every time as agreed. Therefore, he had earned his pay and the slate was clean. Still, he felt he knew Thad and Lou, although Lou was only a voice on the telephone. Finally, he settled on a plan. He would do what Mr. Alasdair asked. The feeling of peace and warmth spread slowly over him and he opened his eyes and relaxed as he sipped his beer.

Fontana stared at Heather, a young, nubile girl. If no rush of customers came and Mr. Alasdair did not object, he planned to chat her up, if possible.

"Walther, here is what we plan for Thad. You will get us in to see Thad. Once there, we will neutralize Lou and the other guard. When we leave you will leave enough of your good explosives and accelerant to clear up the mess, but not enough to destroy the building. Although Thad owns the building, there are innocent people there."

"I would prefer that you not accompany me to see Thad, Mr. Alasdair. If something happened to both you and me, who would look after Maddie? I can handle Thad alone. Certainly, Fontana and I can handle him. You need not risk yourself."

"No, hell no! The bastard tried to kill me and I intend to tell him I do not accept such actions. I intend to shoot the bastard. Clear?"

"Yes, sir."

"I think you should let Walther and me handle this, Mr. Alasdair," Fontana said. "You are too important a man to do this yourself. Too many people depend on you."

"Hell's the matter with everybody? The son of a bitch sent that guy, Casale, down to the islands to finish up what his first frigging group failed to do. He hasn't looked a gun in the face in a long time, and I think he deserves to see me holding it."

"Everyone says I'm crazy but I'm not," Fontana said. "Fucked up, yeah. I'll go along with that. But I'm right about this. Just think about what we say. Let Walther do it. He knows how. I'll help him."

"Gentlemen, you ready for another round? Beginning to look empty. Your glasses, I mean." It was Heather.

"Damn, you scared the hell out of me," Alasdair said. "Yeah, bring another." He turned back to his conversation. "Fontana, call Smitty and get him down here so we can talk about what he found out this morning. He did go over and check out Thad's office, didn't he?"

"Yeah, sure. I'll call him."

"While Smitty is on his way," Alasdair said to Walther, "I have thought about what you have said and you may be right. Maybe I should leave Thad to you and Fontana. Doesn't seem quite right though. Makes me no better than the ass hole who hired a bunch of Latinos to kill me. Ain't much of a man won't do his own dirty work. I'll wait until we talk to Smitty to make a final decision."

"I make my living doing other men's dirty work," Walther said. "There is no shortage of work, but I only take four or five jobs a year. Pick and choose, I do. Your situation is different from most of my clients. You have not attacked anyone, someone has attacked you and you are only retaliating. Thad is only a link in the chain, the third

link, actually. We took care of the fourth link today and you participated. The third link we sever in the morning. I will make a plan.
The final link is yours. Me and Fontana will help, but his ass is
yours."

"Your drinks, gentlemen. You want some snacks, some chips or
something? No, I guess not. Thanks."

"Sit down, Smitty, and tell us what you found out, or what you
saw."

"Hey, lady, over here," Smitty called. "A glass of your very ordinary red wine, please." He turned back to Alasdair. "It is your normal
office building, concrete and glass with a little marble in the lobby to
give it some class. No security. Big chunk of granite in the middle of
the lobby with a list of people in the building. Four elevators, two on
each side. Only two offices on the eleventh floor. A travel agency has
one side and Thad has the other. Reliable Services, Inc. is what's on
the door. Big heavy wood door, no glass anywhere on this side. Camera above the door gets you when you step off the elevator. You'll
never get in unless they know you or you have an appointment."

"What time did you go?"

"I got there at 6:30. The building was open. Your man showed up
at seven. They got no inside parking so he came to the front door in a
big Lincoln Town Car. Tall skinny guy, lots of white hair, and two
bodyguards. Looks like he gets there every morning at seven. Guy
showed up with his newspaper about two minutes to seven. He gave
him the paper and one of the bodyguards gave him a tener. Old ratty
looking lady with a white carnation for him. She got a tener from the
same bodyguard. Cost him twenty bucks to get in the building."

"Any other people around? What about other tenants?"

Walther leaned forward, intent, his expression tense. "They are his
watchers. Did you see them before the car arrived? No. I didn't think
so. Where did they go afterwards? No, I didn't think so. In my country we have watchers for everything. We even have watchers for the
watchers. They signaled him. The newspaper, the way it was folded,

the hand that held it. The flower, the way it was presented, whether or not it was placed in his buttonhole or just handed to him. You were reported. Unless words were spoken to the guards you were given a pass: insignificant person passing by. I know the setup. I must plan and I will tonight."

"Hey, look. Here come the women," Alasdair said. "OK, business is over."

❧   ❧   ❧

September 1, 1970, 10:00 p.m. GMT–5, The Wayward Wind Inn

Walther pressed his back against the wall of the shower stall, enjoying the prickles of the hot shower beating on his shoulders and chest. His plan was complete. The tide of warmth and peace flowed over him much as the shower water. Without knowing what he was looking for, Smitty had discovered exactly the information Walther needed for his plan. The watchers. Watch the watchers. Many times that had worked for him in Africa and Europe. Walther smiled. He felt peaceful. Walther liked that feeling.

"Maddie, I must go speak with Mr. Alasdair. Go with me and keep that woman in another room while we talk. I am old fashioned. I like my discussions to be private."

"You mean, you are not interested in having women at your meetings, especially that woman. I'll take her away while you lay out your plan to Alasdair. It will be a good plan, as are all your plans. I love you, Walther. I want you to finish this work and us to leave forever, go somewhere far away."

"We will, my love. Far away. Mr. Alasdair promised me anywhere we want to go, as long as it is what you want to do. If you do not want to go with me, he will not let me take you. I want you to know that. You have the option of not going away with me."

"I will go anywhere with you, Walther. Plan on it. We will go see Alasdair now, OK?"

Walther explained the details of his plan to Alasdair. He needed one more day to make sure everything would work and that Fontana understood his role. Alasdair agreed. Early on Thursday morning Walther would meet Thad Rosamiro for one final time.

🍁   🍁   🍁

September 3, 1970, 6:00 a.m. GMT–5, City Café, Camden N.J.

Walther munched on a chocolate-covered donut and sipped the strong tea he had made himself with the hot water and tea bag furnished, reluctantly, by the staff of the City Café. Although almost a block away from the office building, the huge window next to the booth gave Walther an unobstructed view of the front of the Reliable Building, home of Reliable Insurance, Inc., Reliable Scavenger, Inc., Reliable Trucking Company, and a myriad of others. From the information given by Smitty about his visit to the building yesterday, Walther knew the old woman, poorly dressed and in need of a bath, would pass the café on her way to deliver her message and a white carnation. He planned to meet her before she crossed Main Street to the Reliable Building.

While he could not see Fontana, he knew him to be about the same distance away from the building, further up Main Street. Fontana intended to meet the newspaper man if he came the way they expected. If he came from a different direction it did not matter with Walther's plan. Alasdair wanted to be sure the poor old bag lady was not injured. Walther remembered the meeting last evening, and smiled while thinking of the concern Alasdair expressed for what he termed 'innocent persons'. Dealing with Thad's group left little room for 'innocent persons'.

Alasdair had agreed to the new plan without enthusiasm only because it reminded him of how he and his New Orleans associates evaded people following them. The Continental Bank in New Orleans was the key in much the same way that the Reliable Building would be here. The Reliable Building spanned the block between Main Street and 37th Street, with a secondary entrance fronting on 37th Street. Although the stock brokerage firm occupying most of the first floor did not open until 9:00 a.m., the doors on 37th opened at 6:00 a.m., as did the Main Street entrance.

Walther explained to Alasdair and Fontana how the morning would go, what they needed to do, and when. Walther needed to know where the carnation lady and the newspaperman waited each morning for Thad to arrive. When the pair began to move out, that would indicate the imminent arrival of Thad and his two guards. When Thad arrived, Walther and Fontana would be in the building at the elevators near the huge block of granite bearing the Directory of Occupants. The Main Street entrance lobby housed the directory and the elevators to the tower. A wide hall led from that lobby to the lobby for the stock brokerage company and the 37th Street entrance. The hall was lined on either side with fake trees and shrubs in large containers. Several trees were twenty or more feet tall in containers covered with what appeared to be Spanish moss overflowing onto the floor. At the 37th Street entrance, there was a passenger drop-off and pick-up lane with a ten-minute waiting area for automobiles. The rented Lincoln Town Car would be there waiting for them.

Once they located the two watchers, Fontana and Walther would enter the building a few minutes before Thad arrived. The watchers could report, if they chose, that two men had entered the building a few minutes earlier, one a businessman of some sort and the other a maintenance person from Jason Office Equipment Company.

A sudden commotion at the entrance of the café captured Walther's attention. The cause of the disturbance was an old woman, shabbily dressed, carrying a handful of white carnations wrapped in green florist's tissue paper. It soon became evident he was in some way involved in the argument going on between the old woman and the cashier-waitress.

"Is my breakfast ready and why is that repairman sitting in my booth? Don't he know who I am?"

"I doubt he does, madam, and for that matter I don't know who you are either?"

"Well, by God, you better know who I am. I eat here every morning at 6:30 and that is my table. Always is my table. Who the hell are you anyway, ducks? I never saw you here before. Where the hell is Gretta? She'll get that bastard out of my booth. Hey where is my breakfast, you painted puss? I don't have time to screw around with you bunch of fuck-ups. Get that cooking hand out here. Roscoe, the black bastard from Atlanta. He knows who I am and knows I gotta have my food at 6:30."

"Madam, I do not know who you think you are but that gentleman was here before you and wanted that booth, and as far as I…"

"Never mind, miss," Walther interrupted. "I am leaving. I have no desire to occupy a seat that this wretch has been near. She can have the booth with my blessings. If she continues to bother you, I will be glad to pitch her out the door on her ancient and ample ass."

"No, sir, you do not have to leave…"

Roscoe the cook rushed in from the kitchen. "What is going on? Mandy is you showing your ass again? Just because you know some gangster, why do you think you is such hot shit. Look at the customers. They all ready to leave. Just get back to the booth and shut up. Your food be there in one minute. I'm sorry, sir. Hell he gone. It's OK, folks, everything is OK. Relax, please. I just trying to make a living here and sometimes Mandy ain't all that nice. Don't mean nothing by it; just can't help being an old bat. Now relax and I send you some fresh coffee."

Outside the café, Walther leaned against the building and studied the street and adjacent buildings. He glanced at his watch and saw the time to be 6:40. A town full of late risers, Walther thought, as he looked for any signs of automobiles or people. The few people in the restaurant were, seemingly, the only people in the area. He wondered about Fontana. He must be nearby, probably in the car park toward the end of the block. He switched the toolbox he was carrying to his left hand and crossed the street diagonally toward the office building. A yellow cab raced by. Some people were beginning to move.

Walther thought about the woman and decided he really detested her. He found her fat, ugly, profane, and, most likely, dirty. None of these traits appealed to Walther's sensitive nature. He wished the waitress, hostess or whatever, had allowed him to throw the old bat out of the restaurant. There was no reason for her to exist in the beautiful and serene world Walther saw. Unfortunately, there was no time for him to make a plan for her.

Inside the building, Walther punched the up button and the elevator nearest the entrance opened almost immediately. He stepped into the empty elevator and placed the toolbox against the edge of the door, holding it open. He removed the Jason Office Machine Equipment Company jacket, folded it neatly, and placed it on the floor near the back of the elevator. His shirt, clean and neatly pressed, with black letters on the back, indicated the wearer was an employee of the Otis Elevator Company. After opening the toolbox, he placed an out-of-order sign on the cigarette ash stand between the elevators, and began removing the plate covering the buttons for the different floors.

At 6:55 Walther saw the obnoxious old woman leaving the City Café and slowly crossing the street on her way to meet Thad. At the same time Fontana, wearing his new black suit, white shirt, and black tie, came through the 37th Street entrance. When he arrived at Walther's elevator, a black Lincoln Town Car pulled up to the Main Street entrance.

"Like we suspected," Fontana said, "the newspaper guy was in the car park watching 37th Street. I left when he did so he should be at the front about now."

"Come over closer, Fontana," Walther said, and handed him a 9mm English-made machine pistol with noise suppresser and fifteen-round clip in place. Walther removed his own weapon from the box and held it beside his leg. He continued working with the control panel while Fontana peered into the elevator as though he was asking about the nature of the problem

Outside, the watchers were giving their reports. "No sign of anyone near the 37th entrance, nor in the parking area," the newspaperman said.

"One repairman of some sort went in a few minutes ago. Other than him you are the first arrival on this side," reported the female watcher. She and the newspaperman accepted their money from Lou.

The Lincoln Town Car moved into the empty street and headed toward the car park. Thad walked to the door beside the second bodyguard and, when the door opened automatically, he started into the lobby one step ahead of the bodyguard. Lou rushed to catch up. When they were barely inside the lobby and before the automatic doors closed, Walther and Fontana fired a third of a clip into each of the three men bunched together at the doors. The only sounds from the Panther machine pistols were low thumps and the clank of gun actions slamming machine-like back and forth. The bullets, worked on earlier by Walther, ripped into the men but did not exit. Instead they spread open and splintered, ripping vital organs. The shots hammered all three men to the floor. They writhed and twitched for half a minute before all movement ceased.

The newspaperman spun on his toes and was halfway across the street while the carnation bag lady stood frozen. She screamed. Walther disliked screaming and he disliked the carnation lady. He stepped across Thad's body, shoved a new clip into the pistol, and shot the woman twice in the face. He felt better immediately. Outside, all was quiet except for the fleeing newspaperman. Walther returned to the elevator and shoved the toolbox to the rear of it. He shucked off the Otis Elevator shirt and threw it into the elevator. Leaning inside the door, he punched the button for the top floor and walked toward the stock brokerage office wearing a white shirt and tie. Close examination would have revealed sweat splotches on the shirt and around the collar. It was hot wearing two shirts and a jacket.

At the first of the artificial trees, Walther and Fontana lifted the Spanish moss and dropped the Panthers into the containers. After carefully replacing the moss, they walked outside where a black Lincoln Town Car picked them up and drove quickly away. Alasdair drove them to Teterboro Airport. Smitty met them, and after the three men departed, drove the car to the rental office where he had rented it the night before. When his cab brought him back to the terminal, everyone walked together to the plane and were airborne in fifteen minutes.

Three days later, in a follow-up story, the newspaper reported the death of Thad Rosamiro to be a mob hit resulting from internal differences. Younger men wanted Rosamiro to retire but he insisted on retaining his power and position. Obviously his obstinacy did not sit well with the younger element. The police, the newspaper reported, had, through interviews with the few witnesses who saw bits and pieces of the event, developed a theory of what had happened. The black Lincoln automobile dropped Rosamiro and the bodyguards off at the Main Street entrance to the Reliable Building as usual. It then circled the block and was observed parking at the 37th Street entrance. It waited until a man dressed in a black suit and tie, and another man, believed to have been a fake repairman, exited the building. They entered the black Lincoln and drove away.

The police detained Jocko Spallino, Rosamiro's driver. Despite repeated protestations of innocence, Spallino remained in police custody. He had, he said, driven to the Lincoln dealer in Trenton for routine maintenance. While the dealer backed up his story, Spallino had not arrived at the dealer's garage until 10:30, some three and a half hours after the carnage in Camden. Further complications in the Spallino matter were persistent rumors that Rosamiro's successor would be Spallino's cousin, Vince del Maestro.

❧   ❧   ❧

September 3, 1970, 12:30 p.m. GMT-6, Regas Restaurant, Knoxville, Tenn.

Cheshire Brown leaned back in the corner booth and stretched his legs beneath the large round table. He sipped Kentucky bourbon while scowling at Charlie Cook, seated across the table. Brown was a big man, maybe six feet four, two hundred forty or fifty pounds, mid fifties, wearing a western-cut shirt with an orange UT on the left side pocket, blue jeans with a permanent crease, and cowboy boots. His face was tan, weathered by the sun, and smoothly shaven. The auburn hair, receding slightly, was pushed forward in a futile attempt to disguise the beginning of baldness.

Normally an ill-tempered man, today he was an enraged and frustrated man. Nothing was going right today, nor the last three days. Now, with the University of Tennessee football team's opening game only a week away, he would miss his first game since returning from Europe after World War II because of a government shutdown of his mattress manufacturing facility in Monterey, Mexico. The huge facility assembled more than fifty percent of the store and private label mattress coils and frames sold in the United States. A shut down of two weeks would cost Brown's company hundreds of thousands of dollars. The Mexico shutdown was only one of his problems. Construction of the president's palace addition in Panama lagged two months behind schedule, the large office building for the bank in Pittsburgh was on hold because of high interest rates, and he had been told only yesterday that the airport renovation in Panama would be awarded to Empire Contractors.

Empire Industries and its subsidiaries had for the past four years stabbed and re-stabbed Brown's back. First in Kenya, then Kentucky, Jamaica, England, Belize, and now Panama. Why did the bank need to borrow money to build an office building for itself in Pittsburgh? Brown did not understand. In his mind he knew the man at Empire Industries had a hand in that somewhere.

Brown, a product of the coal mines and steel mills of Pennsylvania, managed to acquire a good education by earning a football scholarship from the University of Tennessee. The war more or less wreaked havoc with his football career by giving him a four-year break between his sophomore and junior years. The university treated him and all other veterans fairly and earned his enduring appreciation. He occupied the bench for most of his junior and senior years, not because he was a poor player but because there were better players on the team. He enthusiastically participated in university life, and after graduation, returned to Pennsylvania, but neither to the steel mills nor the coal mines. He turned to banking. His career flourished, giving him opportunities to invest in businesses doing business with the bank. First was the mattress company in Philadelphia. They needed money and he made them a loan, provided he was allowed to buy an interest in the business for a token amount. Later he bought it all with a loan from the bank. With the profits from the mattress company he purchased stock in the bank. Now he controlled the bank and the mattress company, which he had moved to Mexico, enjoying the fruits of cheap labor. Sometimes he wondered if the shipping costs were eating up the labor savings.

With the U.S. pouring money into Europe and Africa for construction and reconstruction, Brown partnered with an old classmate in a construction business. Their aim was to do as much of the construction work as possible. Success bred success, their money multiplied, and all the businesses grew. But suddenly Brown began to lose business. Other companies came on the scene, paying bigger bribes and taking the work. The worst of the lot was Empire Industries, run, by N. J. Alasdair. In a period of six months, Alasdair beat him out on construction work totaling one hundred million U.S. dollars, wrecked his control of most of the banking in the Caribbean, and had designs on his mattress company in Mexico. He was without a doubt, in Brown's mind, the cause of his problems with the government in Monterey.

When he struck a deal with the greedy banker, Devoe, it all seemed so simple. One gigantic sweep of Alasdair and his associates would end him for all time. Devoe assured him that the people he knew would handle everything with ease and expedience. Now all was a shamble. Alasdair was alive, his wife was alive, the man in London, Keaton, who Brown wanted to hire to run his construction operations, was dead. Brown had no doubt he could have hired Keaton after Alasdair's death, but now Alasdair was alive and Keaton dead. The bloodthirsty bomber set off the bomb when he saw Keaton and Dobbins pause to look at the car. Another of the many mistakes of the week was using the IRA. Over one hundred thousand dollars spent, and only a few useless bodies to show for it. He rubbed his eyes with his knuckles. His head began to hurt.

As his wealth increased, the weather in Philadelphia seemed to worsen each year. Moving to Knoxville to be near Big Orange football seemed a better idea. The mattress company was in Mexico, the construction company could be anywhere, with most of its work in Africa, Mexico, and Central America. That left only the bank in Pennsylvania. He was not involved in the day-to-day operation of the bank. Sales offices for the mattress company really did all the work and only needed a central accounting center. Knoxville would do fine for that.

From the eighth floor of the Bank of Knoxville building, he could look out the windows to the Tennessee River and Neyland Stadium, home of the University of Tennessee Volunteers. Brown bought a large house with a boat dock, on the Alcoa Highway southeast of Knoxville and across the river. The river became his road to the Vol's football games. He acquired a private slip for his boat only a few yards from the stadium. His pre-game parties became the talk of a certain section of Knoxville society, although the Kingston Pike and Cherokee Hills society people shunned him as they would a communicable disease.

"Tell me, Cook, what is the problem in Mexico?" Brown said.

"I have spoken with Mabe several times and always it is the same story," Cook replied. "The general thinks we should hire more men. We are not using all the unemployed people near the plant."

"They are stumbling all over themselves now. What does Mabe suggest?"

"More bribes. A ten percent raise to all the government bastards and the problem will go away. For fifteen percent we can probably let a bunch go."

"Dammit, Cook, why has this come up? It's that damn Alasdair, isn't it? The son of a bitch isn't satisfied with what he did to me in the islands and Belize, he wants to screw up Panama and Mexico. I hate the arrogant bastard and his fucking Vanderbilt friends."

"Mr. Brown, you are paranoid on the subject of Alasdair. He is not doing anything to us in Mexico or Panama. What he did in the Caribbean, I do not know. That was an accident, I think."

"Well you think wrong. He is paying off that General Noriega in Panama to cause me problems. Noriega is taking more and more power and running Torrijos like a puppet. I don't like that pockmarked Noriega and he knows it. Torrijos can't control him and a few bucks from Alasdair is all he needs to run me out of Panama. I won't have it! I won't!"

"Mr. Brown, my investigations show Alasdair has never been to Panama. Carlotta has only been twice. They are not the problem. We are two months behind on the president's house. That is the problem. That so-called engineer you got in charge of Panama projects is the problem. He couldn't build a dog house for that damn mutt, Smokey, the Vols' mascot."

"Don't talk about Helton. He played football at UT with me, made the block that sprung me for the Alabama touchdown. Damn good man."

"Possibly, but a piss-poor engineer. Too bad he didn't take wood-working or sheet metal or something we can use."

"Shut up about him. We gonna eat anything? It's nearly 2:30. Order us something while I try Devoe on the pay phone. I told the office to call here if he called."

On the way to the pay phone near the entrance, Brown saw Berry, the office manager, rush through the door. The mousy little 'yes man', sweating and ruffled, saw Brown and rushed to him, breathless, with consternation showing on his rodent-like face.

"Mr. Brown, I must talk with you. Where is your table? Same as always, I assume."

"Yes, Berry, calm down and go over to the table with Cook. I'm just on my way to call Devoe. I'll be there in a minute."

"No, no, that's what I came to tell you. There's been an accident, Mr. Devoe…"

"Wait, come on over to the table. Get him a drink out of my bottle, Cook. He's in a lather. Now what is it?"

"Its Mr. Devoe. He's in the hospital. He may die. The bank manager called for you and I ended up with the call because he insisted on talking to somebody. A highway maintenance worker found Mr. Devoe just before noon today in a dry creek bed fifty feet below the road."

"What do you mean found him in a dry creek?"

"That's what I mean. Somebody threw him off the bridge or something and he rolled down the rip-rap to the creek bed, all cut up and bleeding everywhere."

"How the hell? Why do you think somebody threw him off a bridge?"

Berry extended a trembling hand holding an empty glass in the direction of the waiter standing near the table listening. Not getting his attention quickly enough, Berry shook the ice noisily.

"Get him another drink, Billy, then get your ass back to the kitchen."

The pacified Berry continued. "They said his hands were taped together with duck tape and so were his feet. His mouth was hanging open cause his jaws were broken and his hands are a mess. Rolling down the rip-rap really worked on him. Cut him all over. The manager said the fall did not break his jaws. He thinks a hammer did that. His fingers same way. Each finger broken at least twice and most are crushed. Probably never use them again."

"Damn, who would have done that, Mr. Brown?" Cook asked.

Brown was not listening. Neither Cook nor Berry knew about Devoe and his involvement with St. Croix, Belize, and London. He offered no answer, but he knew. Alasdair! Somehow Alasdair found Devoe and now he knew about him. Brown understood that the kind of questioning used by Alasdair would get truthful answers. Devoe knew everything, and now Alasdair knew as well.

"Did the manager tell you anything more?"

"Oh, yes, he did. The doctors say someone stuck an iron rod part way up his ass, maybe a piece of square iron. It's horrible, just horrible."

"Damn sure is."

Back at his office, a stunned and shaken Cheshire Brown sat at his desk staring out the window at his beloved Neyland Stadium. Moving to Knoxville was a way of reliving his college football days, the happiest time of his life. Each passing year increased the glory days of his UT football experience. Though his football career consisted mostly of sitting on the bench, there was the one dash from the ten-yard line for a touchdown against the Crimson Tide of Alabama. Through the ensuing years quite a large number of players scored touchdowns against mighty Alabama. Still, his touchdown was enough for memories and without a wife and family, it was the best he had. During the years he came to think of UT as his family and the past year had made the last payment on his pledge of one million dollars to the University of Tennessee, becoming, in his mind, the first player to make such a contribution. First or not, it qualified him to stand on the fifty-yard line at half time of the home coming game and have his picture made with the president of the university and the football coach. An almost life-sized enlargement of the picture hung on the wall behind his desk. From time to time he considered moving it to the wall in front of him. Brown enjoyed looking at the picture.

Today he began to regret his attack on Alasdair, but only because the people Devoe recruited botched the incident in St. Croix. Now he faced the possibility of a counterattack by Alasdair. From the outline of Devoe's condition given him by Berry, there seemed to be no doubt it was Alasdair's work, nor did Brown harbor any doubt about Alasdair's intentions. "Well, the die is cast," he thought. "What will be will be. Now I've got to get to Mexico."

Brown punched the intercom button and barked into his telephone to the secretary out front, "Get Helton for me." He banged the telephone onto its hook and pressed his knuckles hard against his teeth.

🍁   🍁   🍁

September 3, 1970, 12:38 p.m. GMT–4, Police Station, St. Croix

Chief Halfpenny sorted through the stuffed drawers of the huge wooden desk in his office, trying to decide what to keep and what to throw away. Most of what he found he had not seen in years. Drawers in desks tend to fill with items important on a particular day and never again. He studied a 1967 appointment book, still wrapped in cellophane. He had not needed it in 1967 but had thought it too nice for the trash bin. Now, three years later, he wondered if he should keep it. The buzz of the intercom on his desk postponed the decision.

"Yes?"

"That FBI agent is on the phone for you."

"Which one?"

"I'll ask."

"You do that, Officer Wamble." During the ensuing wait, Halfpenny tossed the appointment book into the trashcan with other remnants of his past nine years as chief.

"It is Agent Edward Edwards."

"Thank you, Officer Wamble."

"Good morning, Agent Edwards. How may I assist you?"

"Just a few questions, Chief. Have you spoken to Alasdair since our meeting last Saturday?"

"No."

"Have you sent him the report I left with you?"

"No."

"Umm, uh, where is he?"

"I do not know. He left here going to Nashville to check on his wife. If everything is found to be satisfactory there, she wanted to go to Atlanta for the weekend. He planned a visit with the families of his employees who were killed in London. One lived in Oklahoma, I believe, and the other in California somewhere. I would think you might find him at one or the other of those places. The office in Nashville is closed until the shooting and bombing ceases. May I assist you?"

"I don't know, Chief. I am just gonna pass on to you what my office told me a few minutes ago. There is in Camden, New Jersey, one Thad Rosamiro, a businessman in the trash and junk business, insurance, and who knows what else. Thad is reputed, rumored, no evidence, to run an international murder-for-hire business. None of our investigations ever turned up anything other than a coincidence or two. In any event, he had an unexpected meeting at his office this morning. When he went into his office building at 7:00 a.m. two men were waiting for him and blew his ass away, along with two bodyguards and an old bag lady. Hit him up at a bad time, the bag lady I mean. Just my natural curiosity made me wonder where Alasdair is."

"Agent Edwards, surely you don't see any connection with Alasdair. Why would you think…Because of this man's reputation as a—Oh, I see. You think he might be the one back of all this. Why?"

"Well, Chief, sit your big ass down and I will tell you. You can't take this standing up. It seems Thad always traveled light, no ID, no wallet, no money. Only thing in his pockets was a crumpled note from his secretary. It said a Mr. Devoe from the bank called about setting up a meeting to discuss the Scavenger account."

"Holy shit."

"Exactly what I said. If Alasdair knew of that connection he would be in Camden this very moment."

Halfpenny thought it best not to mention that Alasdair did know about Devoe, that he planned to speak with Devoe. He decided to let the matter rest but needed the answer to one more question. "Have the police interviewed Devoe?"

"They went by but he had not come in when they were there. Going back this afternoon. Curious about that note, eh?"

"I don't know, Edwards. Bankers have lots of customers."

"Bullshit, Chief. It's the circle and you know it; Brown to Devoe to Rosamiro to Alasdair and back to Brown. Please hold that report until I can do a little more checking. Meanwhile keep your mouth shut and I will do likewise."

"I have no one to talk to and neither do you, Edwards. Alasdair is not involved in the Rosamiro incident. That is not his style. He is busy with family and employees' families. In the unlikely event he learned of Rosamiro's existence he has had no time to give it any consideration, let alone plan an assassination. It is ridiculous."

"The colonel has had time."

"There is no colonel."

Agent Edwards did not think Halfpenny was certain. Halfpenny himself did not think he sounded sure.

❦   ❦   ❦

September 3, 1970, 4:30 p.m. GMT–4, Police Station, St. Croix

Both physically and mentally tired, Halfpenny looked at the clock on the booking room wall. He was there in search of some brawn to move the trash from his office and load the boxes into his van. His office would then be clean, his last day as chief complete. Where, he wondered, was he going and how long would it last? It was there that Officer Wamble located him with a message from Agent Edwards. "Edwards," she said, "is waiting for you in the bar at the Caravelle Hotel. He said it is important and for you to come ASAP."

"ASAP my ass. I don't jump every time the FBI calls."

"I'm sure that's true, Chief, but I've got your car out front waiting."

"Thank you, Officer Wamble."

"We all gonna miss you, you know that? We sort of fond of you. My husband says whoever takes your place won't be half the man you are. I told him there ain't no man that's half the man you are, not even a third the man you are. Hee hee."

"I'll give you some advice, Officer Wamble, take a look at that butt of yours before old Stan Wamble takes a look at one of those normal-sized butts at Little Switzerland where he works."

Chief Halfpenny lowered himself gingerly into one of the captain's chairs across the table from Agent Edwards. The agent seemed eager to impart his message to Halfpenny, commencing the story before the Cruzan tea arrived.

"Not all the excitement is in St. Croix," Edwards said. "They are beginning to get some up in my area. I told you the Camden cops went to Philly to see Devoe and he hadn't come in. Well, the Philly cops called them about an hour ago. Devoe left the office about noon Tuesday and has not returned and will not for some time. A highway department maintenance guy doing a routine dry season check of interstate highway bridges found old Devoe..."

"Found Devoe, found Devoe? What do you mean, found Devoe?"

That is what I mean, Chief. He found Devoe. The police think somebody threw his ass off a bridge or at least rolled him down a fifty-foot rip-rap embankment into a dry creek bed. He is not dead, but damn near."

"Holy shit! This is Thursday. They think he's been out there two days?"

"Yep. That's what they think. Like I said, he is damn near dead."

"Son of a bitch. Why are you smiling like that? What is going on? You don't think—You do think, don't you?"

"I don't think anything, Chief, but let me explain. The cops think Devoe landed in the creek bed shortly before noon, or maybe shortly after noon, Tuesday. If the highway people didn't look at bridges during the dry season he would still be there. Let me tell you, the SOB was bound hand and foot with duct tape. Amazing stuff that duct tape. Both his jaws were broken, his hands beaten to a pulp, a real mess he is. May not live. Once they got him in the hospital the police searched the area thoroughly and found a three-pound hammer and a spike. The doctors believe his jaws were broken with the hammer and his hands beaten with it. Now get this, a metal object of some kind was shoved up his ass and the odds-on favorite is the spike. The man was asked a few questions and I am thinking he answered them all. Your man Alasdair don't waste time. I don't know how he found Devoe, but I can hear the questions: 'Who did this to me?' Pause, tap the spike with the hammer. 'OK, who paid him?' Pause, tap the spike with the hammer. 'OK. Throw his ass off the bridge.'"

"Edwards, an interesting theory, but only a theory. The man is in Nashville with his wife, or they are visiting his employees' families. It appears strange to you and me, but that is just a result of what we know. All of this is totally unrelated."

"Bullshit. I am now officially on vacation and this is not a federal case and I am not involved and I do not plan to share my theories with anyone. If I had proof I would have to come forward, but everyone can have a private theory, even an FBI agent. Just find Alasdair and urge him to stay away from Knoxville and Brown. Go to Mexico, anywhere, but not in the U.S. I'll order you some fresh tea. You have let the ice melt."

CHAPTER 9

September 3, 1970, 12:13 p.m. GMT–6, Cornelia Fort Airport, Nashville

Less than five minutes after the blue Aero Commander belonging to Mullican Construction Company braked to a stop in front of the small Cornelia Fort terminal, its six passengers piled into a big Buick station wagon and roared through the main gate. Although in a hurry, Alasdair decided to avoid the ferry across Stones River in favor of the less obvious long way to Donelson, near the municipal airport. From downtown Nashville, where Shelby Street crossed the river, he followed Lebanon Road through Donelson, turning onto Donelson Pike to the private terminal at Nashville's Berry Field. He drove through the gate and out onto the apron as the Sabreliner taxied to a stop, its body between the terminal and the passenger exit from the plane. Alasdair pulled the Buick to a stop near the plane's door and the passengers in the plane exchanged places with the occupants of the Buick. Wallace Locke explained to airport personnel they needed no assistance and were just letting off a passenger.

Mrs. Alasdair noticed a few minutes later, as she turned the wagon back onto Donelson Pike, that the Sabreliner already was streaking down the runway. At the Airport Hilton she transferred the Buick to Sue, retrieved her Mercedes, and drove to her home in West Nashville. Sue turned the Buick over to Jean and the number crunchers, and drove her Mustang to the long-term parking lot near the main terminal. At the Eastern Airlines counter she fished her passport and her American Express card from her voluminous shoulder bag and purchased a ticket to Belize. "Alasdair will be upset," she said to herself while waiting for the ticket, "but I don't care. I am tired of being left behind. He will get over it when he sees me."

Her flight would leave Atlanta at 1:30 p.m. tomorrow. She checked the first available flight to Atlanta and found one leaving in twenty minutes if she would like to take it, or another at 8:25 a.m. the next day. Quickly she decided. It was no problem. Mrs. Alasdair is not the only person who likes the Ritz Carlton in Buckhead. Tonight I will live like that bitch and eat in the dining room of the Ritz Carlton.

Rusty Lawrence leveled off the Sabreliner, having reached altitude, and pointed it due south as Wallace Locke switched off the 'No Smoking' and 'Fasten Seat Belt' signs. Locke realized Alasdair probably already was tearing at the cellophane wrapper on a huge Macanudo cigar. Lawrence, a confirmed coffeeholic, almost punched the stewardess button to call Reggie for a cup when he thought better. He knew Reggie was breaking out the Scotch for Alasdair and lighting his cigar, if she was quick enough. Reggie made no excuses for her blatant pursuit of Alasdair. Usually he ignored her as he would an extra piece of furniture. She was not deterred. Only when Jean and Sue, either or both, were on the plane did she show signs of concern. Both were at least her equal in looks and charm, and both had greater access to Alasdair. More than once when both women were on board, Lawrence had seen Reggie pull up her uniform skirt and roll the waistband under to keep the skirt higher and expose more of her legs. Why she and the other two thought Alasdair would dump his wife and take on one of those schemers, was a mystery to Lawrence.

"Hey, Wally, do you think that bitch Reggie will take a break from fawning over the boss and get us some coffee?"

"I doubt it. She is in a funk over spending three days with Sue and Jean. It was either them or the CPAs. Boy, a couple of embalmers. They fit right in at the funeral homes. Before it was over they were saying goodbye to people leaving and opening the door for people arriving."

"Here's your coffee, Rusty," Reggie said before slamming the cockpit door closed. "I know you are bitching about having to wait ten seconds. Did you see that blonde bitch back there? Looks at me like I am trying to get that red-headed freak away from her. God, what a bitch! You notice her hair? Dull, it's really dull, no shine at all. Gad."

"Reggie, get off it. There is nothing wrong with that woman, no flaw, none. She is perfect and you need to get used to it. Dull hair? Shit."

"Reggie, go back there and look after Smitty. He doesn't fit in with that crowd. He needs a little attention."

"Forget it, Wally. That Fontana character looks at me like I am his next meal. Is he a crazy man or something? Where the hell did he come from? What is with Jim, hauling around a flock of loony birds? I swear he and Smitty are the only ones back there not certifiable."

"Jim is it now? I'd be careful with that word were I you."

"Stuff it, Rusty. What's going on back there? Every time I get near them conversation stops, and as soon as I leave they are back whispering to each other. Strange. I don't blab everything I know."

"There goes your buzzer, Reggie. 'Jim' wants another Scotch."

"Bastard."

"Hee hee."

Alasdair, seated on the leather-covered sofa, leaned forward to speak directly to Walther and Maddie. Smitty and Fontana feigned inattention while missing nothing. Shaking the ice in his empty glass, Alasdair looked at Smitty, who immediately pressed the buzzer to summon Reggie. Again conversation ceased until the glass was refilled. Fontana squinted, then stared at Reggie, causing Smitty to nudge him rather vigorously with an elbow. It was Maddie who broke the silence.

"May I please have a spritzer, Reggie?"

"And me, Regg" It was Smitty with an unusual request. "No, no, not a spritzer. How about a glass of that Dewars the boss likes so well? It's a long ride to Belize City." Reggie gave him a look of disgust really meant for Maddie and stomped into the galley.

"Walther, when we get to Belize, you and Maddie are free to go where ever you wish. I doubt that jerk in New Jersey sent you your money, so I will pay you what he owes you and give you enough to last you and Maddie a couple of years. By then you will have worked out your future. Satisfactory?"

"What do you plan to do about the other man, the one in Knox-ville?"

"I'll take care of him. No need for you to worry about him."

"I have not yet made a plan for the future. I have quite a lot of money saved over the years from my business and do not have to worry about that," Walther said. "I do feel a strong obligation to you for what you have done for Maddie. Perhaps I need to stay with you for a few months, until all your loose ends are cleared up. Maddie and I are not only willing but anxious to assist you in tying up your loose ends."

Reggie arrived with Scotch for Smitty and shoved a spritzer at Maddie who responded to her insolence by flashing one of her big beautiful smiles. Reggie spun on her toes and stomped toward the cabin without a word to anyone.

"I can't take you back to the States, neither you nor Maddie. And both of you need to stay away from the islands. You have repaid all my favors and owe me nothing. I owe you and Fontana a debt I can-not pay with money. Go back to Botswana and make a new life. I have a friend in Tanzania who will eventually show up and help me and Fontana with Brown."

"Perhaps we should discuss this later, Mr. Alasdair. Let me think about what we want to do. I will discuss it with Maddie. I will make a plan."

❧   ❧   ❧

September 3, 1970, 7:30 p.m. GMT–5, Knoxville

The rain had stopped earlier in the evening, but the humidity was heavy in the air. Cheshire Brown, oblivious to both heat and humidity, nursing straight bourbon, sat on the deck overlooking the river, watching the fog move in like a silver-gray wall, obliterating the view of everything in its path. His thoughts rumbled through his muddled mind, jumping from worry to anger, then to stupid people, and finally settling on the banker Devoe. The trust he had placed in Devoe stood as a monument to his own stupidity. "I know to get something done right you have to do it yourself," he thought, "I relied on Devoe and his connections, and now I've got botched jobs both in London and the islands. The Belize job, I handled that myself, and the Mexicans did everything they were hired to do plus getting themselves killed, leaving the authorities without a clue."

It was not the authorities who worried Brown. He suddenly realized that his clothes were soaked from humidity and fog and, worse, his glass was empty. Those worries and worries about the authorities were dwarfed by the Alasdair worry. No authorities would be involved when Alasdair arrived in Knoxville, and his arrival was imminent. Brown knew Alasdair would not wait and probably was on his way now. But no matter, the Mexican workers' strike demanded his attention. Upon his return, he vowed, he would deal with Alasdair personally and straight away.

"That ass hole Alasdair is a mean, vicious, and evil man, a man with an unbridled arrogance, too egomaniacal to describe," Brown said to himself. "That man is arrogant enough to go into African countries almost simultaneously with the revolutions ridding them of the imperial colonialists, and call his companies Empire Industries, Empire Construction Co., Empire Consultants. The speed with which the African revolutionaries sold out their convictions disgusts me almost as much as the bribe-paying bastards who preyed on them with bags full of dollars. Those people are the scum of the business world. That Alasdair prick ruined me in Africa and the Caribbean, and is now moving on me in Panama. No decent man with scruples and ethics would stand for such treatment by scum. Neither will I. Once I rid the world of Alasdair, an international medal from the countries of the world would be appropriate."

. Inside the house he began to make plans for Mexico. However, he found it impossible to overcome the anger he felt toward Alasdair and his ilk. Bad plans were worse than no plans, so he enjoyed his anger and another glass of bourbon without including plans for dealing with Alasdair.

🍁   🍁   🍁

September 3, 1970, 8:30 p.m.GMT-6, Santa Rita Hotel, Belize City, Belize

"Walther, I believe we must stay with Alasdair until he gets rid of the Brown problem. I think Brown is a nasty man deserving of punishment. No one is better at punishing than you. You must stay and take care of Mr. Alasdair. I will help."

Walther moved his eyes from Maddie and they took in the entire room in a clockwise direction before returning to Maddie's lovely face. He felt himself blessed with this beautiful, loving woman. Why it had happened exceeded his depth of understanding. Walther never questioned a blessing. On the surface it appeared she had known him for years and had waited patiently for his return to rescue her from the sordid mess she had created. How long will it last? Will she suddenly revert to Maddie, the much put-upon banker? What to do?

Walther's mind spun wildly and without a plan. Walther needed a plan.

"Is that what you want to do, Maddie?"

"Yes, Walther, that is what I want to do. I hope you will do it for me."

"Very well, I will make a plan."

꙳   ꙳   ꙳

September 6, 1970, 8:30 a.m. GMT-6, Monterey, Mexico

"Mabe, listen to me. That plane we saw landing as we passed the airport was a Sabreliner and it belongs to that damn Alasdair. He is here to ruin me in Mexico. Don't give me any more of that bullshit about being paranoid. Alasdair is after me and you know it. His goal is to ruin me and I don't know why. I never did anything to him. He's just a mean bastard who, for some reason, hates me. Probably hates UT too."

"Mr. Brown, that man is no different from a dozen others doing business all over the world, just as you do. I have never heard of him in Mexico. Don't yell at me for saying it again, but you need to forget Alasdair and concentrate on your work. Neglect of the big boys here is causing our problem, not Alasdair."

"Neglect, hell. What have you been doing? You are supposed to take care those bastards. You are here all the time. If they have been neglected it is because you haven't been doing your job. Why don't you pass that junk heap ahead of us? He's been drag-assing for the last ten miles."

"I'll pass when there is a wide spot in the road. This is no interstate you know; just a semi-paved path. You know I have been doing my job. It's just that I'm looked at as your flunky and a flunky can't deal with generals and vice presidents. They want to see the big cheese, and that is you, not me"

"Self important little pricks. At home they'd be raking leaves in some apartment house parking lot. Ze GEN-e-ROWL-ee my ass. Pompous little grease ball. We haven't met another vehicle in thirty minutes. Pass this junker if you have to run him over. I am tired of his drag-assing around."

Mabe cursed under his breath as he down shifted the Toyota Land Cruiser and shoved the accelerator to the floor. Bouncing and clawing, the Land Cruiser negotiated the crumbling verge. "Dammit, here comes a truck." Banging into the decrepit junker, Mabe shoved it aside before sliding between it and the only other vehicle they had met in half an hour. The truck, loaded with crate upon crate of chickens, took the ditch on the left and the junker hit the ditch on the right. Only the Land Cruiser took the open road. In his mirror Mabe saw crates of chickens bouncing on the narrow strip of pavement, the verge and the ditch. One crate landed on the hood of the decrepit vehicle he had just passed.

"Good show, Mabe. Shoulda done that a long time ago," Brown said. "Might have been better if you had waited till the chickens passed. Now we can get on to Santa Rosa. Hey! What the hell you doing?"

"I'm stopping to help those people I ran off the road."

"You get your foot off the brake and get moving. We ain't stopping. I have important work to get done. It was their choice to run off the road. Let them handle their own problems, after all they caused them. Get going now! Damn it, Mabe, get this truck going. I told you we are not stopping."

Reluctantly Mabe continued toward the Madres beyond Santa Rosa. As he watched the mountains looming ahead he mumbled to himself, "The Generale is not the only self-important little prick in Mexico." To relieve some of his anger Mabe pushed the Land Cruiser to unsafe speed on the lonely so-called roadway. Conversation no longer existed between the two men. There was only an occasional snort from Brown until Santa Rosa, almost a ghost town, appeared on the dusty horizon.

"I dream about Alasdair. You know that, Mabe? In my dreams he is always sneaking about spying on me. Several times I have awakened with a clear impression of him being in my bedroom. I check the closet, the bath, even under the bed. I know he is there, somewhere. I will have to kill him to save my businesses. He's after me, Mabe, big time after me."

The lines in Mabe's forehead tightened and his eyebrows squeezed together and became one. Mabe did not look at Brown but clinched the wheel harder. "That is not something you should say, Mr. Brown. Someone might think you are serious."

"I am serious, Mabe, serious as a heart attack. He is trying to ruin my businesses and then ruin me personally. He is jealous of my football record at UT. He envies my business success. He is after me and I know it. That was his plane coming in when we left Monterey. Trying to overbid me on the gold concessions. Look out! Armadillo.

"You know, Mabe, sometimes the fog comes up the river by my house and hovers out there like a curtain. Yeah, like somebody just pulled a curtain all round me. In that fog, just at the edge where you must look closely, there is a boat. It is Alasdair. I can see him peering at me through night goggles, trying to see if I'm home. If I am, he shovels off to Panama or Africa or England, and dallies with my business. If he finds me gone, he rifles my office and house. Oh, he is a sneaky bastard."

Mabe rolled his eyes back and thought, "He's loosing it. Crazy as old St. Vitas." Not knowing what else to do he pushed the accelerator to the floor. It was a long, tedious climb up a steep trail to the gold mine near the top of an unnamed mountain. He hoped Brown would calm himself by looking at the view, or change the subject.

"You don't believe me, do you? Well, I know he is there or has been there. Smell the damn cigar smoke. I will kill the bastard if I catch him in my house or the mattress factory or snooping around the gold mines. He's here, you know, seen his plane landing."

. "We don't know it was his plane." Mabe said. "It was just a plane like his. Could be anybody from anywhere. Before we start up this mountain I want to be sure the two generators in the back are secure. I'll stop at the gate and signal we are on the way up so no one will be on the road coming down. Barely wide enough for one vehicle and I sure don't want to back down this mountain."

"It's his plane all right. He is after me, the sorry bastard. I can almost see him now, peeking out of some hole, behind some bush. I can feel him staring at me. I can feel it."

Mabe pushed his ample belly against the Land Cruiser and pulled with all his might to tighten the straps holding two generators and the two fifty-five gallon drums of diesel fuel in place. He faced a drive of twenty-five minutes creeping up the steep road. One miscalculation and it would be a long roll back to the bottom. He didn't look at Brown. Instead he stared for a long minute at the "worm" snaking in and out of the gaping mine adit near the top of the mountain.

He manhandled and finessed the overloaded Land Cruiser up the long, little-used road as it snaked around and up and down on the rugged climb of five thousand feet. Both men were silent until they passed the heap-leaching facility. "Damn, Mabe, how many acres you got scraped off down there?"

"Don't ask me questions about this stuff. I make springs for mattresses."

"It must be five or six acres. One acre is concrete. How the hell they get that concrete up here?"

"About a jillion trips in all the trucks they could beg or borrow," Mabe said. "That was to get the cement up here and the water. Had to haul it up, too. Plenty of crushed stone up here to use to mix with the cement."

"What is that on the ground? Looks like plastic."

"That's what it is. During the leaching process a lot of liquid comes out and is collected and filtered through carbon filters. Gold treated with cyanide sticks to the carbon and most of the other crap goes on through. That's' all I know, Mr. Brown."

"Well, you are right about the liquid, Mabe. That is what leaching is, getting the liquid out. Look at that creek, Mabe. The water is copper-colored. Why is that?"

"All the stuff that passes through the filters runs down the mountain and into the creek. Water, cyanide, copper. Anything drinks that water is dead. This place was mined from 1919 by the British and closed in the '30s or '40s, so that shit been running in that creek for ten, maybe twenty years before shut down. Now your operation is beginning to do the same thing."

"What is that block house over there? Looks like a bunker."

"I told you I make mattress springs. Should've brought Hector with you. He knows about this shit," Mabe said. "But I think it is a bunker. That's where they store cyanide, dynamite, fertilizer, and some TNT."

"That fucking Alasdair shows up here, I'll put his ass in there and blow him to hell and back."

"Mr. Brown, Alasdair is not coming here. He doesn't give a damn about mattress springs or gold mines. It is not his style. You gonna say something like that and the wrong person hears, and you in trouble. I know a—"

"Watch out, big chunk of road slid out on this side."

"I see it. Anyhow, the guy I know had a word battle with some neighbor and ended the conversation by saying 'I hope your dog dies.' Next morning the dog is dead. Bastard insists my buddy did in the dog and now they in court. Hell, the dog just died, maybe a heart attack. Still in court. Could happen to you. Don't keep saying you gonna kill Alasdair."

"I am going to kill the lousy bastard. He's fucked with my business for the last time."

Mabe mouthed an obscenity and rolled his eyes skyward.

❧   ❧   ❧

September 9, 1970, 10:00 p.m. GMT–6, Panama City, Panama

Moses King Helton read and re-read the telex as it clicked and clattered its way into his combination home and office. "What is Mabe talking about? The boss ain't crazy, a little strange but not crazy. So what if he's upset about Alasdair and wants me to come to Mexico. That don't mean he's loosing it. I'll take Gomez with me. He was some kind of a shrink before he became a drunk. Now he's a teetotaler and wants everybody to be like him. Boring bastard, but maybe he can talk to Cheshire if he really does have a problem. Depression, my guess."

Helton had met Brown his freshman year at UT and they became fast friends. The four years they shared during World War II brought them even closer, almost like brothers. Back at UT after the war to play football, not very well, they were back to where they had left off after Pearl Harbor. The lucky block Helton made to sprang Brown for a touchdown against Alabama was their crowning moment.

After graduation Brown went back to Pittsburgh and proceeded to make a fortune while Helton bounced from architecture to engineering, never quite making it to the big time. In desperation he called Brown after ten years of floundering, and admitted he wasn't making it as an architect or engineer. Brown bought him an engineering company and put him in business.

"If he has a problem mentally or physically, I will help him whatever way I can. He is a mean, greedy bastard but never to me. To me he is a brother. A good brother. This damn palace for the presidente is not going too well so I look forward to passing it along to that young jackass sent in from Knoxville. Thinks he knows everything. Let him have a go at dealing with the bastard's wife or wives. Change this, change that. Drives me up the wall." Suddenly Helton realized he was talking to the wall. "Damn, be glad to get out of this place."

He was a happy man thinking of Mexico, no Panamanian dictators, no building he did not know how to build.

✤   ✤   ✤

September 18, 1970, 10:30 p.m. GMT-7, Hidalgo de Parral, Mexico

"It was a lovely meal, Walther," Maddie said. "I am glad we were able to be alone tonight. We seldom have an evening alone anymore. I am glad Mr. Alasdair wanted to drive to Santa Maria del Oro, and I am glad Smitty and Fontana went with him. Where is the plane? The pilots and that woman are nowhere around. Did they go somewhere?"

"Maddie, my love with a thousand questions, I am trying to think and need a bit of time to work things out in my mind." Walther plodded along at his normal pace while Maddie pouted ever so slightly as she pretended to enjoy the walk in the moonlight and the warm breeze.

"Walther, did you see those girls sitting on the steps in back of the restaurant? I counted seven. It's 10:30. Why aren't they home? Can't be more than twelve or maybe fourteen years old. Ought to be home. Do they work for the motel? Well, they are too young to have to work. Ought to be home."

"Maddie, Maddie. They are at home, as much home as they have. Those girls are trying to make some money. They do the same type work Auntie Monica did."

"Oh, Walther, that can't be true. They are just babies."

"Babies without decent homes, money, hope. It's the same the world over. Get used to it, Maddie."

"OK."

Walther glanced at Maddie and shook his head to dislodge an unwanted thought. "What is the future with Maddie? I must make a plan."

❧   ❧   ❧

September 18, 1970, 10:30 p.m. GMT-7, Santa Maria del Oro, Durango, Mexico

Informe de la vista a la mina Santa Ana en el municipo de Santa Maria del Oro.Durango, Mexico.

"Hell's this, Smitty?"

"The directions to the Santa Ana mine. If we are going there, we need to know how to get there. I got these from that engineer down at the mining office. He doesn't speak American."

"How we gonna get there if we can't read the directions?" Alasdair sounded a bit testy. Smitty shrugged it off. "We can make out enough to find the place."

"OK, let me look at it again." Alasdair snatched the note from Smitty's hand.

La mina Santa Ana se localiza en el Estado de Durango, a 230 kilometros al N 15° W. De la Capital del Estado de Durango, particularmente a 2.5 kilometros al Norte del poblado de Santa Maria del Oro, Dgo.
El Acceso a la Zona minera es por carretera #45 de Durango a Hidalgo del Parral, Chih.; a la altura del Km. #281 se encuentra la desvicaion que conduce al Poblado de Santa Maria del Oro y las minas. El recorrido total del tray ecto es de aproximadamente 325 kilometros, que se cubren en un tiempo de 4.30 horas en camioneta pick up.

Handing the paper back to Smitty, Alasdair announced there would be a new driver from that moment: Smitty. "If you can read that crap then you can drive the roads." He snatched up the bottle of Dewars and a glass before he collapsed into a rickety chair facing Fontana, who slouched on the sofa. "You are a mountain man, Fontana. How are we going to dig that bastard out of his hole? He's dug in on top of that mountain, which is good for us, but we've got to move. He won't be up there forever. Been there for a week already. How you suggest we get to him? Damn mountain is ten thousand feet high."

"Easy, Mr. Alasdair. Smitty and I get some guns, climb the mountain, and shoot his ass and them two guys that came in yesterday. Anyway, it ain't near ten thousand."

CHAPTER 10

Jim Alasdair pondered what Fontana had been saying, that he and Smitty simply would climb the mountain and terminate Mr. Cheshire Brown and associates. Alasdair did not like it. He did not care for simple plans for complex operations. They didn't account for all possibilities, all the unexpected things that go wrong. They didn't cover the plans the other side might have. They depended on people not privy to the plan, such as targets, acting in a prescribed manner. People don't do that. You never know what people might do. Plans need to include every possible preparation and reaction by the other side, every possible eventuality, everything conceivable that could turn sour. Then there was the matter of force. It had to be overwhelming, more than the opponent possibly could anticipate and prepare for, sudden, crushing, and devastating, such as the force used in the Buccaneer Bar and against Thad. Those plans had worked, even if not fully prepared and developed. But this was the end game. This was winning or losing. This was the last fight in the war, the only one anybody has to win. If you don't plan for every possible outcome, and if you don't employ enough power, you have problems like the Japanese had at Midway in 1942. You get your ass kicked. You wind up losing the war. No, only fools go into a final fight they are not certain they will win. This would be the final fight in this whole bloody little war started by Cheshire Brown. Old Jim

Alasdair would be certain. Brown had taken up a defensive position on top of a hill. That was a mistake. You don't win by hunkering down. That gives all the initiative to your opponent and he can plan and gather the force he needs. You can't. And, while Fontana was an overwhelming force by himself, he always could be taken down by a stray bullet or some accident. Hell, he could fall off the mountain or break a leg climbing it. And Smitty might not be up to backing him up. This wasn't his kind of operation. Walther was good at planning. Maybe Walther would plan. Anyway, Fontana's simple plan had something in it that Alasdair simply could not accept. One could not know, plan and plan again and it might go exactly like Fontana suggested.

"Probably won't be that easy," Alasdair said to Fontana. "Besides that, I'm shooting his ass myself."

"No, man, you too important for that. We do it for you and it will be fun. Walther will go with us and blow his ass up if that is what you want. I know Smitty ain't never killed anyone but he is pissed off about Keaton. They were friends. Your friends in Idaho never forgive me if I let you get hurt or involved in killing somebody else." Fontana finished his longest speech ever, then noticed Smitty's disapproving glare. Their eyes clashed briefly, and Fontana continued.

"OK, OK. I know Smitty don't want to kill nobody and that's OK. He don't have to. Just carry some of the stuff and Walther and me do it."

"Hell's the matter with you, Fontana? Didn't you hear me say I'm gonna shoot the bastard?"

"I heard you, but we have to climb the backside of that mountain. We can't use the road because they'd kill us with rifles when they see us. It is wide open all the way to the top. Not even a bush to hide behind. Yeah, we have to climb the backside of that mountain, and you ain't no spring chicken any more, boss man."

"Hell's that you said, Fontana? I can climb any fucking hill you can. What you trying to say? I'm over the hill? Give it a rest. You killed a few Mexicans but that don't make you Superman or boss. I'm going to bed. Maybe we'll talk tomorrow if I don't send your ass back to Idaho." Alasdair stomped out of the room muttering to himself.

"You made him mad." Smitty stated the obvious.

"I know, but I'm right. He don't need to even be here when we get Brown. But he will be. I know that."

        ❦   ❦   ❦

September 15, 1970, 10:30 p.m.GMT-7, Santa Ana Mine, Santa Maria del Oro, Mexico

In the owner's suite of the ranch-style bunkhouse, Brown and Helton stood looking through the plate glass window, surveying the bleak and barren landscape. Brown had built the bunkhouse a few months earlier, bowing to his mine foreman's urging. It would keep the mineworkers on the mountain more and reduce the beer talk when they went home. What the workers were finding in the mine was Brown's business and no concern of the town. So far, the schedule of three weeks on and one week off worked well.

Helton's eyes shifted from the ore-crushing machine to the heap-leaching area, piled high with crushed ore, then to the bunker filled with explosives and cyanide. Earlier, a brief look inside the bunker had sent a chill through his body. He was, after all, an engineer and knew something about explosives and their safe storage. Nitro stored in a too-hot bunker with case after case of dynamite surrounded by reels of priming cord and boxes of blasting caps, failed to meet any sensible storage standard. The container of cyanide in with the explosive mix did not ease Helton's mind. Quickly turning his gaze away from the bothersome bunker, he noticed that the huge pile of crushed ore loomed larger in the thickening darkness of the nearly moon less night. It was an ominous sign in Helton's mind. The distant throbbing of the diesel generators created the only sound on the barren mountain.

Walking to the kitchen to replenish his ice and sour mash whiskey, Helton's eyes were drawn to the pile of weapons on the dining table. The ice popped and crackled as he splashed the whiskey over the cubes, sounding louder in the quiet room than in reality. Preoccupation with the weapons caused him to overfill the tumbler and spill whiskey on the floor. He sat the bottle of Jack on the table with the arsenal and took a swig from the glass to lower the liquid level. He ripped a wad of paper towels off the roll over the sink to wipe up the spill. He looked again at the well-armed table and began to think maybe the bitching in Panama was to be preferred over what loomed on the horizon atop this dreary mountain in Mexico.

"Hey, Helton, don't waste the booze. It isn't too easy to come by here. I got plenty, but we don't know how long we gonna be here. If Alasdair wants me he gonna have to come up that mountain road to get me, and when he does I will blow his ass all over this damn mountain." Brown had broken the silence and the spell being spun in Helton's head.

"Damn, Cheshire, you startled me. I had forgotten you were here."

"Don't forget that, Helton. I am not leaving your side. You are my right-hand man. That big-bore sawed-off shotgun got your name on it. Hector know how to shoot a gun? Not likely, the way he looks."

"Forget about shooting, Cheshire, forget about Alasdair. From what I heard in Panama he has more problems in Belize than he can handle. He is not worrying about you. He doesn't know you. Forget him."

"Forget him? Hell, I can't forget him. The problems in Belize are only a tip of the iceberg of problems he has. Maybe I ought to tell you about his problems and why I know he will come here after me. I am the cause of his problems, his problems in London, the Virgin Islands, Belize, and in his own house in Nashville. I caused them. Me, I did it."

Brown was almost screaming, "I did it, I did it." Helton was stunned and alarmed at Brown's outburst.

"What are you saying? You killed those people in Belize? In London? What people in London? We didn't hear about any trouble in London. What are you saying, Cheshire?"

Calm returned as Brown continued in his normal, raspy voice. "No, Helton, I did not kill anyone. I hired me a man to get Alasdair out of my business. But Alasdair won't stop. He messed me up in the islands. In Panama he is dealing with that bastard Noriega. And now he is here after my business in Mexico. He is lusting for my gold mine. He means to get it and kill me in the process." Brown paused briefly to sip his sour mash. That gave Helton time to try to digest what he had heard. He recalled what Mabe had said about Brown and wondered if he was right. He surely sounded crazy. Was Alasdair conducting a campaign to ruin Brown's business? Certainly Brown was under that impression.

"You know that bastard breaks into my house when I am away and rifles through my desk, my closets, and even the kitchen. I know when he has been there because I can smell his damn cigars. Smokes them all the time, even while he rummages through my house. Mean, sorry piece of shit he is. I am gonna kill him, I really am."

"Cheshire, you are overwrought. I know Alasdair is a tough competitor, but burgling your house? I don't think so. Did you really have something to do with that mess in Belize? If you did, it will be some type of cops looking for you, not Alasdair." Moses King Helton was beginning to worry.

"Why do you think I got you here? I need help. I don't need advice or questions. I need you to help me kill Alasdair. You will help me, won't you?"

"You are my brother, Cheshire, and I will help you do anything you ask. I just got to adjust to this, this turn of events. You just got to tell me everything and why we got to do this. OK?"

It was after 3:00 a.m. when the sour mash bottle was empty. Cheshire Brown stopped talking and slept soundly in his chair. Moses King Helton went to bed and wondered if Hector Gomez had ever used a shotgun.

🍁   🍁   🍁

September 19, 1970, 9:30 a.m. GMT-7, Near Santa Maria del Oro, Mexico

"How come there is a gate across the road?" Alasdair said. "You can't just stop a road with a gate."

"You can in Mexico," Smitty said. "Someone has. Hang on and I'll open it." He stomped the parking brake pedal, jerked the gear shifter into neutral, and leaped from the dusty yellow Land Cruiser. "Crap, it's locked." Smitty rattled the metal gate and found it to be stable and firmly fastened to strong metal posts. The rather new cattle fence attached to either post ran as far as could be seen in generally northeast and southwesterly directions. The vehicle idled roughly near the edge of what probably served as a turn around. "Looks like the end of the public road, Mr. Alasdair."

"Can we shove the posts over with the Land Cruiser? Only about a two-inch post. Shove right over, don't you think? Get in and get us moving again."

"Yes, sir," Smitty said while climbing into the vehicle and sliding under the steering wheel. He released the parking brake, pushed in the clutch, and dropped the shifter into the low slot. Using the accelerator pedal, he moved forward and struck the fence post with the heavy metal bumper. The post bent easily but was held momentarily by the fence and gate, but both fence and gate were defeated by the force of the Land Cruiser and the determination of the driver and crew to go as far as possible before walking and climbing.

As the Land Cruiser moved steadily up the rapidly disappearing road Walther thought about Maddie. She was safe in the motel and promised to stay in the room and read until Walther returned. He might be gone overnight, although the plan he worked out in his mind would have him back before midnight. Climbing the backside of the mountain would take until noon in Walther's plan. Their route would put them at the mine entrance by then. They would incapacitate the mineworkers to remove them from the equation. If Brown and the other two men were at the mine it would be over in a matter of minutes. If not, Walther had another plan. Alasdair would rely on Walther and Fontana. Smitty would remain with the vehicle or, if needed, help carry supplies and weapons up the mountain.

Fontana, sprawled across his half of the rear seat, passed the time oblivious to anything except the voice of Dolly Parton. Her voice came to him through the earpiece attached to the Walkman hanging from a clothes hook above the door next to him. His closed eyes did not indicate whether he was awake or asleep. He appeared unconcerned about anything except his music. Walther glanced at him and thought Fontana a very strange person. That did not disturb Walther.

Alasdair remained silent and nearly motionless as he thought his own thoughts and smoked his Macanudo.

The road did not end so much as it just dwindled away. The Land Cruiser continued past an abandoned mine shaft with elevator platform remaining intact. Only site work remained where an ore crusher once stood. Obviously the mine represented the long ago terminus of the road, now a near-forgotten memory. The Madres are honeycombed with closed and forgotten gold mines and haunted by memories.

"I think we better find a place to leave the vehicle, Mr. Alasdair," Smitty said. "We are not making much progress now and it looks worse just ahead. Getting downright steep. Too much for the Land Cruiser. We can walk faster. Sort of a bluff up ahead."

"Pick a spot, Smitty, and we will get this show on the road."

Smitty parked the Land Cruiser five minutes later on a semi-level ledge under a rock bluff.

"Hell's the matter with Fontana? He's alive, isn't he? Damn well looks dead. Spread out all over the back seat like Sunday lunch. Listening to tits and twang again? Come on, Fontana, I am not upset with you. You gave me good advice and I know it, but I plan to ignore it completely."

Walther moved away from the vehicle after retrieving his gear. He began to arrange it more to his liking. He placed the floppy brown hat firmly on his head to protect his white skin from the sun, then checked the backpack to make sure nothing could move out of place during the climb up the mountain. With some difficulty he secured the pack over his enormous shoulders and fastened the bottom of it securely to his belt. The pack contained some rather delicate supplies. Finding everything in place, including weapons on ankle, shoulder, and forearm, Walther looked back over the valley below and allowed his plan to flow over him like a warm mist. All thoughts of Maddie departed for a while as the comforting plan enveloped his being. Refreshed, he joined the others for the difficult climb to the summit.

☙   ☙   ☙

September 19, 1970, 9:10 a.m. GMT-7, Santa Ana Mine, Near the Adit

"Look at that view, Nickel. You can see some trees in the distance. Other side of the valley. Not a house anywhere. This is really the boonies," said the tall man in the Pinkerton uniform. "How can brown and gray be so pretty when you are looking at it from high above and far away?"

"It is nice," the man called Nickel replied. "And there is very little color in this part of Mexico. Still beautiful." Nickel turned to face the other four men, all dressed, as was he, in blue-gray Pinkerton guards' uniforms. "Now that we are away from that bastard Brown, I will explain this gig to you. I think Brown is crazy. He is crazy but rich. He is convinced some international crook is conniving to kill him and take this gold mine from him. Our job is to guard the mine and protect Brown from this multinational, multimillionaire interloper."

Who the hell wants this mine? Move this frigging mountain and what they do with it? Not enough gold here to make a wedding ring."

"The way I see it, Swan, our most dangerous part of this gig is that damn road that runs up here. Going down when we finish may be worse. It is the only way to this mine and we can see anyone on the road an hour before they get here. Brown says they'll come over the backside of this mountain. Crap. You ever see a multimillionaire mountain goat?"

"So, whatta we do now?"

"There is only about three or four hundred yards from where we are to the last place we might expect someone to come up from, the back side. There are half a dozen mountains behind the bunkhouse and leach pile to cross to get there. I studied the map and this strip is about it. Johnson, you and Bonner go over to the edge of the far side of this strip. The rest of us will sort of spread out from here and watch the down side. About every hour you walk over this way and meet us in the center. Be ready for lunch about noon. I brought food from a fast food place in Monterey. It is in the Igloo box. Our shift change is about seven. Meanwhile, keep your eye out for a mad multimillionaire."

"Damn, this gonna be a thrill a minute," Johnson said. "See you for lunch."

Nickel found a shady spot behind a rock outcropping, broke out his camp stool, and made himself comfortable. Johnson and the other three made up the best of his Pinkerton franchise. That is the reason he picked them for this trip, a couple of weeks at double their regular pay doing an easy job for a wealthy nut. Just like a vacation.

Nickel closed his eyes and wished for some trees to look at on the mountain.

❦   ❦   ❦

September 19, 1970, 9:30 a.m. GMT-7, Santa Ana Mine, Bunkhouse

Cheshire Brown fretted and fumed with the telephone with only occasional success. Having strung miles of wire to Santa Maria del Oro, he thought the telephone should work. Mabe had gone to check with the airport about Alasdair's plane. Brown wanted to know if it was there. Mysteriously the telephone dial tone began to hum. Finally he had Mabe on the line. "Yes, sir, I went to the airport and you are right. It is Alasdair's plane. The crew is in town, at one of our best hotels I am sure. The airport person I spoke with did not know which hotel. The flight manifest showed the plane arrived with a crew of three, one female and two males, and five passengers, three females and two males. They are here while Alasdair and his wife are in Atlanta taking a few days off."

"You don't believe that shit do you, Mabe? In Atlanta my ass. He is here, I tell you, and I know he is. You find him and let me know. Then I want to set up a meeting with him. You let me know and I will contact him. You find him. I don't want him coming here. I have guards if he does, but you just find him. Get that damn general and his men looking for him. Hell, get the vice president and his men. I will come in to Monterey sometime, maybe tomorrow, and we will set up a command post. You have him located. You got that, Mabe?"

Brown slammed the telephone down just as he heard the ore crusher engines start. Looking out the office window he saw one of the dump trucks backing up to the chute as another pulled away from the adit. In the next room he was surprised to find Gomez, the thin former psychologist, gleefully plowing through the weapons on the table.

Helton turned toward Brown as he entered the room. "Look at that," he said. "Gomez is a damn gun nut. He knows everything there is to know about that pile of iron. Hell, he was trained as a sniper during the Korean thing but never got to try the real thing. That Alasdair attack us, he be an asset. That is what they called people like him in the army, assets. Hell, during WW II nobody ever called us assets, did they, Brown?"

"Man, we need a bunch of assets like you, brother Gomez." Brown smiled for the first time in weeks. "Things are beginning to look up," he thought.

"Damn, that crusher makes a lot of noise," muttered Gomez.

❧   ❧   ❧

September 19, 1970, 11:50 a.m. GMT-7, Santa Ana Mine, Near the Adit

Fontana led the three men up the steep, boulder-strewn slope as quickly as he dared without unnecessary noise. All were sweaty, dirty, and while not tired, they felt the strain of the climb. He sensed the nearness of the mine before he heard the sounds of trucks being loaded and moving away. The mine opening was to their left, maybe three hundred yards, and a hundred feet above them. Fontana signaled for the others to stop as he sensed movement almost directly above him. Noticing Walther squatting behind a large boulder, Smitty did likewise. Alasdair, squatting beside Fontana, strained to see what Fontana was trying to point out to him. Something above and directly ahead had caught Fontana's eye and he tried to point it out to Alasdair.

Leaning close to Alasdair's left ear, he whispered, "See that little patch of blue up there at about one o'clock? Well what do you make of that? To me it is a serious problem. You see anything blue anywhere on the way up? No, and neither did anyone else. What does that mean? To me it means an officer in a Chinese Advisory Group in

Nam. I ask what are they doing here? Of course, they are not here, but it's something just as bad. We wait."

Alasdair strained to see anything blue between the boulders and the rugged edge of the outcropping above. Then he saw the patch of blue as it began to move, and suddenly a man in uniform loomed above him. No one moved or breathed as the guard brushed dirt and dust off the seat of his pants. "Why blue?" Alasdair wondered. He and his people had the good sense to dress in khaki that blended into the dun-colored mountain. Fontana touched Alasdair's arm and pointed to the guard's left as four other men carrying box lunches joined the first guard.

"Damn," Alasdair muttered under his breath. He raised his rifle and put the sights on the guard in the middle. "Now," he said without looking at either Walther or Fontana. He knew they were ready. The rifle fire lasted only a few seconds before leaving five Pinkertons dead or nearly so, and Smitty in nervous collapse. The three shooters dashed thirty yards to where the guards had fallen. Alasdair and Fontana checked the surrounding area for other guards while Walther used his ankle weapon to end the pain of a gravely wounded man.

Fontana stuck an earphone in place and pressed the play button on his Dolly Parton tape in the Walkman hanging from his belt. With the toe of his boot, Alasdair turned over a Loco-Polo box lunch and said, "Fried chicken." Walther went to check on Smitty.

The shots went unheard in the bunkhouse. The ore crusher made too much noise.

❧   ❧   ❧

September 19, 1970, 12:00 Noon, GMT-7, Santa Ana Mine, Bunkhouse

Pedro Morales, the mine foreman, powered down the ore crusher at exactly twelve o'clock and instructed the workers in charge of the cyanide sprayers to shut down and close up. Working quickly, the crusher and cyanide crews cleaned and stowed their tools and porta-ble equipment in the storage room beneath the bunkhouse. As the men completed the shut down and clean up, most made an obliga-tory pass at the outdoor sink and shower before lining up at the counter in the area outside Brown's office for their pay.

Fidel Morales, Pedro's brother, counted out a sizable stack of money for each man. All smiles and good humor, they began piling into the truck idling near the crusher. When it began the trip down the alleged road Helton counted twelve workers on board. They would return in one week, after all the religious celebration ended.

Before Pedro and Fidel left they explained to Helton how centu-ries ago the Madonna of St. Christie appeared at a tiny church near Santa Maria del Oro. It was during a time of great sickness and much death. All who believed and went to worship with her were cured. Those who did not believe perished. On the anniversary of this event thousands of people come to visit the holy place, a tiny church on an unpaved road surrounded by level acres of smooth parking area. For most of one week every year all spaces are taken. Tomorrow, Sunday, September 20, begins that week. All the workers and their families will be there, many helping in managing the crowd of worshipers

"A blessed event," Fidel said.

Brown chuckled and dug out the sour mash whiskey as the VW van of the brothers Morales bounced and shook down the road. Hector Gomez continued to caress and polish a Winchester 30-30 rifle as he walked through Brown's office out onto the porch. Gomez loaded the rifle with five rounds and jacked two through to check the mechanism. It was flawless. The stock of the rifle felt cool to his jaw and comfortable against his shoulder as he drew a bead on a scrub bush struggling for life along the road. Swinging around, Gomez aimed at the yellow front-end loader parked near the mine entrance. "Must be 200 yards from here," he said to no one in particular as he continued to take aim at non-moving objects.

Next he sighted in on a pile of used truck and tractor tires well beyond the mine entrance, on the edge of the ore loading area. "Damn!" Gomez detected movement. Something popped up on the tires and moved back and forth from one end to the other, then out of sight. "Some furry little animal, maybe a chipmunk or a prairie dog," Gomez thought. When it appeared again, Gomez sent three 30-30 rounds to seek it out.

At the sound of gunfire, Brown ran out of his office and onto the porch, scattering ice cubes and sour mash in his wake. "Don't shoot, don't shoot up there! I've got guards up there. You might hit one of them. Damn, I didn't know you were going to shoot the damn thing."

Helton, looking for lemon in the bottom of the refrigerator, banged his head against the bottom of the freezer compartment door above his head. The sound of gunfire caused him to forget the door was open and the force of the blow dropped him to his knees. The lemon rolled under the stove. Ice cubes and broken glass bits chased the lemon. Helton sat down heavily.

Dashing out of the workers' kitchen, the cook and dishwasher collided forcefully with the five relief guards who abandoned their hearts game to join the confusion on the porch. Two guards and the dishwasher were knocked off the porch and fell onto a pile of dirt and rocks three feet below the edge of the porch.

"Son of a bitch, three fucking shots and we are disabled," Brown said. "What the hell is the matter with you people?" He pointed an agitated finger at the guards "Where the hell are your guns? If we were under attack did you plan to defend us with a deck of cards? Shit, what a mess." Looking directly at Gomez, he yelled, "Have you reloaded or are you finished fucking up for the day?"

❧   ❧   ❧

Smitty cleared a decent flat area behind a pile of old truck and tractor tires and watched as Walther spread his packages across the shelf-like dirt bank. Walther placed them by size with small on left and increasing size as they moved to the right. There were a total of eight packs. He gave Smitty four timers and showed him how to place them on the Velcro pad he had made on each package. Over the shock of seeing five men killed, Smitty was now able to do more than just carry supplies. Alasdair and Fontana were analyzing the situation and planning how best to attack the bunkhouse. The plan had been to use the dump trucks, but the trucks were left at the bunkhouse when the workers quit at noon. Perhaps the front-end loader was a way to cover the open three hundred yards.

"Hell's that Fontana? I know that whine. Somebody is shooting at us." Hearing a noise behind him, Alasdair spun around in time to see Smitty being slammed against the ground by a bullet. The whine of the bullet was followed by the sound of the shot. Walther looked at Smitty, then returned to his work. Fontana was gone. He had snatched up his pack and the AR 180. Now screaming at his loudest, he dashed across the loading area in front of the mine entrance, firing wildly at the cluster of men on the porch of the bunkhouse. Fontana was on his third clip of ammo by the time Alasdair joined him. Alasdair carefully aimed his shots while confusion reigned on the porch. He hit two men before those still standing could scramble into the bunkhouse.

Gomez pleaded that he was sorry to have started all the shooting. "It just felt so good I couldn't resist. I am truly—" At that moment, as if by magic, Gomez's head and throat seemed to explode, spraying Brown with blood, bone, and brains. "Fucking guards are shooting at us," he screamed at a relief guard, who was without a gun of any type.

"That's not our men. They only have shotguns and pistols."

Another sustained blast of gunfire knocked the guard off the porch and into another world. Amid a shower of glass shards and wood splinters, Brown stumbled into his office. Two relief guards stood absolutely still inside, as if in shock, and did not move until bullets slammed through the walls and ripped through their bellies. Another blast of semi-automatic fire swept through the windows and walls of the owner's suite and office.

Cheshire Brown, covered with blood and brains, wounded by innumerable wood splinters, unaware as yet that he also had been hit by something more deadly than wood and glass, snatched a rifle off the table an instant before a volley of fire raked the table, sending weapons spinning.

"What in the hell is happening to me? It's that son of a bitch, Alasdair. How the hell did he do this? Where is the son of a bitch? Ten guards and the bastards have not fired a shot. I think they are all dead."

Turning in circles like a dog searching for a place to lie down, Brown saw Helton sitting on the kitchen floor in front of the refrigerator. Its door was bullet-riddled and hanging from one hinge. Helton turned his head and looked at Brown. "What is the matter with your belly, Cheshire?" Brown looked down and for the first time felt pain. He saw there was a problem with his belly. Things he had never noticed before were hanging out over his belt. He felt confused.

Helton said, "I think I'm dying, Cheshire. I have an awful pain in my chest. Sit here beside me and have a last drink with me. I have the bottle."

Brown crawled over and sat next to Helton and they both took a pull from the bottle. "Tell me again, Cheshire, how my block sprung you for that touchdown against Alabama." Cheshire Brown never answered. If he had, Moses King Helton would not have heard him.

Epilogue

Charlotte Amalie, USVI, July 4, 1980

"Why are you stopping? The story is not over. You never left those bodies scattered over a hill in Mexico. Tell me the rest of the story."

"Why do I have to spell everything out to you, Washburn? Don't you have any imagination? Finish the story to suit yourself."

"Come on, Jim. Out with it."

"OK, here goes.

"When the shooting stopped Fontana and I were behind the John Deere about two hundred yards from the bunkhouse. We didn't know who or how many were left in the bunkhouse. We only knew there was no firing at us. Fontana started the loader and lifted the scoop bucket as a protection for us, and went hell for leather to the bunkhouse. I hung on to the back of the seat more worried about falling off and being run over than getting shot.

"He slid to a stop against the bunkhouse foundation below the big windows, big windows now shot to shit. I ran to the porch and Fontana dashed to the kitchen door on the side opposite where I was. There were dead folks all over the porch and the steps leading up to the porch. I suppose the kitchen door was locked, or at least not open, because I heard Fontana empty half a clip into and through it. I found no one alive and neither did Fontana. Cheshire Brown and his college buddy, Helton, were sitting on the kitchen floor leaning on each other. Both dead. I damn near shot the bastard anyhow.

"Fontana's ear piece was flopping about his ankles but still working, so he shoved it in his ear and listened to tits and twang while we dragged the bodies out to the loader and heaved them into the scoop. There were the five relief guards, two guys wearing aprons that we determined to be cook and dishwasher, a skinny dude missing a head, and Brown and Helton. Ten in all. Made a damn scoop full and took a lot of hot work, moving all those bodies. I found what I think was the skinny dude's head and tossed it on the pile. Fontana drove the John Deere to the mine entrance. I lit a cigar after two or three attempts and walked behind the tractor and puffed on the cigar. That kind of shit makes me a bit nervous after it's over, it does.

"Walther, always neat and methodical, neatly stacked the five Pinkertons in an ore cart, which is part of the worm. He showed care and even concern in the placement and handling of the bodies. I helped him arrange the last body in the cart. All of a sudden the carts began to bounce and shake on the track. I had forgotten about Fontana and the John Deere. He very unceremoniously dumped the ten bodies from the bunkhouse into the last two carts. Then he banged the bucket against the carts to dislodge anything remaining therein. Walther shook his head and commenced placing his packages, which included the timers he and Smitty were attaching when the shooting started.

"I didn't see Smitty's body anywhere and I asked Walther. He nodded toward the mine entrance and there was Smitty sitting on a dynamite box, looking sick and holding a bloody handkerchief against the top of his head. I went over to congratulate him on being alive. For sure I had thought he was dead. He said he had a headache and I didn't doubt that. He has a permanent part in his mass of shaggy brown hair. That bullet left a neat line about four inches long and quarter of an inch wide. Skin and hair surgically removed, the skull exposed, nicely grooved in two places, and scarred the length of the part. Smitty recovered and his eyes uncrossed after a couple of weeks.

"Walther took the John Deere to the storage bunker where the explosives were kept and opened the door, using a tooth on the loader bucket to break the chain holding the door. Damn place must have been a fairyland for Walther. He was in there for twenty minutes, then he started hauling out boxes and stowing them in the loader scoop. He drove the John Deere at what I considered excessive speed. It was like he suddenly got in a hurry.

"Fontana was slouched on a box next to Smitty. He fieldstripped and cleaned the AR 180. It is his friend and he takes care of his friends. Boy, does he. In his pack Fontana found a few new tapes of Dolly and listened to different versions of tits and twang. I helped Walther place his newfound goodies in the carts and up front of the worm.

"Satisfied with his work, Walther dusted his hands on the seat of his pants and gave me what passed for a smile before starting the worm's engine. He drove it several yards to make sure everything was working properly before jumping off and watching as the carts of bodies disappeared into the dark of the mine.

"How far the worm would crawl in fifteen or twenty minutes neither Walther nor I knew. Hell, we didn't know how deep the shaft went back into the mountain. All we knew was there was gonna be a humongous explosion in about twenty minutes. There was.

"When it blew Walther was working at the bunkhouse. The rumble lasted five minutes. I gave him a thumbs up.

"For the next hour I paced, smoked, and wished for a Scotch. Smitty groaned and held his head while Fontana listened to Dolly and polished the 180. Walther wanted no help or advice as he worked out his plan for the bunkhouse and the explosive storage bunker. Later we cleaned up all evidence of our presence on the mountain except for the brass that Fontana and I scattered over the road. I ran the loader over the road with the scoop down and dumped a few loads of what I could scrape up. Waste of time, but I had nothing better to do at the moment.

"I looked at my watch. The time was 3:18 p.m. Walther set the timers for two hours to give us time to put distance between the bunkhouse and us. We did."

❧   ❧   ❧

"Hell's that you are scribbling, Washburn?"

"Just a few points you have not covered, James. Take a look at this and fill me in."

Thoughts To Ponder

Did Sue ever get out of Belize?

Did the colonel ever get out of Africa?

What did Mabe do with the mattress springs plant?

Did Jean ever get naked and into a pile?

Did the Alasdairs remain together?

What was the future for Maddie and Walther?

Did Chief Halfpenny ever meet the colonel?

Did Cosgrove get to spend the second half of the money?

"Next time, Washburn, next time. No more today. Maybe I'll tell the rest another day. But first I need to make a plan."

###
Until next time.

About the Author

During a career in manufacturing, construction, and international consulting he left his footprints from Sweden to Wales, England, Europe, Lebanon, Syria, Spain, Africa, USVI, Mexico The United States, and Canada. Now semi-retired he lives in Nashville, TN where he is finishing his next book;

I killed A Bluebird

In mid 2003, he expects to publish an epic novel of murder and intrigue in Africa. The author may be reached at his website **www.jimtraveler.com**

0-595-65153-4

Printed in the United States
1252300002B/104